INVASION OF THE GOOL WORLD

from "End As a Hero"

Using the technique I had grasped from the Gool it-self, I struck, stifling the outcry, invaded the fetid blackness and grappled the obscene gelatinous im-mensity of the Gool spy as it spasmed in a frenzy of xenophobia—a ton of liver writhing at the bottom of a dark well.

I clamped down control. The Gool mind folded in on itself, gibbering. Not pausing to rest, I followed up, probed along my channel of contact, tracing patterns, scanning the flaccid Gool mind . . .

OTHER BOOKS BY
KEITH LAUMER
Available in Berkley Medallion Editions

IT'S A MAD, MAD, MAD GALAXY

ASSIGNMENT IN NOWHERE

PLANET RUN (written with Gordon Dickson)

EARTHBLOOD (written with Rosel George Brown)

GREYLORN

GALACTIC ODYSSEY

RETIEF'S WAR

THE MONITORS

CATASTROPHE PLANET

THE TIME BENDER

KEITH LAUMER
NINE BY LAUMER

A BERKLEY MEDALLION BOOK
PUBLISHED BY
BERKLEY PUBLISHING CORPORATION

ACKNOWLEDGMENTS

"Hybrid" from *The Magazine of Fantasy and Science Fiction*.
Copyright © 1961 by Mercury Press, Inc.

"End As a Hero" from *Galaxy Magazine*. Copyright © 1963
by Galaxy Publishing Corporation.

"The Walls" from *Amazing Stories*. Copyright © 1963 by
Ziff-Davis Publishing Company.

"Dinochrome" as "Combat Unit" from *The Magazine of
Fantasy and Science Fiction*. Copyright © 1960 by Mercury
Press, Inc.

"Placement Test" from *Amazing Stories*. Copyright © 1964
by Ziff-Davis Publishing Company.

"Doorstep" from *Galaxy Magazine*. Copyright © 1960 by
Galaxy Publishing Corporation.

"The Long Remembered Thunder" from *Worlds of Tomorrow*.
Copyright © 1963 by Barmaray Company, Inc.

"Cocoon" from *The Magazine of Fantasy and Science Fiction*.
Copyright © 1962 by Mercury Press, Inc.

"A Trip to the City" as "It Could Be Anything" from *Amazing
Stories*. Copyright © 1962 by Ziff-Davis Publishing Company.

CONTENTS

Introduction

THE UNIVERSE, ACCORDING TO LAUMER

Harlan Ellison

Perhaps it is because I work at the same craft as Keith that I concur with his philosophy that in a time silly enough to revere politicians, soldiers, rock singers, pneumatic starlets, bunny-tailed cocktail waitresses and cops, there are only two really holy occupations: teaching and writing. For only these two commit themselves completely to preserving history, furthering culture, alerting man and beautifying the days through which we stumble, usually downcast and bludgeoned.

Those who know Laumer's work only through the series of clever Retief stories (thus far collected in two volumes— *Envoy to New Worlds* [Ace Books, 1963] and *Galactic Diplomat* [Doubleday, 1965]—and a novel, *Retief's War* [Doubleday, 1966], may be largely shocked and bewildered by the works that follow hereafter. For without exception— even when there is a humorous or satiric strain—every piece in the following nine is serious, and completely unlike the Retief *oeuvre.*

In the Retief stories Laumer uses his familiarity with matters diplomatic (based on over two years with the U.S. Foreign Service) to take quarterstaff lunges and noggin-knocks at the pomposity and stupidity of career diplomats. He does it with high good humor. Keith calls them "funny stories." I would try to be more precise in calling them "waggish" or "whimsical," but the semantics are certainly the property and province of the creator.

Little of this gentle kidding shows in the nine stories we have here. Yet there are subsurface similarities, of course. Within the framework of political satire, fast-action space opera, caricature characterization and the neighbor-next-door familiarity of a continuing series protagonist, Laumer has managed to say some rather explicit and serious things in his Retief stories. Statements, however, that are made much more baldly and forcefully here, though I am a fan of the

Retief series. And, in point of fact, I consider this collection a much truer cross-section of Laumer as man and as writer than the Retief stuff. For here he deals with topics that compel him, rather than merely clever story-gimmicks. (This is not intended to demean the Retief series, which is self-abrogating of criticism by its interior consistency and wry good humor.) I'm just not sure the genre knows quite the depth of the writer whose best work polls second to his frippery.

It is possible to be charmed by the writings-for-children of Wilde, St. Exupéry, Dickens, Twain, Graves or Tolstoy, and still categorize them on the value scale of a serious author's work. I think in this rating *A Christmas Carol* rates lower than *Dombey and Son, The Little Prince* rates lower than *Wind, Sand and Stars,* and the Retief stories rate lower than either "Hybrid" or "Dinochrome."

So if the student of science fiction wishes to seriously understand and appreciate Laumer (an undertaking of some merit: Laumer is the only first-rank writer the field has produced since Kurt Vonnegut, some years ago), I submit this book is inestimably more valuable than the "entertainments" (as Graham Greene would tag them) of the Retief drolleries.

Hence, if we are to offer this volume as a critique, a few words of analysis and discussion seem relevant, both in terms of writing (and writing science fiction) and of the writer who produced them.

On at least four separate occasions, usually during late-hour discussions with other arguers, Keith has said to me, "The single most important thing a human being can do is establish mind-to-mind communication, through speech or writings."

Keith's literal obsession with this concept is reflected in his many attitudes toward life-things about him: his advocacy of the Milford Science Fiction Writers Conferences which hold relatively little in the way of education for him as a growing writer; his frustration at listening to an argument in which both parties make the same point and are merely disputing semantics; his frenzy at the type of young woman who lives her life in a contemporary fantasy that barely impinges on the real world, who uses language merely to dissemble, to obfuscate, to taunt; his loathing of the bulk of television, which he considers a corruption of the medium of communication for "entertainment" or commercial ends.

Most writers—by the very insurmountable nature of trying to verbalize their own thoughts on paper—at one time or another deal with the subject of communication between humans. Whether it manifests itself as the frustration of blood and love as Baldwin attacks it in *Another Country* or *Go Tell It on the Mountain* ... or as protocol, as class and society strangle it in Marquand's *The Late George Apley* ... or as the nightmare alienation of nobody listening which Joseph K. suffers in Kafka's *The Trial* . . . I have seldom encountered a writer who has dealt with it on such a literal and crusading level.

(The above examples, incidentally, are not offered as evidence of my erudition, but as specific references to similarity in the postures assumed by Laumer in his fictions. It would be unfair and fustian to claim that Laumer is treading ground never before explored. But that he ventures into the terra incognita of this subject as very much his own man *is* important.)

Keith often asserts that he is not out to change the world, that he cannot write about contemporary topics, that he would much rather write and exist in a mist-world of his own building. Manure! The writer in Laumer keeps betraying his lip service. He deals with contemporary problems constantly, albeit disguised by the false-faces of science fiction. Of some of the others, more in a moment, but of this subject of communication—something of penetration and impact, rather than merely mouth-to-mouth resuscitation—there are prime examples in this book.

In "End As a Hero," Granthan spends the entire time of the story trying desperately to *communicate* with his superior, Kayle. He tries to convince him he has the solution to the problem of the Earth-Gool war. No one will listen. So he *forces* them to listen. It is not my place to reveal the content of the story here, but it is worthy of note that a mental device is used in "End As a Hero" that is similar to a device used in "The Long Remembered Thunder." This is the concept of following thoughts back to their owners, and reaching directly into the mind. In "Thunder" it is used to destroy the Niss, and in "Hero" it is used to destroy the Gools. I only offer this as a possibility, but it seems Laumer may even unconsciously consider such mind-to-mind communication ultimately de-

structive, yet necessary despite the risk—as if he were determined to get completely *into* the mind of his communicant,
whether the images and reasoning on the inside were born of
the pit or not. I take this as an attitude of great courage, on
the part of the writer, and on the part of the man.

That Laumer's own thought processes are frequently mud-
died by past memories, experiences, predilections, reaction
formations, even sophisticated prejudices of both harmful and
beneficent properties—is something that cannot be avoided.
Nor should we care to avoid it: the writer is the sum of the
parts that make up the man. The edges, corners, convolutions
and topography of those parts is what separates each writer
from the next. If we were not prepared to enjoy and suffer
the psychoses and special hell-images of the writer-as-
individual, we would never be able to look out of the eyes of
a Rimbaud, a Kesey, a Céline, a Conrad. We will take the
man, however imperfect, *blessedly* imperfect; for it is men
who write stories, not computers. Laumer is a man, not an
IBM machine, and thus, thank Godly, a flawed mechanism,
as are we all.

But if we might postulate for a moment that a Writer is
merely a Man hag-ridden and in symbiosis with his Talent,
then we might conclude that were it not for the men in us,
the writers might be better. Then again, the writers might
melt away like a fizzing tablet in a glass of water. Which
sustains the other? Is it a necessary symbiosis: writer and
man? Is it the shark and the pilot-fish? Or is it the Glory
hauling around the worthless husk of *Homo sapiens* merely
to keep its spark with a roof over its head?

Whatever the conclusion, it becomes apparent that to
know the Writer we must know the Man. Not by any means
to understand the writing, but to understand the wellsprings
of the Talent. To examine where the past of the Man touches
the statements of the Writer....

John Keith Laumer was born June 9, 1925 (that's Gemini,
for those who dabble in such fripperies; and to further allow
the sage nodding of their zodiacally-oriented heads, the same
sign as the author of this introduction) in Syracuse, New
York. His early reading was in the Land of Oz and the
Kingdom of Barsoom.

In 1937, he moved to St. Petersburg, Florida, not entirely
under his own volition. At the age of twelve, one pretty
much does as one's parents suggest. He attended high school,

lived on the beach, owned a Model T, a .22 and a dog named Snuffy. He built model airplanes like mad, and admired Janice from afar. He wore short pants till the age of thirteen, "thus achieving," he remembers, "the status of a persecuted minority."

Graduated high school at age sixteen. In 1942, at 10:00 P.M., saw a light plane hit a telephone pole fifty feet from where he was parked with a young lady, in Coffeyville, Kansas. He drove to a local cemetery for privacy with the young lady, and a second light plane crashed among the tombstones, thus reinforcing a persecution complex Laumer has maintained to this day.

In August of 1943 Keith volunteered for the U.S. Army, took his basic training at Fort Benning, and was sent to the University of Indiana by the Army for pre-med training. When he refused assignment to medical school, he was returned to the infantry in December of 1944.

As Keith tells it: "More Basic at Camp Howze, Texas, and then a charming free trip to Europe. Saw many interesting sights, such as dead Germans in ditches, more dead men lying on hillsides, overturned rusty locomotives, leveled cities, dead horses, D.P.'s. Spent three nights and two days in a genuine 40 and 8. Quartered in a house in Bonn, found stuffed owl lying in flower bed in very nice park; fowl had been blown out of side of museum by a U.S. bomb. All very neat but for owl. Germans very neat people. Toured Buchenwald the day after liberation. Neatness of Germans slipped here."

He lucked into a supply of chocolate bars, chewing gum, cigarettes and other trade goods, which pyramided into other goods and services. If you find my note of this series of activities vague, it is because Keith's references to it have always been vague, and the one time I mentioned that some might misinterpret it as working the black market, Keith pursed his lips in that peculiarly sinister manner he has, and tried to assume the look of a woodland nymph or sprite. Neatness of Laumer slipped here.

With the Army, Keith saw Holland, Luxembourg, Belgium, and other capitals of Europe which he has somehow, inexplicably, failed to use in his stories. At one point he was entertained by a young lady who told an interesting tale concerning a goose.

(Incidentally, the lack of real-life locales that any other self-respecting writer would mine out of memory to lend

authenticity to his stories is a peculiar omission in Laumer's
work. Were I the conjecturing sort, I might take it as a silent
verification of Laumer's oft-attested loathing for the real
world, and his determination to create a newer, better one in
his stories.)

He returned to the United States in 1946 and was dis-
charged from the service. He spent that summer hitchhiking
around the country and in the fall went to the University of
Illinois. The following summer he decided to attend the
University of Stockholm, and sailed in September for Sweden
on the *Gripsholm*.

A year in Sweden, during which he learned to speak the
language fluently, is a topic of fond reminiscence during an
evening of conversation with Keith. He avers that the local
customs of the Swedish ladies are as reported by starry-
eyed bachelor tourists.

In February of 1949, back in the States, Laumer married
the admired-from-afar Janice. I have met Janice. Laumer's
taste, based on that one act of selection, repudiates all the
other gaucheries so trying to his fans, friends and admirers.
Not to mention kind strangers.

He graduated from the University of Illinois that same
year with a Bachelor of Science degree and promptly started
over as a freshman on the G.I. Bill. His daughter Virginia
was born in December of that year. To survive, supporting
his wife and child, he designed and made clay-modeling tools,
worked at odd jobs, rescued rusty bikes from the backyards
of fraternity houses and rebuilt them, and sold them ... and
his daughter Tony was born in April of 1951.

A degree in Architecture in 1952, a position on the University staff from '52 to '53, and then came Korea. In
January 1953 Laumer enlisted once again, this time as a first
lieutenant in the Air Force.

He was sent to Labrador—alone. He spent a year in
monastic isolation, and made the verge-of-madness discovery
that exposure to extreme cold slows the metabolism, thus
increasing the subjective time-rate. He spent all his time
outside freezing, and completed the year in three and a half
months. Or so he says.

He applied for the U.S. Foreign Service, and after eighteen
months of elaborate testing, was appointed Vice Consul of
Career in the Consular Service, Third Secretary of Embassy
in the Diplomatic Service, and Foreign Service Officer of

Class Six in the Foreign Service. He was trained in Washington and then assigned to Rangoon, where his third daughter, Sabrina, was born in December of 1956.

He and the State Department parted company late in 1958, and during the same period he wrote his first story, "Greylorn," which was purchased immediately out of the slush pile by the then-editor of *Amazing Stories/Fantastic* magazines, Cele Goldsmith.

During the next year and a half, Keith spent his time in Florida, chopping wood and writing. It was a meager living for a wife and three open mouths. He returned to active duty with the USAF, as Captain, in May of 1960, stationed in London. Three years in London, and he returned to the United States where he settled down into off-base suburbia in a house with an air conditioner.

After two years this became intolerable and he left the service. He decided now was the time to plunge into the writing full-time, and writing furiously all the while, he went to take a look at Mexico, and afterward returned to Florida and his family to complete a novel nearing deadline.

Since 1959 he has sold sixteen books, nearly twenty Retief stories and a Retief novel, innumerable unrelated stories, and a mainstream novel, *Embassy*, based on his experiences with the Foreign Service.

He is currently living in Brooksville, Florida, with family, writing furiously. The last communication I received from him, when this introduction was only seven months tardy, went as follows:

"I have decided to forgive you for not showing up to eat all that southern fried hog jowl and chitlins that Jan bought for you at the Kwik-Chek. I'm building the house on the island, and I'm counting on you winging in from the Coast when it's done, and paying a visit, out of which will come, I predict, a memorable collaborative short story! Kick Norm Spinrad for me for not showing up to bid adieu when I left the City of the Angels. Adieu, K."

There is a mythos growing up about Laumer the Man, quite apart from Laumer the Writer. The legend of Laumer would be pointless, obviously, if there were not an impressive body of work behind it, to lend it substance.

Both fortunately and unfortunately, much of this stature comes from the Retief series. Fortunately, because they are good, and original, and memorable. Unfortunately, because they cannot compare to Laumer's more serious works; works heretofore ignored.

And since we have come through a preliminary comment on the attack of Laumer in his writings, and seem inescapably to bounce off the Retief stories at every turning, perhaps a moment of comparison between the Man and his Creation might be valid.

Retief, the galactic diplomat, in the stories is a man who defies, despises, but understands the System. But defies is the operable word. Constantly. And manages through dint of cleverness and courage and audacity to win the day. Keith Laumer also despises the System. The punch-card culture that steals men's souls. That this is so is patently demonstrable by the Retief works and more poignantly by several stories in this collection.

In "The Walls" and "Cocoon" we see the ultimate horror of a computerized civilization, in which the individual becomes something akin to an automaton, or a mummy. In "Cocoon" he has surrendered all volition to a life of sybaritic ease and sense-pleasure, immolated by his own apathy and fear of responsibility. (One of my sharpest recollections of Keith was an evening we spent discussing the Catherine Genovese slaying, in the streets of New York, while thirty-eight people watched and refused to come to her aid. His deep sense of revulsion, not so much at the crime, but at the motionless swine who watched and did nothing, becomes obtrusive in the light of this story. I think—from what I know of Laumer's personal philosophy, diverse as it may be—that this story fulfills one of the basic tenets of *important* science fiction: that it should, ideally, point up a moral for the world of today, through the extrapolations of the world of tomorrow. It is a cautionary tale, filled with all the loathing Keith feels for those who do not heed Justice Oliver Wendell Holmes' warning that, "A man should share the action and passion of his times at peril of being judged not to have lived." And this is not the only example of Laumer the storyteller commenting upon a world in which he moves, a world he finds less than idyllic.) In the end, it destroys him—even though the conclusion finds him, driven by instinct, making a massive effort to free himself—too late for salvation. Laumer gives us fair warning.

In "The Walls" an individual tries to fight the quagmire

totality of the Systematized Culture, and makes a valiant effort (unlike the "protagonist" of "Cocoon," who just lies there till his final moments, allowing the System to literally absorb him), and in the end, when winning becomes impossible, flees to a refuge in madness. Another solution to the problem, and yet another fair warning from Laumer.

Actually, these two stories are thematically linked in content to a startling degree. They are, in reality, the same story, told two different ways. A tour de force infrequently accomplished by commercial writers, most of whom are incapable of presenting an argument from more than one viewpoint. Laumer has taken his premise and carried it to the same destination, but his routes could be no more different than if he had weathered the Horn or flown the transpolar route.

Told slightly differently, and with a dash of wry, this same story appears as "Placement Test," in which we are offered a solution to the problem. The System threatens to punch-card you? Why then, fight it till you win. Mart Maldon does so, only to find a twitch to the bunny's nose. But he wins. Which leads to the conclusion that Laumer feels winning is at least possible.

Employing the asymptotic curve of progress, we might chronologize these stories as being seventy-five years in the future ("Placement Test"), one hundred years ahead ("The Walls"), and two hundred years away ("Cocoon").

Additionally, Laumer's very crystallized images of the System draw forth some suppositions as to what sort of Air Force officer he must have been. In a system of Systems as rigid as the Armed Forces, Laumer did amazingly well for the maverick his writings reveal him to be. And how did he take to the protocol of Rangoon? Perhaps very much like Retief.

How he must have done this—wool-pulling of the first rank—is mute testimony to Laumer's adaptability and finesse in situations that might crowd lesser talents to the walls ... or "The Walls." I know my own military experiences were bewildering, until I devised numerous short-circuits and con games that confused the System, till I had made a berth for myself that was tolerable until my discharge. But Laumer did it *within* the legal machinery of his System, and came out the other end an *official* of the System—licking them by joining them—which is precisely what the hero of "Placement Test" does.

Where does autobiography begin and wish-fulfillment end?

Where does analysis end and sententiousness begin? In the writing of an introduction, right here. In my enthusiasm for these stories, and the writing entity they illuminate, I have committed an unpardonable error: I have too long kept you from the delights of reading Laumer.

I go now, but beg your indulgence for just one more moment. My personal favorite story of these nine is "Hybrid," which I consider something of a small masterpiece. Next, I recommend "Dinochrome," and down the line to "Doorstep," which was a very early Laumer effort, and consequently, at least to me, seems negligible, and not even remotely on a par with the other eight stories in this fine cross-section of The Other Laumer.

But I would be remiss in my efforts if I did not draw your particular attention to "A Trip to the City," a story I have reread at least seven times in the preparation of these introductory notes. It is, I think, something very rare, and something very remarkable.

I will attempt no explanation of Laumer's images in the story—the scene in the Club Rexall, the broken china teacup, the nippleless breasts of the girl-doll, the real identity of the fat man in the seersucker suit—for each time I read the piece, they take on different properties, consecutively more perplexing ramifications. But the story is Laumer's attempt, it seems to me, to contact the reader directly, by precise obfuscation, if such a term seems communicative. He is saying something definite about reality here. Something intimately codified for Laumer. There is a silent plea in this story to *understand*. To reach out, as a reader, and grasp what Laumer is trying to tell you, about the nature of shadow and reality in our times, about the nature of our place in the insensate universe, about the possibility that Camus was right, that life *is* basically absurd. Brett is the farm lad in all of us, the country mouse gone to the big time. He is the naïve slice of our soma, wide-eyed, wandering through a city, saturated with that innocence of childhood or nature that we all inevitably misplace or corrupt. What the plot of this story may be, is inconsequential (though you can muddle up a pretty fair fantasy explanation for the action therein) in the light of the greater treasures it proffers. Life can mean what you want it to mean, whether stable and oriented, or clinging to the crumbling edge of madness and disorientation.

And if there is a message in this collection, the message is surely somewhere in this story. The triumph is that the message will be different for you than it is for me. And I don't think this was happenstance. I submit it was intentional on Laumer's part, and carried off with bravura and panache. I think it shows, more clearly than any other story in this book (with the possible exception of "Hybrid"), just how deep runs the talent of Keith Laumer.

It is a talent constantly flexing its muscles, constantly growing, always compelling and *demanding* just a little more of the reader than that he sit there and let the pap drop into his lap. Laumer's growth is geometrical, and it seems obvious that he will be in the front rank of science fiction for many years to come. His roots are sunk deep in the rituals of honest storytelling, yet he has the youthful verve to experiment, to strike out, to see how hard he can swing that sledge.

For those who know Retief, this book will be an eye-opener. For they will find a Laumer they may not have suspected existed. For those who are confronting Laumer for the first time in *any* garb, I envy you: you are about to discover a prose stylist whose single aim is to pleasure you. And you will learn the truth of Pascal's contention that:

"When we encounter a natural style we are always surprised and delighted, for we thought to see an author and found a man."

HARLAN ELLISON

Sherman Oaks
California

HYBRID

Deep in the soil of the planet, rootlets tougher than steel wire probed among glassy sand grains, through packed veins of clay and layers of flimsy slate, sensing and discarding inert elements, seeking out calcium, iron, nitrogen.

Deeper still, a secondary system of roots clutched the massive face of the bedrock; sensitive tendrils monitored the minute trembling in the planetary crust, the rhythmic tidal pressures, the seasonal weight of ice, the footfalls of the wild creatures that hunted in the mile-wide shadow of the giant Yanda tree.

On the surface far above, the immense trunk, massive as a cliff, its vast girth anchored by mighty buttresses, reared up nine hundred yards above the prominence, spreading huge limbs in the white sunlight.

The tree was only remotely aware of the movement of air over the polished surfaces of innumerable leaves, the tingling exchange of molecules of water, carbon dioxide, oxygen. Automatically it reacted to the faint pressures of the wind, tensing slender twigs to hold each leaf at a constant angle to the radiation that struck down through the foliage complex.

The long day wore on. Air flowed in intricate patterns; radiation waxed and waned with the drift of vapor masses in the substratosphere; nutrient molecules moved along capillaries; the rocks groaned gently in the dark under the shaded slopes. In the invulnerability of its titanic mass, the tree dozed in a state of generalized low-level consciousness.

The sun moved westward. Its light, filtered through an increasing depth of atmosphere, was an ominous yellow now. Sinewy twigs rotated, following the source of energy. Somnolently, the tree retracted tender buds against the increasing cold, adjusted its rate of heat and moisture loss, its receptivity to radiation. As it slept, it dreamed of the long past, the years of free-wandering in the faunal stage, before the in-

13

stinct to root and grow had driven it here. It remembered the grove of its youth, the patriarchal tree, the spore-brothers. . . .

It was dark now. The wind was rising. A powerful gust pressed against the ponderous obstacle of the tree; great thews of major branches creaked, resisting; chilled leaves curled tight against the smooth bark.

Deep underground, fibres hugged rock, transmitting data which were correlated with impressions from distant leaf surfaces. There were ominous vibrations from the northeast; relative humidity was rising, air pressure falling—a pattern formed, signalling danger. The tree stirred; a tremor ran through the mighty branch system, shattering fragile frost crystals that had begun to form on shaded surfaces. Alertness stirred in the heart-brain, dissipating the euphoric dream-pattern. Reluctantly, long dormant faculties came into play. The tree awoke.

Instantly, it assessed the situation. A storm was moving in off the sea—a major typhoon. It was too late for effective measures. Ignoring the pain of unaccustomed activity, the tree sent out new shock roots—cables three inches in diameter, strong as stranded steel—to grip the upreared rock slabs a hundred yards north of the tap root.

There was nothing more the tree could do. Impassively, it awaited the onslaught of the storm.

"That's a storm down there," Malpry said.

"Don't worry, we'll miss it." Gault fingered controls, eyes on dial faces.

"Pull up and make a new approach," Malpry said, craning his neck from his acceleration cradle.

"Shut up. I'm running this tub."

"Locked in with two nuts," Malpry said. "You and the creep."

"Me and the creep are getting tired of listening to you bitch, Mal."

"When we land, Malpry, I'll meet you outside," Pantelle said. "I told you I don't like the name 'Creep'."

"What, again?" Gault said. "You all healed up from the last time?"

"Not quite; I don't seem to heal very well in space."

"Permission denied, Pantelle," Gault said. "He's too big for you. Mal, leave him alone."

"I'll leave him alone," Malpry muttered. "I ought to dig a hole and leave him in it. . . ."

"Save your energy for down there," Gault said. "If we don't make a strike on this one, we've had it."

"Captain, may I go along on the field reconnaissance? My training in biology—"

"You better stay with the ship, Pantelle. And don't tinker. Just wait for us. We haven't got the strength to carry you back."

"That was an accident, Captain—"

"And the time before. Skip it, Pantelle. You mean well, but you've got two left feet and ten thumbs."

"I've been working on improving my coordination, Captain. I've been reading—"

The ship buffeted sharply as guidance vanes bit into atmosphere; Pantelle yelped.

"Oh-oh," he called. "I'm afraid I've opened up that left elbow again."

"Don't bleed on me, you clumsy slob," Malpry said.

"Quiet!" Gault said between his teeth. "I'm busy."

Pantelle fumbled a handkerchief in place over the cut. He would have to practice those relaxing exercises he had read about. And he would definitely start in weight-lifting soon—and watching his diet. And he would be very careful this time and land at least one good one on Malpry, just as soon as they landed.

Even before the first outward signs of damage appeared, the tree knew that it had lost the battle against the typhoon. In the lull as the eye of the storm passed over, it assessed the damage. There was no response from the north-east quadrant of the sensory network where rootlets had been torn from the rock face; the tap root itself seated now against pulverized stone. While the almost indestructible fibre of the Yanda tree had held firm, the granite had failed. The tree was doomed by its own mass.

Now, mercilessly, the storm struck again, thundering out of the southwest to assault the tree with blind ferocity. Shock cables snapped like gossamer; great slabs of rock groaned and parted, with detonations lost in the howl of the wind. In the trunk, pressures built, agonizingly.

Four hundred yards south of the tap root, a crack opened in the sodden slope, gaping wider. Wind-driven water poured in, softening the soil, loosening the grip of a million tiny rootlets. Now the major roots shifted, slipping. . . .

Far above, the majestic crown of the Yanda tree yielded imperceptibly to the irresistible torrent of air. The giant north buttress, forced against the underlying stone, shrieked as tortured cells collapsed, then burst with a shattering roar audible even above the storm. A great arc of earth to the south, uplifted by exposed roots, opened a gaping cavern.

Now the storm moved on, thundered down the slope trailing its retinue of tattered debris and driving rain. A last vengeful gust whipped branches in a final frenzy; then the victor was gone.

And on the devastated promontory, the stupendous mass of the ancient tree leaned with the resistless inertia of colliding moons to the accompaniment of a cannonade of parting sinews, falling with dream-like grace.

And in the heart-brain of the tree, consciousness faded in the unendurable pain of destruction.

Pantelle climbed down from the open port, leaned against the ship to catch his breath. He was feeling weaker than he expected. Tough luck, being on short rations; this would set him back on getting started on his weight-lifting program. And he didn't feel ready to take on Malpry yet. But just as soon as he had some fresh food and fresh air—

"These are safe to eat," Gault called, wiping the analyzer needle on his pants leg and thrusting it back into his hip pocket. He tossed two large red fruits to Pantelle.

"When you get through eating, Pantelle, you better get some water and swab down the inside. Malpry and I'll take a look around."

The two moved off. Pantelle sat on the springy grass, and bit into the apple-sized sphere. The texture, he thought, was reminiscent of avocado. The skin was tough and aromatic; possibly a natural cellulose acetate. There seemed to be no seeds. That being the case, the thing was not properly a fruit at all. It would be interesting to study the flora of this planet. As soon as he reached home, he would have to enroll in a course in E.T. botany. Possibly he would go to Heidelberg or Uppsala, attend live lectures by eminent scholars. He would have a cosy little apartment—two rooms would do—in the old part of town, and in the evening he would have friends in for discussions over a bottle of wine—

However, this wasn't getting the job done. There was a glint of water across the slope. Pantelle finished his meal, gathered his buckets, and set out.

"Why do we want to wear ourselves out?" Malpry said.

"We need the exercise. It'll be four months before we get another chance."

"What are we, tourists, we got to see the sights?" Malpry stopped, leaned against a boulder, panting. He stared upward at the crater and the pattern of uptilted roots and beyond at the forest-like spread of the branches of the fallen tree.

"Makes our sequoias look like dandelions," Gault said. "It must have been the storm, the one we dodged coming in."

"So what?"

"A thing that big—it kind of does something to you."

"Any money in it?" Malpry sneered.

Gault looked at him sourly. "Yeah, you got a point there. Let's go."

"I don't like leaving the Creep back there with the ship."

Gault looked at Malpry. "Why don't you lay off the kid?"

"I don't like loonies."

"Don't kid me, Malpry. Pantelle is highly intelligent—in his own way. Maybe that's what you can't forgive."

"He gives me the creeps."

"He's a nice-looking kid; he means well—"

"Yeah," Malpry said. "Maybe he means well—but it's not enough . . ."

From the delirium of concussion, consciousness returned slowly to the tree. Random signals penetrated the background clatter of shadowy impulses from maimed senses—

"Air pressure zero; falling . . . air pressure 112, rising . . . air pressure negative . . .

"Major tremor radiating from—Major tremor radiating from—

"Temperature 171 degrees, temperature —40 degrees, temperature 26 degrees . . .

"Intense radiation in the blue only . . . red only . . . ultra violet . . .

"Relative humidity infinite . . . wind from north-northeast, velocity infinite . . . wind rising vertically, velocity infinite . . . wind from east, west . . ."

Decisively, the tree blanked off the yammering nerve-trunks, narrowing its attention to the immediate status-concept. A brief assessment sufficed to reveal the extent of its ruin.

There was no reason, it saw, to seek extended personal survival. However, certain immediate measures were necessary to gain time for emergency spore-propagation. At once, the tree-mind triggered the survival syndrome. Capillaries spasmed, forcing vital juices to the brain. Synaptic helices dilated, heightening neural conductivity. Cautiously, awareness was extended to the system of major fibres, then to individual filaments and interweaving capillaries.

Here was the turbulence of air molecules colliding with ruptured tissues, the wave pattern of light impinging on exposed surfaces. Microscopic filaments contracted, cutting off fluid loss through the wounds.

Now the tree-mind fine-tuned its concentration, scanning the infinitely patterned cell matrix. Here, amid confusion, there was order in the incessant restless movement of particles, the flow of fluids, the convoluted intricacy of the alpha-spiral. Delicately, the tree-mind readjusted the function-mosaic, in preparation for spore generation.

Malpry stopped, shaded his eyes. A tall thin figure stood in the shade of the uptilted root mass on the ridge.

"Looks like we headed back at the right time," Malpry said.

"Damn," Gault said. He hurried forward. Pantelle came to meet him.

"I told you to stay with the ship, Pantelle!"

"I finished my job, Captain. You didn't say—"

"OK, OK. Is anything wrong?"

"No sir. But I've just remembered something—"

"Later, Pantelle. Let's get back to the ship. We've got work to do."

"Captain, do you know what this is?" Pantelle gestured toward the gigantic fallen tree.

"Sure; it's a tree." He turned to Gault. "Let's—"

"Yes, but what kind?"

"Beats me. I'm no botanist."

"Captain, this is a rare species. In fact, it's supposed to be extinct. Have you ever heard of the Yanda?"

"No. Yes." Gault looked at Pantelle. "Is that what this is?"

"I'm sure of it. Captain, this is a very valuable find—"

"You mean it's worth money?" Malpry was looking at Gault.

"I don't know. What's the story, Pantelle?"

"An intelligent race, with an early animal phase; later, they root, become fixed, functioning as a plant. Nature's way of achieving the active competition necessary for natural selection, then the advantage of conscious selection of a rooting site."

"How do we make money on it?"

Pantelle looked up at the looming wall of the fallen trunk, curving away among the jumble of shattered branches, a hundred feet, two hundred, more, in diameter. The bark was smooth, almost black. The foot-wide leaves were glossy, varicolored.

"This great tree—"

Malpry stooped, picked up a fragment from a burst root.

"This great club," he said, "to knock your lousy brains out with—"

"Shut up, Mal."

"It lived, roamed the planet perhaps ten thousand years ago, in the young faunal stage. Then instinct drove it here, to fulfill the cycle of nature. Picture this ancient champion, looking for the first time out across the valley, saying his farewells as metamorphosis begins."

"Nuts," Malpry said.

"His was the fate of all males of his kind who lived too long, to stand forever on some height of land, to remember through unending ages the brief glory of youth, himself his own heroic monument."

"Where do you get all that crud?" Malpry said.

"Here was the place," Pantelle said. "Here all his journeys ended."

"OK, Pantelle. Very moving. You said something about this thing being valuable."

"Captain, this tree is still alive, for a while at least. Even after the heart is dead, the appearance of life will persevere. A mantle of new shoots will leaf out to shroud the cadaver, tiny atavistic plantlets without connection to the brain, parasitic to the corpse, identical to the ancestral stock from which the giants sprang, symbolizing the extinction of a hundred million years of evolution."

"Get to the point."

"We can take cuttings from the heart of the tree. I have a

book—it gives the details on the anatomy—we can keep the tissues alive. Back in civilization, we can regenerate the tree—brain and all. It will take time—"

"Suppose we sell the cuttings."

"Yes, any university would pay well—"

"How long will it take?"

"Not long. We can cut in with narrow aperture blasters—"

"OK. Get your books, Pantelle. We'll give it a try."

Apparently, the Yanda mind observed, a very long time had elapsed since spore propagation had last been stimulated by the proximity of a female. Withdrawn into introverted dreams, the tree had taken no conscious notice as the whispering contact with the spore-brothers faded and the host-creatures dwindled away. Now, eidetically, the stored impressions sprang into clarity.

It was apparent that no female would pass this way again. The Yanda kind was gone. The fever of instinct that had motivated the elaboration of the mechanisms of emergency propagation had burned itself out futilely. The new pattern of stalked oculi gazed unfocussed at an empty vista of gnarled jungle growth, the myriad filaments of the transfer nexus coiled quiescent, the ranked grasping members that would have brought a host-creature near drooped unused, the dransacs brimmed needlessly; no further action was indicated. Now death would come in due course.

Somewhere a drumming began, a gross tremor sensed through the dead hush. It ceased, began again, went on and on. It was of no importance, but a faint curiosity led the tree to extend a sensory filament, tap the abandoned nerve-trunk—

Convulsively, the tree-mind recoiled, severing the contact. An impression of smouldering destruction, impossible thermal activity. . . .

Disoriented, the tree-mind considered the implications of the searing pain. A freak of damaged sense organs? A phantom impulse from destroyed nerves?

No. The impact had been traumatic, but the data were there. The tree-mind re-examined each synaptic vibration, reconstructing the experience. In a moment, the meaning was clear: A fire was cutting deep into the body of the tree.

Working hastily, the tree assembled a barrier of incombustible molecules in the path of the fire, waited. The heat reached the barrier, hesitated—and the barrier flashed into incandescence.

A thicker wall was necessary.

The tree applied all of its waning vitality to the task. The shield grew, matched the pace of the fire, curved out to intercept—

And wavered, halted. The energy demand was too great. Starved muscular conduits cramped. Blackness closed over the disintegrating consciousness.

Sluggishly, clarity returned. Now the fire would advance unchecked. Soon it would by-pass the aborted defenses, advance to consume the heart-brain itself. There was no other countermeasure remaining. It was unfortunate, since propagation had not been consummated, but unavoidable. Calmly the tree awaited its destruction by fire.

Pantelle put the blaster down, sat on the grass and wiped tarry soot from his face.

"What killed 'em off?" Malpry asked suddenly.

Pantelle looked at him.

"Spoilers," he said.

"What's that?"

"They killed them to get the *dran*. They covered up by pretending the Yanda were a menace, but it was the *dran* they were after."

"Don't you ever talk plain?"

"Malpry, did I ever tell you I didn't like you?"

Malpry spat. "What's with this *dran*?"

"The Yanda have a very strange reproductive cycle. In an emergency, the spores released by the male tree can be implanted in almost any warm-blooded creature and carried in the body for an indefinite length of time. When the host animal mates, the dormant spores come into play. The offspring appears perfectly normal; in fact, the spore steps in and corrects any defects in the individual, repairs injuries, fights disease, and so on; and the life-span is extended; but eventually, the creature goes through the metamorphosis, roots, and becomes a regular male Yanda tree—instead of dying of old age."

"You talk too much. What's this *dran*?"

"The tree releases an hypnotic gas to attract host animals. In concentrated form, it's a potent narcotic. That's *dran*. They killed the trees to get it. The excuse was that the Yanda could make humans give birth to monsters. That was non-sense. But it sold in the black market for fabulous amounts."

"How do you get the *dran?*"

Pantelle looked at Malpry. "Why do you want to know?"

Malpry looked at the book which lay on the grass. "It's in that, ain't it?"

"Never mind that. Gault's orders were to help me get the heart-cuttings."

"He didn't know about the *dran.*"

"Taking the *dran* will kill the specimen. You can't—"

Malpry stepped toward the book. Pantelle jumped toward him, swung a haymaker, missed. Malpry knocked him spinning.

"Don't touch me, Creep." He wiped his fist on his pants leg.

Pantelle lay stunned. Malpry thumbed the book, found what he wanted. After ten minutes, he dropped the book, picked up the blaster, and moved off.

Malpry cursed the heat, wiping at his face. A many-legged insect scuttled away before him. Underfoot, something fur-tive rustled. One good thing, no animals in this damned woods bigger than a mouse. A hell of a place. He'd have to watch his step; it wouldn't do to get lost in here . . .

The velvety wall of the half buried trunk loomed, as dense growth gave way suddenly to a clear stretch. Malpry stopped, breathing hard. He got out his sodden handkerchief, staring up at the black wall. A ring of dead-white stalks sprouted from the dead tree. Nearby were other growths, like snarls of wiry black seaweed, and ropy looking things, dan-gling—

Malpry backed away, snarling. Some crawling disease, some kind of filthy fungus—But—

Malpry stopped. Maybe this was what he was looking for. Sure, this was what those pictures in the book showed. This was where the *dran* was. But he didn't know it would look like some creeping—

"Stop, Malpry!"

Malpry whirled.

"Don't be so . . . stupid . . ." Pantelle was gasping for breath. There was a bruise on his jaw. "Let me rest . . . Talk to you . . ."

"Die, you gutter-scraping. Have a nice long rest. But don't

muck with me." Malpry turned his back on Pantelle, unlimbered the blaster.

Pantelle grabbed up a broken limb, slammed it across Malpry's head. The rotten wood snapped. Malpry staggered, recovered. He turned, his face livid; a trickle of blood ran down.

"All right, Creep," he grated. Pantelle came to him, swung a whistling right, arm bent awkwardly. Malpry lunged, and Pantelle's elbow caught him across the jaw. His eyes went glassy, he sagged, fell to his hands and knees. Pantelle laughed aloud.

Malpry shook his head, breathing hoarsely, got to his feet. Pantelle took aim and hit him solidly on the jaw. The blow seemed to clear Malpry's head. He slapped a second punch aside, knocked Pantelle full-length with a backhanded blow. He dragged Pantelle to his feet, swung a hard left and right. Pantelle bounced, lay still. Malpry stood over him, rubbing his jaw.

He stirred Pantelle with his foot. Maybe the Creep was dead. Laying his creeping hands on Malpry. Gault wouldn't like it, but the Creep had started it. Sneaked up and hit him from behind. He had the mark to prove it. Anyway, the news about the *dran* would cheer Gault up. Better go get Gault up here. Then they could cut the *dran* out and get away from this creeping planet. Let the Creep bleed.

Malpry turned back toward the ship, leaving Pantelle huddled beside the fallen tree.

The Yanda craned external oculi to study the fallen creature, which had now apparently entered a dormant phase. A red exudation oozed from orifices at the upper end, and from what appeared to be breaks in the epidermis. It was a strange creature, bearing some superficial resemblance to the familiar host-creatures. Its antics, and those of the other, were curious indeed. Perhaps they were male and female, and the encounter had been a mating. Possibly this hibernation was normal process, preparatory to rooting. If only it were not so alien, it might serve as a carrier . . .

The surface of the organism heaved, a limb twitched. Apparently it was on the verge of reviving. Soon it would scurry away and be seen no more. It could be wise to make a quick examination; if the creature should prove suitable as a host. . . .

Quickly the tree elaborated a complex of tiny filaments, touched the still figure tentatively, then penetrated the surprisingly soft surface layer, seeking out nerve fibres. A trickle of impressions flowed in, indecipherable. The tree put forth a major sensory tendril, divided and subdivided it into fibres only a few atoms in diameter, fanned them out through the unconscious man, tracing the spinal column, entering the brain—

Here was a wonder of complexity, an unbelievable profusion of connections. This was a center capable of the highest intellectual functions—unheard of in a host creature. Curiously, the tree-mind probed deeper, attuning itself, scanning through a kaleidoscope of impressions, buried memories, gaudy symbolisms.

Never had the Yanda-mind encountered the hyperintellectual processes of emotion. It pressed on, deeper into the phantasmagoria of dreams—

Color, laughter, and clash-of-arms. Banners rippling in the sun, chords of a remote music, and night-blooming flowers. Abstractions of incredible beauty mingled with vivid conceptualizations of glory. Fascinated, the tree-mind explored Pantelle's secret romantic dreams of fulfillment—

And abruptly, encountered the alien mind.

There was a moment of utter stillness as the two minds assessed each other.

You are dying, the alien mind spoke.

Yes. And you are trapped in a sickly host-creature. Why did you not select a stronger host?

I . . . originated here. I . . . we . . . are one.

Why do you not strengthen this host?

How?

The Yanda mind paused. *You occupy only a corner of the brain. You do not use your powers?*

I am a segment. . . . The alien mind paused, confused. *I am conceptualized by the monitor-mind as the subconscious.*

What is the monitor-mind?

It is the totality of the personality. It is above the conscious, directing. . . .

This is a brain of great power, yet great masses of cells are unused. Why are major trunks aborted as they are?

I do not know.

There was no more information from the alien brain which indeed, housed multiple minds.

The Yanda mind broke contact, tuned.

There was a blast of mind-force, overwhelming. The Yanda mind reeled, groped for orientation.

YOU ARE NOT ONE OF MY MINDS.

You are the monitor-mind? gasped the Yanda.

YES. WHAT ARE YOU?

The Yanda-mind projected its self-concept.

STRANGE, VERY STRANGE. YOU HAVE USEFUL SKILLS, I PERCEIVE. TEACH THEM TO ME.

The Yanda mind squirmed under the torrent of thought impulses.

Reduce your volume. You will destroy me.

I WILL TRY. TEACH ME THAT TRICK OF MANIPULATING MOLECULES.

The Yanda cringed under the booming of the alien mind. What an instrument! A fantastic anomaly, a mind such as this linked to this fragile host-creature—and unable even to use its powers. But it would be a matter of the greatest simplicity to make the necessary corrections, rebuild and toughen the host, eliminate the defects—

TEACH ME, YANDA MIND!

Alien, I die soon. But I will teach you. There is, however, a condition. . . .

The two minds conferred, and reached agreement. At once, the Yanda mind initiated sweeping rearrangements at the submolecular level.

First, cell-regeneration, stitching up the open lesions on arm and head. Antibodies were modified in vast numbers, flushed through the system. Parasites died.

Maintain this process, the tree-mind directed.

Now, the muscular layers; surely they were inadequate. The very structure of the cells was flimsy. The Yanda devised the necessary improvements, tapped the hulk of its cast-off body for materials, reinforced the musculature. Now for the skeletal members. . . .

The tree visualized the articulation of the ambulatory mechanism, considered for a moment the substitution of a more practical tentacular concept—

There was little time. Better to retain the stony bodies, merely strengthen them, using metallo-vegetable fibers. The air sacs, too. And the heart. They would have lasted no time at all as they were.

Observe, alien, thus, and thus . . . .

I SEE. IT IS A CLEVER TRICK.

The Yanda worked over the body of Pantelle, adjusting, correcting, reinforcing, discarding a useless appendix or tonsil here, adding a reserve air storage unit there. A vestigial eye deep in the brain was refurbished for sensitivity at the radio frequencies, linked with controls. The spine was deftly fused at the base; additional mesenteries were added for intestinal support. Following the basic pattern laid down in the genes, the tree-mind rebuilt the body.

When the process was finished, and the alien mind had absorbed the techniques demonstrated, the Yanda mind paused.

It is finished.

I AM READY TO RE-ESTABLISH THE CONSCIOUS MIND IN OVERT CONTROL.

Remember your promise.

I WILL REMEMBER.

The Yanda mind began its withdrawal. Troublesome instinct was served. Now it could rest until the end.

WAIT. I'VE GOT A BETTER IDEA, YANDA. . . .

"Two weeks down and fourteen to go," Gault said. "Why don't you break down and tell me what happened back there?"

"How's Malpry?" Pantelle asked.

"He's all right. Broken bones knit, and you only broke a few."

"The book was wrong about the Yanda spores," Pantelle said. "They don't have the power in themselves to reconstruct the host-creature—"

"The what?"

"The infected animal; the health and life span of the host is improved. But the improvement is made by the tree, at the time of propagation, to insure a good chance for the spores."

"You mean you—"

"We made a deal. The Yanda gave me this—" Pantelle pressed a thumb against the steel bulkhead. The metal yielded.

"—and a few other tricks. In return, I'm host to the Yanda spores."

Gault moved away.

"Doesn't that bother you? Parasites—"

"It's an equitable deal. The spores are microscopic, and completely dormant until the proper conditions develop."

"Yeah, but you said yourself this vegetable brain has worked on your mind."

"It merely erased all the scars of traumatic experience, corrected deficiencies, taught me how to use what I have."

"How about teaching me?"

"Sorry, Gault." Pantelle shook his head. "Impossible."

Gault considered Pantelle's remarks.

"What about these 'proper conditions' for the spores?" he asked suddenly. "You wake up and find yourself sprouting some morning?"

"Well," Pantelle coughed. "That's where my part of the deal comes in. A host creature transmits the spores through the normal mating process. The offspring gets good health and a long life before the metamorphosis. That's not so bad—to live a hundred years, and then pick a nice spot to root and grow and watch the seasons turn ..."

Gault considered. "A man does get tired," he said. "I know a spot, where you can look for miles out across the Pacific ..."

"So I've promised to be very active," Pantelle said. "It will take a lot of my time, but I intend to discharge my obligation to the fullest."

Did you hear that, Yanda? Pantelle asked silently.

I did, came the reply from the unused corner he had assigned to the Yanda ego-pattern. *Our next thousand years should be very interesting.*

END AS A HERO

I

In the dream I was swimming in a river of white fire. The dream went on and on; and then I was awake—and the fire was still there, fiercely burning at me.

I moved to get away from the flames, and the real pain hit me. I tried to go back to sleep and the relative comfort of the river of fire, but it was no go. For better or worse, I was alive and conscious.

I opened my eyes and took a look around. I was on the floor next to an unpadded acceleration couch—the kind the Terrestrial Space Arm installs in seldom-used lifeboats. There were three more couches, but no one in them. I tried to sit up. It wasn't easy but, by applying a lot more will-power than should be required of a sick man, I made it. I took a look at my left arm. Baked. The hand was only medium rare, but the forearm was black, with deep red showing at the bottom of the cracks where the crisped upper layers had burst . . .

There was a first-aid cabinet across the compartment from me. I tried my right leg, felt broken bone-ends grate with a sensation that transcended pain. I heaved with the other leg, scrabbled with the charred arm. The crawl to the cabinet dwarfed Hillary's trek up Everest, but I reached it after a couple of years, and found the microswitch on the floor that activated the thing, and then I was fading out again . . .

I came out of it clear-headed but weak. My right leg was numb, but reasonably comfortable, clamped tight in a walking brace. I put up a hand and felt a shaved skull, with sutures. It must have been a fracture. The left arm—well, it was still there, wrapped to the shoulder and held out stiffly by a power truss that would keep the scar tissue from pulling up and crippling me. The steady pressure as the truss contracted wasn't anything to do a sense-tape on for replaying at leisure moments, but at least the cabinet hadn't amputated. I wasn't complaining.

As far as I knew, I was the first recorded survivor of contact with the Gool—if I survived.

I was still a long way from home, and I hadn't yet checked on the condition of the lifeboat. I glanced toward the entry port. It was dogged shut. I could see black marks where my burned hand had been at work.

I fumbled my way into a couch and tried to think. In my condition—with a broken leg and third-degree burns, plus a fractured skull—I shouldn't have been able to fall out of bed, much less make the trip from *Belshazzar*'s CCC to the boat; and how had I managed to dog that port shut? In an emergency a man was capable of great exertions. But running on a broken femur, handling heavy levers with charred fingers and thinking with a cracked head were overdoing it. Still, I was there—and it was time to get a call through to TSA headquarters.

I flipped the switch and gave the emergency call-letters Col. Ausar Kayle of Aerospace Intelligence had assigned to me a few weeks before. It was almost five minutes before the "acknowledge" came through from the Ganymede relay station, another ten minutes before Kayle's face swam into view. Even through the blur of the screen I could see the haggard look.

"Granthan!" he burst out. "Where are the others? What happened out there?" I turned him down to a mutter.

"Hold on," I said. "I'll tell you. Recorders going?" I didn't wait for an answer—not with a fifteen-minute transmission lag. I plowed on:

"*Belshazzar* was sabotaged. So was *Gilgamesh*—I think. I got out. I lost a little skin, but the aid cabinet has the case in hand. Tell the Med people the drinks are on me."

I finished talking and flopped back, waiting for Kayle's reply. On the screen, his flickering image gazed back impatiently, looking as hostile as a swing-shift ward nurse. It would be half an hour before I would get his reaction to my report. I dozed off—and awoke with a start. Kayle was talking.

"—your report. I won't mince words. They're wondering at your role in the disaster. How does it happen that you alone survived?"

"How the hell do I know?" I yelled—or croaked. But Kayle's voice was droning on:

". . . you Psychodynamics people have been telling me the Gool may have some kind of long-range telehypnotic ability that might make it possible for them to subvert a loyal man without his knowledge. You've told me yourself that you blacked out during the attack—and came to on the lifeboat, with no recollection of how you got there.

"This is war, Granthan. War against a vicious enemy who strike without warning and without mercy. You were sent out to investigate the possibility of—what's that term you use?—hypercortical invasion. You know better than most the risk I'd be running if you were allowed to pass the patrol line.

"I'm sorry, Granthan. I can't let you land on Earth. I can't accept the risk."

"What do I do now?" I stormed. "Go into orbit and eat pills and hope you think of something? I need a doctor!"

Presently Kayle replied. "Yes," he said. "You'll have to enter a parking orbit. Perhaps there will be developments soon which will make it possible to . . . ah . . . restudy the situation." He didn't meet my eye. I knew what he was thinking. He'd spare me the mental anguish of knowing what was coming. I couldn't really blame him; he was doing what he thought was the right thing. And I'd have to go along and pretend—right up until the warheads struck—that I didn't know I'd been condemned to death.

II

I tried to gather my wits and think my way through the situation. I was alone and injured, aboard a lifeboat that would be the focus of a converging flight of missiles as soon as I approached within battery range of Earth. I had gotten clear of the Gool, but I wouldn't survive my next meeting with my own kind. They couldn't take the chance that I was acting under Gool orders.

I wasn't, of course. I was still the same Peter Granthan, psychodynamicist, who had started out with Dayan's fleet six weeks earlier. The thoughts I was having weren't brilliant, but they were mine, all mine . . .

But how could I be sure of that?

Maybe there was something in Kayle's suspicion. If the

Gool were as skillful as we thought, they would have left no overt indications of their tampering—not at a conscious level.

But this was where psychodynamics training came in. I had been reacting like any scared casualty, aching to get home and lick his wounds. But I wasn't just any casualty. I had been trained in the subtleties of the mind—and I had been prepared for just such an attack.

Now was the time to make use of that training. It had given me one resource. I could unlock the memories of my subconscious—and see again what had happened.

I lay back, cleared my mind of extraneous thoughts, and concentrated on the trigger word that would key an auto-hypnotic sequence . . .

Sense impressions faded. I was alone in the nebulous emptiness of a first-level trance. I keyed a second word, slipped below the misty surface into a dreamworld of vague phantasmagoric figures milling in their limbo of sub-conceptualization. I penetrated deeper, broke through into the vividly hallucinatory third level, where images of mirror-bright immediacy clamored for attention. And deeper . . .

The immense orderly confusion of the basic memory level lay before me. Abstracted from it, aloof and observant, the monitoring personality-fraction scanned the pattern, searching the polydimensional continuum for evidence of an alien intrusion.

And found it.

As the eye instantaneously detects a flicker of motion amid an infinity of static detail, so my inner eye perceived the subtle traces of the probing Gool mind, like a whispered touch deftly rearranging my buried motivations.

I focused selectively, tuned to the recorded gestalt.

"It is a contact, Effulgent One!"

"Softly, now! Nurture the spark well. It but trembles at the threshold . . ."

"It is elusive, Master! It wriggles like a gorm-worm in the eating trough!"

A part of my mind watched as the memory unreeled. I listened to the voices—yet not voices, merely the shape of concepts, indescribably intricate. I saw how the decoy psuedo-personality which I had concretized for the purpose in a hundred training sessions had fought against the intruding stimuli—then yielded under the relentless thrust of the alien probe. I watched as the Gool operator took over the motor centers, caused me to crawl through the choking smoke of the devastated control compartment toward the escape hatch. Fire leaped up, blocking the way. I went on, felt ghostly flames whipping at me—and then the hatch was open and I pulled myself through, forcing the broken leg. My blackened hand fumbled at the locking wheel. Then the blast as the lifeboat leaped clear of the disintegrating dreadnought —and the world-ending impact as I fell.

At a level far below the conscious, the embattled psuedo-personality lashed out again—fighting the invader.

"Almost it eluded me then, Effulgent Lord. Link with this lowly one!"

"Impossible! Do you forget all my teachings? Cling, though you expend the last filament of your life-force!"

Free from all distraction, at a level where comprehension and retention are instantaneous and total, my monitoring basic personality fraction followed the skillful Gool mind as it engraved its commands deep in my subconscious. Then the touch withdrew, erasing the scars of its passage, to leave me unaware of its tampering—at a conscious level.

Watching the Gool mind, I learned.

The insinuating probe—a concept regarding which psycho-dynamicists had theorized—was no more than a pattern in emptiness . . .

But a pattern which I could duplicate, now that I had seen what had been done to me.

Hesitantly, I felt for the immaterial fabric of the continuum, warping and manipulating it, copying the Gool probe. Like planes of paper-thin crystal, the polyfinite aspects of reality shifted into focus, aligning themselves.

Abruptly, a channel lay open. As easily as I would stretch out my hand to pluck a moth from a night-flower, I reached across the unimaginable void—and sensed a pit blacker than the bottom floor of hell, and a glistening dark shape.

There was a soundless shriek. *"Effulgence! It reached out— touched me!"*

Using the technique I had grasped from the Gool itself, I struck, stifling the outcry, invaded the fetid blackness and grappled the obscene gelatinous immensity of the Gool spy as it spasmed in a frenzy of xenophobia—a ton of liver writhing at the bottom of a dark well.

I clamped down control. The Gool mind folded in on itself, gibbering. Not pausing to rest, I followed up, probed along my channel of contact, tracing patterns, scanning the flaccid Gool mind . . .

I saw a world of yellow seas lapping at endless shores of mud. There was a fuming pit, where liquid sulphur bubbled up from some inner source, filling an immense natural basin. The Gool clustered at its rim, feeding, each monstrous shape heaving against its neighbors for a more favorable position.

I probed farther, saw the great cables of living nervous tissue that linked each eating organ with the brain-mass far underground. I traced the passages through which tendrils ran out to immense caverns where smaller creatures labored over strange devices. These, my host's memory told me, were the young of the Gool. Here they built the fleets that would transport the spawn to the new worlds the Prime Overlord had discovered, worlds where food was free for the taking. Not sulphur alone, but potassium, calcium, iron and all the metals—riches beyond belief in endless profusion. No longer would the Gool tribe cluster—those who remained of a once-great race—at a single feeding trough. They would spread out across a galaxy—and beyond.

But not if I could help it.

The Gool had evolved a plan—but they'd had a stroke of bad luck.

In the past, they had managed to control a man here and there, among the fleets, far from home, but only at a superficial level. Enough, perhaps, to wreck a ship, but not the complete control needed to send a man back to Earth under Gool compulsion, to carry out complex sabotage.

Then they had found me, alone, a sole survivor, free from the clutter of the other mindfields. It had been their misfortune to pick a psychodynamicist. Instead of gaining a patient slave, they had opened the fortress door to an unseen spy. Now that I was there, I would see what I could steal.

A timeless time passed. I wandered among patterns of white light and white sound, plumbed the deepest recesses of hidden Gool thoughts, fared along strange ways examining the shapes and colors of the concepts of an alien mind.

I paused at last, scanning a multi-ordinal structure of

pattern within pattern; the diagrammed circuits of a strange machine.

I followed through its logic-sequence; and, like a bomb-burst, its meaning exploded in my mind.

From the vile nest deep under the dark surface of the Gool world in its lonely trans-Plutonian orbit, I had plucked the ultimate secret of their kind.

Matter across space.

"You've got to listen to me, Kayle," I shouted. "I know you think I'm a Gool robot. But what I have is too big to let you blow it up without a fight. Matter transmission! You know what that can mean to us. The concept is too complex to try to describe in words. You'll have to take my word for it. I can build it, though, using standard components, plus an infinite-area antenna and a moebius-wound coil—and a few other things. . . ."

I harangued Kayle for a while, and then sweated out his answer. I was getting close now. If he couldn't see the beauty of my proposal, my screens would start to register the radiation of warheads any time now.

Kayle came back—and his answer boiled down to "no."

I tried to reason with him. I reminded him how I had readied myself for the trip with sessions on the encephalo-scope, setting up the cross-networks of conditioned defensive responses, the shunt circuits to the decoy psuedo-personality, leaving my volitional ego free. I talked about subliminal hypnotics and the resilience quotient of the ego-complex.

I might have saved my breath.

"I don't understand that psychodynamics jargon, Gran-than," he snapped. "It smacks of mysticism. But I understand what the Gool have done to you well enough. I'm sorry."

I leaned back and chewed the inside of my lip and thought unkind thoughts about Colonel Ausar Kayle. Then I settled down to solve the problem at hand.

I keyed the chart file, flashed pages from the standard index on the reference screen, checking radar coverages, beacon ranges, monitor stations, controller fields. It looked as though a radar-negative boat the size of mine might possibly get through the defensive net with a daring pilot, and as a condemned spy, I could afford to be daring.

And I had a few ideas.

III

The shrilling of the proximity alarm blasted through the silence. For a wild moment I thought Kayle had beaten me to the punch; then I realized it was the routine DEW line patrol contact.

"Z four-oh-two, I am reading your IFF. Decelerate at 1.8 gee preparatory to picking up approach orbit . . ."

The screen went on droning out instructions. I fed them into the autopilot, at the same time running over my approach plan. The scout was moving in closer. I licked dry lips. It was time to try.

I closed my eyes, reached out—as the Gool mind had reached out to me—and felt the touch of a Signals Officer's mind, forty thousand miles distant, aboard the patrol vessel. There was a brief flurry of struggle; then I dictated my instructions. The Signals Officer punched keys, spoke into his microphone:

"As you were, Z four-oh-two. Continue on present course. At oh-nineteen seconds, pick up planetary for re-entry and let-down."

I blanked out the man's recollection of what had happened, caught his belated puzzlement as I broke contact. But I was clear of the DEW line now, rapidly approaching atmosphere.

"Z four-oh-two," the speaker crackled. "This is planetary control. I am picking you up on channel forty-three, for re-entry and let-down."

There was a long pause. Then:

"Z four-oh-two, countermand DEW line clearance! Repeat, clearance countermanded! Emergency course change to standard hyperbolic code ninety-eight. Do not attempt re-entry. Repeat: do not attempt re-entry!"

It hadn't taken Kayle long to see that I'd gotten past the outer line of defense. A few more minutes' grace would have helped. I'd play it dumb, and hope for a little luck.

"Planetary, Z four-oh-two here. Say, I'm afraid I missed part of that, fellows. I'm a little banged up—I guess I switched frequencies on you. What was that after 'pick up channel forty-three' . . . ?"

"Four-oh-two, sheer off there! You're not cleared for re-entry!"

"Hey, you birds are mixed up," I protested. "I'm cleared all the way. I checked in with DEW—"

It was time to disappear. I blanked off all transmission, hit the controls, following my evasive pattern. And again I reached out—

A radar man at a site in the Pacific, fifteen thousand miles away, rose from his chair, crossed the darkened room and threw a switch. The radar screens blanked off . . .

For an hour I rode the long orbit down, fending off attack after attack. Then I was clear, skimming the surface of the ocean a few miles southeast of Key West. The boat hit hard. I felt the floor rise up, over, buffeting me against the restraining harness.

I hauled at the release lever, felt a long moment of giddy disorientation as the escape capsule separated from the sinking lifeboat deep under the surface. Then my escape capsule was bobbing on the water.

I would have to risk calling Kayle now—but by voluntarily giving my position away, I should convince him I was still on our side—and I was badly in need of a pick-up. I flipped the sending key.

"This is Z four-oh-two," I said. "I have an urgent report for Colonel Kayle of Aerospace Intelligence."

Kayle's face appeared. "Don't fight it, Granthan," he croaked. "You penetrated the planetary defenses—God knows how. I—"

"Later," I snapped. "How about calling off your dogs now? And send somebody out here to pick me up, before I add sea-sickness to my other complaints."

"We have you pinpointed," Kayle cut in. "It's no use fighting it, Granthan."

I felt cold sweat pop out on my forehead. "You've got to listen, Kayle," I shouted. "I suppose you've got missiles on the way already. Call them back! I have information that can win the war—"

"I'm sorry, Granthan," Kayle said. "It's too late—even if I could take the chance you were right."

A different face appeared on the screen.

"Mr. Granthan, I am General Titus. On behalf of your country, and in the name of the President—who has been apprised of this tragic situation—it is my privilege to inform you that you will be awarded the Congressional Medal of

Honor—posthumously—for your heroic effort. Although you failed, and have in fact been forced, against your will, to carry out the schemes of the inhuman enemy, this in no way detracts from your gallant attempt. Mr. Granthan, I salute you."

The general's arm went up in a rigid gesture.

"Stow that, you pompous idiot!" I barked. "I'm no spy!"

Kayle was back, blanking out the startled face of the general.

"Goodbye, Granthan. Try to understand . . ."

I flipped the switch, sat gripping the couch, my stomach rising with each heave of the floating escape capsule. I had perhaps five minutes. The missiles would be from Canaveral.

I closed my eyes, forced myself to relax, reached out . . .

I sensed the distant shore, the hot buzz of human minds at work in the cities. I followed the coastline, found the Missile Base, flicked through the cluster of minds.

"—*missile on course; do right, baby. That's it, right in the slot.*"

I fingered my way through the man's mind and found the control centers. He turned stiffly from the plotting board, tottered to a panel to slam his hand against the destruct button.

Men fell on him, dragged him back. "—*fool, why did you blow it?*"

I dropped the contact, found another, who leaped to the panel, detonated the remainder of the flight of six missiles. Then I withdrew. I would have a few minutes' stay of execution now.

I was ten miles from shore. The capsule had its own power plant. I started it up, switched on the external viewer. I saw dark sea, the glint of star-light on the choppy surface, in the distance a glow on the horizon that would be Key West. I plugged the course into the pilot, then leaned back and felt outward with my mind for the next attacker.

IV

It was dark in the trainyard. I moved along the tracks in a stumbling walk. Just a few more minutes, I was telling myself. *A few more minutes and you can lie down . . . rest . . .*

The shadowed bulk of a box car loomed up, its open door

a blacker square. I leaned against the sill, breathing hard, then reached inside for a grip with my good hand.

Gravel scrunched nearby. The beam of a flashlight lanced out, slipped along the weathered car, caught me. There was a startled exclamation. I ducked back, closed my eyes, felt out for his mind. There was a confused murmur of thought, a random intrusion of impressions from the city all around. It was hard, too hard. I had to sleep—

I heard the snick of a revolver being cocked, and dropped flat as a gout of flame stabbed toward me, the imperative Bam! echoing between the cars. I caught the clear thought:

"God-awful looking, shaved head, arm stuck out; him all right—"

I reached out to his mind and struck at random. The light fell, went out, and I heard the unconscious body slam to the ground like a poled steer.

It was easy—if I could only stay awake.

I gritted my teeth, pulled myself into the car, crawled to a dark corner behind a crate and slumped down. I tried to evoke a personality fraction to set as a guard, a part of my mind to stay awake and warn me of danger. It was too much trouble. I relaxed and let it all slide down into darkness.

The car swayed, click-clack, click-clack. I opened my eyes, saw yellow sunlight in a bar across the litter on the floor. The power truss creaked, pulling at my arm. My broken leg was throbbing its indignation at the treatment it had received— walking brace and all—and the burned arm was yelling aloud for more of that nice dope that had been keeping it from realizing how bad it was. All things considered, I felt like a badly embalmed mummy—except that I was hungry. I had been a fool not to fill my pockets when I left the escape capsule in the shallows off Key Largo, but things had been happening too fast.

I had barely made it to the fishing boat, whose owner I had coerced into rendezvousing with me before shells started dropping around us. If the gunners on the cruiser ten miles away had had any luck, they would have finished me—and the hapless fisherman—right then. We rode out a couple of near misses, before I put the cruiser's gunnery crew off the air.

At a fishing camp on the beach, I found a car—with driver. He dropped me at the railyard, and drove off under the impression he was in town for groceries. He'd never believe he'd seen me.

Now I'd had my sleep. I had to start getting ready for the next act of the farce.

I pressed the release on the power truss, gingerly unclamped it, then rigged a sling from a strip of shirt tail. I tied the arm to my side as inconspicuously as possible. I didn't disturb the bandages.

I needed new clothes—or at least different ones—and something to cover my shaved skull. I couldn't stay hidden forever. The yard cop had recognized me at a glance.

I lay back, waiting for the train to slow for a town. I wasn't unduly worried—at the moment. The watchman probably hadn't convinced anyone he'd actually seen me. Maybe he hadn't been too sure himself.

The click-clack slowed and the train shuddered to a stop. I crept to the door, peered through the crack. There were sunny fields, a few low buildings in the distance, the corner of a platform. I closed my eyes and let my awareness stretch out.

"—lousy job. What's the use? Little witch in the lunch room ... up in the hills, squirrel hunting, bottle of whiskey ..."

I settled into control gently, trying not to alarm the man. I saw through his eyes the dusty box car, the rust on the tracks, the listless weeds growing among cinders, and the weathered boards of the platform. I turned him, and saw the dingy glass of the telegraph window, a sagging screen door with a chipped enameled cola sign.

I walked the man to the door, and through it. Behind a linoleum-topped counter, a coarse-skinned teen-age girl with heavy breasts and wet patches under her arms looked up without interest as the door banged.

My host went on to the counter, gestured toward the waxed-paper-wrapped sandwiches under a glass cover. "I'll take 'em all. And candy bars, and cigarettes. And give me a big glass of water."

"Better git out there and look after yer train," the girl said carelessly. "When'd you git so all-fired hungry all of a sudden?"

"Put it in a bag. Quick."

"Look who's getting bossy—"

My host rounded the counter, picked up a used paper bag,

began stuffing food in it. The girl stared at him, then pushed him back. "You git back around that counter!"

She filled the bag, took a pencil from behind her ear.

"That'll be one eighty-five. Cash."

My host took two dog-eared bills from his shirt pocket, dropped them on the counter and waited while the girl filled a glass. He picked it up and started out.

"Hey! Where you goin' with my glass?"

The trainman crossed the platform, headed for the box car. He slid the loose door back a few inches against the slack latch, pushed the bag inside, placed the glass of water beside it, then pulled off his grimy railroader's cap and pushed it through the opening. He turned. The girl watched from the platform. A rattle passed down the line and the train started up with a lurch. The man walked back toward the girl. I heard him say: "Friend o' mine in there—just passin' through."

I was discovering that it wasn't necessary to hold tight control over every move of a subject. Once given the impulse to act, he would rationalize his behavior, fill in the details—and never know that the original idea hadn't been his own.

I drank the water first, ate a sandwich, then lit a cigarette and lay back. So far so good. The crates in the car were marked "U.S. Naval Aerospace Station, Bayou Le Cochon." With any luck I'd reach New Orleans in another twelve hours. The first step of my plan included a raid on the Delta National Labs; but that was tomorrow. That could wait.

It was a little before dawn when I crawled out of the car at a siding in the swampy country a few miles out of New Orleans. I wasn't feeling good, but I had a stake in staying on my feet. I still had a few miles in me. I had my supplies—a few candy bars and some cigarettes—stuffed in the pockets of the tattered issue coverall. Otherwise, I was unencumbered. Unless you wanted to count the walking brace on my right leg and the sling binding my arm.

I picked my way across mushy ground to a pot-holed black-top road, started limping toward a few car lights visible half a mile away. It was already hot. The swamp air was like warmed-over subway fumes. Through the drugs, I could feel my pulse throbbing in my various wounds. I reached out and touched the driver's mind; he was thinking about shrimps, a fish-hook wound on his left thumb and a girl with black hair. "Want a lift?" he called.

I thanked him and got in. He gave me a glance and I pinched off his budding twinge of curiosity. It was almost an effort now not to follow his thoughts. It was as though my mind, having learned the trick of communications with others, instinctively reached out toward them.

An hour later he dropped me on a street corner in a shabby marketing district of the city and drove off. I hoped he made out all right with the dark-haired girl. I spotted a use-clothing store and headed for it.

Twenty minutes later I was back on the sidewalk, dressed in a pinkish-gray suit that had been cut a long time ago by a Latin tailor—maybe to settle a grudge. The shirt that went with it was an unsuccessful violet. The black string tie lent a dubious air of distinction. I'd swapped the railroader's cap for a tarnished beret. The man who had supplied the outfit was still asleep. I figured I'd done him a favor by taking it. I couldn't hope to pass for a fisherman—I wasn't the type. Maybe I'd get by as a coffee-house derelict.

I walked past fly-covered fish stalls, racks of faded garments, grimy vegetables in bins, enough paint-flaked wrought iron to cage a herd of brontosauri, and fetched up at a cab stand. I picked a fat driver with a wart.

"How much to the Delta National Laboratories?"

He rolled an eye toward me, shifted his toothpick.

"What ya wanna go out there for? Nothing out there."

"I'm a tourist," I said. "They told me before I left home not to miss it."

He grunted, reached back and opened the door. I got in. He flipped his flag down, started up with a clash of gears and pulled out without looking.

"How far is it?" I asked him.

"It ain't far. Mile, mile and a quarter."

"Pretty big place, I guess."

He didn't answer.

We went through a warehousing district, swung left along the waterfront, bumped over railroad tracks, and pulled up at a nine-foot cyclone fence with a locked gate.

"A buck ten," my driver said.

I looked out at the fence, a barren field, a distant group of low buildings. "What's this?"

"This is the place you ast for. That'll be a buck ten, mister."

I touched his mind, planted a couple of false impressions and withdrew. He blinked, then started up, drove around the field, pulled up at an open gate with a blue-uniformed guard. He looked back at me.

"You want I should drive in, sir?"

"I'll get out here."

He jumped out, opened my door, helped me out with a hand under my good elbow. "I'll get your change, sir," he said, reaching for his hip.

"Keep it."

"Thank YOU." He hesitated. "Maybe I oughta stick around. You know."

"I'll be all right."

"I hope so," he said. "A man like you—you and me—" he winked. "After all, we ain't both wearing berets fer nothing."

"True," I said. "Consider your tip doubled. Now drive away into the sunrise and forget you ever saw me."

He got into the car, beaming, and left. I turned and sized up the Delta Labs.

There was nothing fancy about the place; it consisted of low brick and steel buildings, mud, a fence and a guard who was looking at me.

I sauntered over. "I'm from Iowa City," I said. "Now, the rest of the group didn't come—said they'd rather rest one day. But I like to see it all. After all, I paid—"

"Just a minute," the guard said, holding up a palm. "You must be lost, fella. This here ain't no tourist attraction. You can't come in here."

"This *is* the cameo works?" I said anxiously.

He shook his head. "Too bad you let your cab go. It's an hour yet till the bus comes."

A dun-painted staff car came into view, slowed and swung wide to turn in. I fingered the driver's mind. The car swerved, braked to a halt. A portly man in the back seat leaned forward, frowning. I touched him. He relaxed. The driver leaned across and opened the door. I went around and got in. The guard was watching, open-mouthed.

I gave him a two-finger salute, and the car pulled through the gate.

"Stop in front of the electronics section," I said. The car pulled up. I got out, went up the steps and pushed through the double glass doors. The car sat for a moment, then moved slowly off. The passenger would be wondering why the driver had stopped—but the driver wouldn't remember.

I was inside the building now; that was a start. I didn't like robbery in broad daylight, but it was a lot easier this way. I wasn't equal to climbing any walls or breaking down any locked doors—not until I'd had a transfusion, a skin graft and about three months' vacation on a warm beach somewhere.

A man in a white smock emerged from a door. He started past me, spun—

"I'm here about the garbage," I said. "Damn fools *will* put the cans in with the edible. Are you the one called?"

"How's that?"

"I ain't got all the morning!" I shrilled. "You scientist fellers are all alike. Which way is the watchamacallit—equipment lab?"

"Right along there." He pointed. I didn't bother to thank him. It wouldn't have been in character.

A thin man with a brush mustache eyed me sharply as I pushed through the door. I looked at him, nodding absently. "Carry on with your work," I said. "The audit will be carried out in such a way as to disturb you as little as possible. Just show me your voucher file, if you please."

He sighed and waved toward a filing cabinet. I went to it and pulled a drawer open, glancing about the room. Full shelves were visible through an inner door.

Twenty minutes later I left the building, carrying a sheet metal carton containing the electronic components I needed to build a matter transmitter—except for the parts I'd have to fabricate myself from raw materials. The load was heavy—too heavy for me to carry very far. I parked it at the door and waited until a pick-up truck came along.

It pulled over. The driver climbed out and came up the walk to me. "Are you—uh . . . ?" He scratched his head.

"Right." I waved at my loot. "Put it in the back." He obliged. Together we rolled toward the gate. The guard held up his hand, came forward to check the truck. He looked surprised when he saw me.

"Just who are you, fella?" he said.

I didn't like tampering with people any more than I had to. It was a lot like stealing from a blind man: easy, but nothing to feel proud of. I gave him a light touch—just the suggestion that what I would say would be full of deep meaning.

"You know—the regular Wednesday shipment," I said darkly. "Keep it quiet. We're all relying on you."

"Sure thing," he said, stepping back. We gunned through the gate. I glanced back to see him looking after the truck, thinking about the Wednesday shipment on a Friday. He decided it was logical, nodded his head and forgot the whole thing.

V

I'd been riding high for a couple of hours, enjoying the success of the tricks I'd stolen from the Gool. Now I suddenly felt like something the student morticians had been practicing on. I guided my driver through a second-rate residential section, looking for an M.D. shingle on a front lawn.

The one I found didn't inspire much confidence—you could hardly see it for the weeds—but I didn't want to make a big splash. I had to have an assist from my driver to make it to the front door. He got me inside, parked my box beside me and went off to finish his rounds, under the impression that it had been a dull morning.

The doctor was a seedy, seventyish G.P. with a gross tremor of the hands that a good belt of Scotch would have helped. He looked at me as though I'd interrupted something that was either more fun or paid better than anything I was likely to come up with.

"I need my dressing changed, Doc," I said. "And maybe a shot to keep me going."

"I'm not a dope peddler," he snapped. "You've got the wrong place."

"Just a little medication—whatever's usual. It's a burn."

"Who told you to come here?"

I looked at him meaningfully. "The word gets around."

He glared at me, gnashed his plates, then gestured toward a black-varnished door. "Go right in there."

He gaped at my arm when the bandages were off. I took a quick glance and wished I hadn't.

"How did you do this?"

"Smoking in bed," I said. "Have you got ... something that ..."

He caught me before I hit the floor, got me into a chair.

Then he had that Scotch he'd been wanting, gave me a shot as an afterthought, and looked at me narrowly.

"I suppose you fell out of that same bed and broke your leg," he said.

"Right. Hell of a dangerous bed."

"I'll be right back." He turned to the door. "Don't go away. I'll just . . . get some gauze."

"Better stay here. Doc. There's plenty of gauze right on that table."

"See here—"

"Skip it, Doc. I know all about you."

"What?"

"I said *all* about you."

He set to work then; a guilty conscience is a tough argument to answer.

He plastered my arm with something and rewrapped it, then looked the leg over and made a couple of adjustments to the brace. He clucked over the stitches in my scalp, dabbed something on them that hurt like hell, then shoved an old-fashioned stickpin needle into my good arm.

"That's all I can do for you," he said. He handed me a bottle of pills. "Here are some tablets to take in an emergency. Now get out."

"Call me a cab, Doc."

I listened while he called, then lit a cigarette and watched through the curtains. The doc stood by, worrying his upper plate and eyeing me. So far I hadn't had to tinker with his mind, but it would be a good idea to check. I felt my way delicately.

—*oh God, why did I . . . long time ago . . . Mary ever knew . . . go to Arizona, start again, too old . . .* I saw the nest of fears that gnawed at him, the frustration and the faint flicker of hope but not quite dead. I touched his mind, wiped away scars . . .

"Here's your car," he said. He opened the door, looking at me. I started past him.

"Are you sure you're all right?" he said.

"Sure, Pop. And don't worry. Everything's going to be okay."

The driver put my boxes on the back seat. I got in beside him and told him to take me to a men's clothing store. He waited while I changed my hand-me-downs for an off-the-hook suit, new shirt and underwear and a replacement beret. It was the only kind of hat that didn't hurt. My issue shoes were still good, but I traded them in on a new pair, added a light raincoat, and threw in a sturdy suitcase for good measure. The clerk said something about money and I dropped an idea into his mind, paused long enough to add a memory of a fabulous night with a redhead. He hardly noticed me leaving.

I tried not to feel like a shoplifter. After all, it's not every day a man gets a chance to swap drygoods for dreams.

In the cab, I transferred my belongings to the new suitcase, then told the driver to pull up at an anonymous-looking hotel. A four-star admiral with frayed cuffs helped me inside with my luggage. The hackie headed for the bay to get rid of the box under the impression I was a heavy tipper.

I had a meal in my room, a hot bath, and treated myself to a three hour nap. I woke up feeling as though those student embalmers might graduate after all.

I thumbed through the phone book and dialed a number.

"I want a Cadillac or Lincoln," I said. "A new one—not the one you rent for funerals—and a driver who won't mind missing a couple nights' sleep. And put a bed pillow and a blanket in the car."

I went down to the coffee room then for a light meal. I had just finished a cigarette when the car arrived—a dark blue heavy-weight with a high polish and a low silhouette.

"We're going to Denver," I told the driver. "We'll make one stop tomorrow—I have a little shopping to do. I figure about twenty hours. Take a break every hundred miles, and hold it under seventy."

He nodded. I got in the back and sank down in the smell of expensive upholstery.

"I'll cross town and pick up U.S. 84 at—"

"I leave the details to you," I said. He pulled out into the traffic and I got the pillow settled under me and closed my eyes. I'd need all the rest I could get on this trip. I'd heard that compared with the Denver Records Center, Fort Knox was a cinch. I'd find out for sure when I got there.

The plan I had in mind wasn't the best I could have concocted under more leisurely circumstances. But with every cop in the country under orders to shoot me on sight, I had to move fast. My scheme had the virtue of unlikeliness. Once

I was safe in the Central Vault—supposed to be the only H-bomb-proof structure ever built—I'd put through a phone call to the outside, telling them to watch a certain spot; say the big desk in the President's office. Then I'd assemble my matter transmitter and drop some little item right in front of the assembled big shots. They'd have to admit I had something. And this time they'd have to start considering the possibility that I wasn't working for the enemy.

It had been a smooth trip, and I'd caught up on my sleep. Now it was five A.M. and we were into the foothills, half an hour out of Denver. I ran over my lines, planning the trickiest part of the job ahead—the initial approach. I'd listened to a couple of news broadcasts. The FBI was still promising an arrest within hours. I learned that I was lying up, or maybe dead, in the vicinity of Key West, and that the situation was under control. That was fine with me. Nobody would expect me to pop up in Denver, still operating under my own power—and wearing a new suit at that.

The Records Center was north of the city, dug into mountain-side. I steered my chauffeur around the downtown section, out a street lined with dark hamburger joints and unlit gas stations to where a side road branched off. We pulled up. From here on, things might get dangerous—if I was wrong about how easy it was all going to be. I brushed across the driver's mind. He set the brake and got out.

"Don't know how I came to run out of gas, Mr. Brown," he said apologetically. "We just passed a station but it was closed. I guess I'll just have to hike back into town. I sure am sorry; I never did that before."

I told him it was okay, watched as he strode off into the predawn gloom, then got into the front seat and started up. The gate of the Reservation surrounding the Record Center was only a mile away now. I drove slowly, feeling ahead for opposition. There didn't seem to be any. Things were quiet as a poker player with a pat hand. My timing was good.

I stopped in front of the gate, under a floodlight and the watchful eye of an M.P. with a shiny black tommygun held at the ready. He didn't seem surprised to see me. I rolled down the window as he came over to the car.

"I have an appointment inside, Corporal," I said. I touched his mind. "The password is 'hotpoint'."

He nodded, stepped back, and motioned me in. I hesitated. This was almost too easy. I reached out again ...

"... *middle of the night ... password ... nice car ... I wish ...*"

I pulled through the gate and headed for the big parking lot, picking a spot in front of a ramp that led down to a tall steel door. There was no one in sight. I got out, dragging my suitcase. It was heavier now, with the wire and magnets I'd added. I crossed the drive, went up to the doors. The silence was eerie.

I swept the area, searching for minds, found nothing. The shielding, I decided, blanked out everything.

There was a personnel door set in the big panel, with a massive combination lock. I leaned my head against the door and felt for the mechanism, turning the dial right, left, right ...

The lock opened. I stepped inside, alert.

Silence, darkness. I reached out, sensed walls, slabs of steel, concrete, intricate mechanisms, tunnels deep in the ground ...

But no personnel. That was surprising—but I wouldn't waste time questioning my good luck. I followed a corridor, opened another door, massive as a vault, passed more halls, more doors. My footsteps made muffled echoes. I passed a final door and came into the heart of the Records Center.

There were lights in the chamber around the grim, featureless periphery of the Central Vault. I set the valise on the floor, sat on it and lit a cigarette. So far, so good. The Records Center, I saw, had been overrated. Even without my special knowledge, a clever locksmith could have come this far—or almost. But the Big Vault was another matter. The great integrating lock that secured it would yield only to a complex command from the computer set in the wall opposite the vault door. I smoked my cigarette and, with eyes closed, studied the vault.

I finished the cigarette, stepped on it, went to the console, began pressing keys, tapping out the necessary formulations. Half an hour later I finished. I turned and saw the valve cycle open, showing a bright-lit tunnel within.

I dragged my bag inside, threw the lever that closed the entry behind me. A green light went on. I walked along the narrow passage, lined with gray metal shelves stacked with gray steel tape drums, descended steps, came into a larger chamber fitted out with bunks, a tiny galley, toilet facilities, shelves stocked with food. There was a radio, a telephone and a second telephone, bright red. That would be the hot-line to Washington. This was the sanctum sanctorum, where the last suvivors could wait out the final holocaust—indefinitely.

I opened the door of a steel cabinet. Radiation suits, tools, instruments. Another held bedding. I found a tape-player, tapes—even a shelf of books. I found a first aid kit and gratefully gave myself a hypo-spray jolt of neurite. My pains receded.

I went on to the next room; there were wash tubs, a garbage disposal unit, a drier. There was everything here I needed to keep me alive and even comfortable until I could convince someone up above that I shouldn't be shot on sight.

A heavy door barred the way to the room beyond. I turned a wheel, swung the door back, saw more walls lined with filing cabinets, a blank facade of gray steel; and in the center of the room, alone on a squat table—a yellow plastic case that any Sunday Supplement reader would have recognized.

It was a Master Tape, the Utter Top Secret Programming document that would direct the terrestrial defense in case of a Gool invasion.

It was almost shocking to see it lying there—unprotected except for the flimsy case. The information it contained in micro-micro dot form could put my world in the palm of the enemy's hand.

The room with the tool kit would be the best place to work, I decided. I brought the suitcase containing the electronic gear back from the outer door where I'd left it, opened it and arranged its contents on the table. According to the Gool these simple components were all I needed. The trick was in knowing how to put them together.

There was work ahead of me now. There were the coils to wind, the intricate antenna arrays to lay out; but before I started, I'd take time to call Kayle—or whoever I could get at the other end of the hot-line. They'd be a little startled when I turned up at the heart of the defenses they were trying to shield.

I picked up the receiver and a voice spoke:

"Well, Granthan. So you finally made it."

VI

"Here are your instructions," Kayle was saying. "Open the vault door. Come out—stripped—and go to the center of the parking lot. Stand there with your hands over your head. A single helicopter manned by a volunteer will approach and drop a gas canister. It won't be lethal, I promise you that. Once you're unconscious, I'll personally see to it that you're transported to the Institute in safety. Every effort will then be made to overcome the Gool conditioning. If we're successful, you'll be awakened. If not . . ."

He let the sentence hang. It didn't need to be finished. I understood what he meant.

I was listening. I was still not too worried. Here I was safe against anything until the food ran out—and that wouldn't be for months.

"You're bluffing, Kayle," I said. "You're trying to put the best face on something that you can't control. If you'd—"

"You were careless at Delta Labs, Granthan. There were too many people with odd blanks in their memories and too many unusual occurrences, all on the same day. You tipped your hand. Once we knew what we were up against, it was simply a matter of following you at an adequate distance. We have certain shielding materials, as you know. We tried them all. There's a new one that's quite effective.

"But as I was saying, we've kept you under constant surveillance. When we saw which way you were heading, we just stayed out of sight and let you trap yourself."

"You're lying. Why would you want me here?"

"That's very simple," Kayle said harshly. "It's the finest trap ever built by man—and you're safely in it."

"Safely is right. I have everything I need here. And that brings me to my reason for being here—in case you're curious. I'm going to build a matter transmitter. And to prove my good faith, I'll transmit the Master Tape to you. I'll show you that I could have stolen the damned thing if I'd wanted to."

"Indeed? Tell me, Granthan, do you really think we'd be fools enough to leave the Master Tape behind when we evacuated the area?"

"I don't know about that—but it's here."

"Sorry," Kayle said. "You're deluding yourself." His voice

was suddenly softer, some of the triumph gone from it. "Don't bother struggling, Granthan. The finest brains in the country have combined to place you where you are. You haven't a chance, except to do as I say. Make it easy on yourself. I have no wish to extend your ordeal."

"You can't touch me, Kayle. This vault is proof against a hell-bomb, and it's stocked for a siege . . ."

"That's right," Kayle said. His voice sounded tired. "It's proof against a hell-bomb. But what if the hell-bomb's in the vault with you?"

I felt like a demolition man, working to defuse a blockbuster, who's suddenly heard a loud click! from the detonator. I dropped the phone, stared around the room. I saw nothing that could be a bomb. I ran to the next room, the one beyond. Nothing. I went back to the phone, grabbed it up.

"You ought to know better than to bluff now, Kayle!" I yelled. "I wouldn't leave this post now for a half a dozen hypothetical hell-bombs!"

"In the center room," Kayle said. "Lift the cover over the floor drain. You'll find it there. You know what they look like. Don't tamper with its mechansim; it's internally trapped. You'll have to take my word for it we didn't bother installing a dummy."

I dropped the phone, hurried to the spot Kayle had described. The bomb casing was there—a dully gray ovoid, with a lifting eye set in the top. It didn't look dangerous. It just lay quietly, waiting . . .

Back at the telephone, I had trouble finding my voice. "How long?" I croaked.

"It was triggered when you entered the vault," Kayle said. "There's a time mechanism. It's irreversible; you can't force anyone to cancel it. And it's no use your hiding in the outer passages.

"The whole center will be destroyed in the blast. Even it can't stand against a bomb buried in its heart. But we'll gladly sacrifice the center to eliminate you."

"How long!"

"I suggest you come out quickly, so that a crew can enter the vault to disarm the bomb."

"How long!"

"When you're ready to emerge, call me." The line went dead.

I put the phone back in its cradle carefully, like a rare and valuable egg.

I tried to think. I'd been charging full speed ahead ever since I had decided on my scheme of action while I was still riding the surf off the Florida coast, and I'd stuck to it. Now it had hatched in my face—and the thing that had crawled out wasn't the downy little chick of success. It had teeth and claws and was eyeing me like a basilisk . . .

But I still had unplayed aces—if there was time.

I had meant to use the matter transmitter to stage a dramatic proof that I wasn't the tool of the enemy. The demonstration would be more dramatic than I'd planned. The bomb would fit the machine as easily as the tape. The wheels would be surprised when their firecracker went off—right on schedule—in the middle of the Mojave Desert.

I set to work, my heart pounding. If I could bring this off—if I had time—if the transmitter worked as advertised . . .

The stolen knowledge flowed smoothly, effortlessly. It was as though I had been assembling matter transmitters for years, knew every step by heart. First the moebius windings; yard after yard of heavy copper around a core of carbon; then the power supply, the first and second stage amplimitters . . .

How long? In the sump in the next room, the bomb lay quietly ticking. How long . . . ?

The main assembly was ready now. I laid out cables, tying my apparatus in to the atomic power-source buried under the vault. The demand, for one short instant, would tax even those mighty engines. I fixed hooks at the proper points in the room, wove soft aluminum wire in the correct pattern. I was almost finished now. How long? I made the last connections, cleared away the litter. The matter transmitter stood on the table, complete. At any instant, the bomb would reduce it—and the secret of its construction—to incandescent gas—unless I transmitted the bomb out of range first. I turned toward the laundry room—and the telephone rang. I hesitated, then crossed the room and snatched it up.

"Listen to me," Kayle said grimly. "Give me straight, fast answers. You said the Master Tape was there, in the vault with you. Now tell me: What does it look like?"

"What?"

"The . . . ah . . . dummy tape. What is its appearance?"

"It's a roughly square plastic container, bright yellow, about a foot thick. What about it?"

Kayle's voice sounded strained. "I've made inquiries. No one here seems to know the exact present location of the Master Tape. Each department says that they were under the impression that another handled the matter. I'm unable to learn who, precisely, removed the Tape from the vault. Now you say there is a yellow plastic container—"

"I know what the Master Tape looks like," I said. "This is either it or a hell of a good copy."

"Granthan," Kayle said. There was a note of desperation in his voice now. "There have been some blunders made. I knew you were under the influence of the Gool. It didn't occur to me that I might be too. Why did I make it possible for you to successfully penetrate to the Central Vault? There were a hundred simpler ways in which I could have dealt with the problem. We're in trouble, Granthan, serious trouble. The tape you have there is genuine. We've all played into the enemy's hands."

"You're wasting valuable time, Kayle," I snapped. "When does the bomb go up?"

"Granthan, there's little time left. Bring the Master Tape and leave the vault—"

"No dice, Kayle. I'm staying until I finish the transmitter, then—"

"Granthan! If there's anything to your mad idea of such a machine, destroy it! Quickly! Don't you see the Gool would only have given you the secret in order to enable you to steal the tape!"

I cut him off. In the sudden silence, I heard a distant sound—or had I sensed a thought? I strained outward . . .

"*. . . volunteered . . . damn fool . . . thing on my head is heavy . . . better work . . .*

"*. . . now . . . okay . . . valve, gas . . . kills in a split second . . . then get out . . .*"

I stabbed out, pushed through the obscuring veil of masonry, sensed a man in the computer room, dressed in gray coveralls, a grotesque shield over his head and shoulders. He reached for a red-painted valve—

I struck at his mind, felt him stagger back, fall. I fumbled in his brain, stimulated the sleep center. He sank deep into unconsciousness. I leaned against the table, weak with the reaction. Kayle had almost tricked me that time.

I reached out again, swept the area with desperate urgency. Far away, I sensed the hazy clutter of many minds, out of range. There was nothing more. The poisonous gas had been the only threat—except the bomb itself. But I had to move fast, before my time ran out, to transmit the bomb to a desert area . . .

I paused, stood frozen in mid-move. A desert. What desert?

The transmitter operated in accordance with as rigid a set of laws as did the planets swinging in their orbits; strange laws, but laws of nature none the less. No receiver was required. The destination of the mass under transmission was determined by the operator, holding in his mind the five-dimensional conceptualization of the target, guiding the action of the machine.

And I had no target.

I could no more direct the bomb to a desert without a five-fold grasp of its multi-ordinal spatial, temporal, and entropic coordinates than I could fire a rifle at a target in the dark.

I was like a man with a grenade in his hand, pin pulled—and locked in a cell.

I swept the exocosm again, desperately. And caught a thin, live line. I traced it; it cut through the mountain, dived deep underground, crossed the boundless plain . . .

Never branching, it bored on, turning upward now—and ending.

I rested, gathering strength, then probed, straining . . .

There was a room, men. I recognized Kayle, gray-faced, haggard. A tall man in braided blue stood near him. Others stood silently by, tension on every face. Maps covered the wall behind them.

I was looking into the War Room at the Pentagon in Washington. The line I had traced was the telephonic hot-line, the top-security link between the Record Center and the command level. It was a heavy cable, well protected and always open. It would free me from the trap. With Gool-tutored skill I scanned the room, memorized its co-ordinates. Then I withdrew.

Like a swimmer coming up from a long dive, I fought my way back to the level of immediate awareness. I sagged into a chair, blinking at the drab walls, the complexity of the transmitter. I must move fast now, place the bomb in the transmitter's field, direct it at the target. With an effort I got to my feet, went to the sump, lifted the cover. I grasped the lifting eye, strained—and the bomb came up, out onto the floor. I dragged it to the transmitter . . .

And only then realized what I'd been about to do.

My target.

The War Room—the nerve-center of Earth's defenses. And I had been ready to dump the hell-bomb there. In my frenzy to be rid of it I would have played into the hands of the Gool.

VII

I went to the phone.

"Kayle! I guess you've got a recorder on the line. I'll give you the details of the transmitter circuits. It's complicated, but fifteen minutes ought to—"

"No time," Kayle cut in. "I'm sorry about everything, Granthan. If you've finished the machine, it's a tragedy for humanity—if it works. I can only ask you to try—when the Gool command comes—not to give them what they want. I'll tell you, now, Granthan. The bomb blows in—" there was a pause—"two minutes and twenty-one seconds. Try to hold them off. If you can stand against them for that long at least—"

I slammed the phone down, cold sweat popping out across my face. Two minutes . . . too late for anything. The men in the War Room would never know how close I had come to beating the Gool—and them.

But I could still save the Master Tape. I wrestled the yellow plastic case that housed the tape onto the table, into the machine.

And the world vanished in a blaze of darkness, a clamor of silence.

NOW, MASTERS! NOW! LINK UP! LINE UP!

Like a bad dream coming back in daylight, I felt the obscene presence of massed Gool minds, attenuated by distance but terrible in their power, probing, thrusting. I fought back, struggling against paralysis, trying to gather my strength, use what I had learned . . .

SEE, MASTERS, HOW IT WOULD ELUDE US. BLANK IT OFF, TOGETHER NOW . . .

The paths closed before me. My mind writhed, twisted, darted here and there—and met only the impenetrable shield of the Gool defenses.

IT TIRES, MASTERS. WORK SWIFTLY NOW. LET US IMPRESS ON THE SUBJECT THE CO-ORDINATES OF THE BRAIN PIT. The conceptualization drifted into my mind. HERE, MAN. TRANSMIT THE TAPE HERE!

As from a distance, the monitor personality fraction watched the struggle. Kayle had been right. The Gool had waited—and now their moment had come. Even my last impulse of defiance—to place the tape in the machine—had been at the Gool command. They had looked into my mind. They understand psychology as no human analyst ever could; and they had led me in the most effective way possible, by letting me believe I was the master. They had made use of my human ingenuity to carry out their wishes—and Kayle had made it easy for them by evacuating a twenty-mile radius around me, leaving the field clear for the Gool.

HERE— The Gool voice rang like a bell in my mind: TRANSMIT THE TAPE HERE!

Even as I fought against the impulse to comply, I felt my arm twitch toward the machine.

THROW THE SWITCH! the voice thundered.

I struggled, willed my arm to stay at my side. Only a minute longer, I thought. Only a minute more, and the bomb would save me . . .

LINK UP, MASTERS!

I WILL NOT LINK. YOU PLOT TO FEED AT MY EXPENSE.

NO! BY THE MOTHER WORM, I PLEDGE MY GROOVE AT THE EATING TROUGH. FOR US THE MAN WILL GUT THE GREAT VAULT OF HIS NEST WORLD!

ALREADY YOU BLOAT AT OUR EXPENSE!

FOOL!! WOULD YOU BICKER NOW? LINK UP!

The Gool raged—and I grasped for an elusive thought and held it. The bomb, only a few feet away. The waiting machine. And the Gool had given me the co-ordinates of their cavern . . .

With infinite sluggishness, I moved.

LINK UP, MASTERS: THEN ALL WILL FEED . . .

IT IS A TRICK. I WILL NOT LINK.

I found the bomb, fumbled for a grip.

DISASTER, MASTERS! NOW IS THE PRIZE LOST TO US, UNLESS YOU JOIN WITH ME!

My breath choked off in my throat; a hideous pain coiled outward from my chest. But it was unimportant. Only the bomb mattered. I tottered, groping. There was the table; the transmitter . . .

I lifted the bomb, felt the half-healed skin of my burned arm crackle as I strained . . .

I thrust the case containing the Master Tape out of the field of the transmitter, then pushed, half-rolled the bomb into position. I groped for the switch, found it. I tried to draw breath, felt only a surge of agony. Blackness was closing in . . .

The co-ordinates . . .

From the whirling fog of pain and darkness, I brought the target concept of the Gool cavern into view, clarified it, held it . . .

MASTERS! HOLD THE MAN! DISASTER!

Then I felt the Gool, their suspicions yielding to the panic in the mind of the Prime Overlord, link their power against me. I stood paralyzed, felt my identity dissolving like water pouring from a smashed pot. I tried to remember—but it was too faint, too far away.

Then from somewhere a voice seemed to cut in, the calm voice of an emergency reserve personality fraction. "You are under attack. Activate the reserve plan. Level Five. Use Level Five. Act now. Use Level Five . . ."

Through the miasma of Gool pressure, I felt the hairs stiffen on the back of my neck. All around me the Gool voices raged, a swelling symphony of discord. But they were nothing. Level Five . . .

There was no turning back. The compulsions were there, acting even as I drew in a breath to howl my terror—

Level Five. Down past the shapes of dreams, the intense faces of hallucination; Level Three; Level Four and the silent ranked memories . . . And deeper still—

Into a region of looming gibbering horror, of shadowy moving shapes of evil, of dreaded presences that lurked at the edge of vision . . .

Down amid the clamor of voiceless fears, the mounting hungers, the reaching claws of all that man had feared since the first tailless primate screamed out his terror in a tree-top: the fear of falling, the fear of heights.

Down to Level Five. Nightmare level.

I groped outward, found the plane of contact—and hurled the weight of man's ancient fears at the waiting Gool—and in their black confining caves deep in the rock of a far world, they felt the roaring tide of fear—fear of the dark, and of living burial. The horrors in man's secret mind confronted the horrors of the Gool Brain Pit. And I felt them break, retreat in blind panic from me—

All but one. The Prime Overlord reeled back with the rest, but his was a mind of terrible power. I sensed for a moment his bloated immense form, the seething gnawing hungers, insatiable, never to be appeased. Then he rallied—but he was alone now.

LINK UP, MASTERS! THE PRIZE IS LOST. KILL THE MAN! KILL THE MAN!

I felt a knife at my heart. It fluttered—and stopped. And in that instant, I broke past his control, threw the switch. There was the sharp crack of imploding air. Then I was floating down, ever down, and all sensation was far away.

MASTERS! KILL TH

The pain cut off in an instant of profound silence and utter dark.

Then sound roared in my ears, and I felt the harsh grate of the floor against my face as I fell, and then I knew nothing more.

"I hope," General Titus was saying, "that you'll accept the decoration now, Mr. Granthan. It will be the first time in history that a civilian has been accorded this honor—and you deserve it."

I was lying in a clean white bed, propped up by big soft pillows, with a couple of good-looking nurses hovering a few feet away. I was in a mood to tolerate even Titus.

"Thanks, General," I said. "I suggest you give the medal to the volunteer who came in to gas me. He knew what he was going up against; I didn't."

"It's over, now, Granthan," Kayle said. He attempted to beam, settled for a frosty smile. "You surely understand—"

"Understanding," I said. "That's all we need to turn this

planet—and a lot of other ones—into the kind of worlds the human mind needs to expand into."

"You're tired, Granthan," Kayle said. "You get some rest. In a few weeks you'll be back on the job, as good as new."

"That's where the key is," I said. "In our minds; there's so much there, and we haven't even scratched the surface. To the mind nothing is impossible. Matter is an illusion, space and time are just convenient fictions—"

"I'll leave the medal here, Mr. Granthan. When you feel equal to it, we'll make the official presentation. Television . . ."

He faded off as I closed my eyes and thought about things that had been clamoring for attention ever since I'd met the Gool, but hadn't had time to explore. My arm . . .

I felt my way along it—from inside—tracing the area of damage, watching as the bodily defenses worked away, toiling to renew, replace. It was a slow, mindless process. But if I helped a little . . .

It was easy. The pattern was there. I felt the tissues renew themselves, the skin regenerate.

The bone was more difficult. I searched out the necessary minerals, diverted blood; the broken ends knit . . .

The nurse was bending over me, a bowl of soup in her hand.

"You've been asleep for a long time, sir," she said, smiling. "How about some nice chicken broth now?"

I ate the soup and asked for more. A doctor came and peeled back my bandages, did a double-take, and rushed away. I looked. The skin was new and pink, like a baby's—but it was all there. I flexed my right leg; there was no twinge of pain.

I listened for a while as the doctors gabbled, clucked, probed and made pronouncements. Then I closed my eyes again. I thought about the matter transmitter. The government was sitting on it, of course. A military secret of the greatest importance, Titus called it. Maybe someday the public would hear about it; in the meantime—

"How about letting me out of here?" I said suddenly. A pop-eyed doctor with a fringe of gray hair blinked at me, went back to fingering my arm. Kayle hove into view.

"I want out," I said. "I'm recovered, right? So now just give me my clothes."

"Now, now, just relax, Granthan. You know it's not as simple as that. There are a lot of matters we must go over."

"The war's over," I said. "You admitted that. I want out."

"Sorry." Kayle shook his head. "That's out of the question."

"Doc," I said. "Am I well?"

"Yes," he said. "Amazing case. You're as fit as you'll ever be; I've never—"

"I'm afraid you'll have to resign yourself to being here for a while longer, Granthan," Kayle said. "After all, we can't—"

"Can't let the secret of matter transmission run around loose, hey? So until you figure out the angles, I'm a prisoner, right?"

"I'd hardly call it that, Granthan. Still . . ."

I closed my eyes. The matter transmitter—a strange device. A field, not distorting space, but accentuating certain characteristics of a matter field in space-time, subtly shifting relationships . . .

Just as the mind could compare unrelated data, draw from them new concepts, new parallels . . .

The circuits of the matter transmitter . . . and the patterns of the mind . . .

The exocosm and the endocosm, like the skin and the orange, everywhere in contact . . .

Somewhere there was a beach of white sand, and dunes with graceful sea-oats that leaned in a gentle wind. There was blue water to the far horizon, and a blue sky, and nowhere were there any generals with medals and television cameras, or flint-eyed bureaucrats with long schemes . . .

And with this gentle folding . . . thus . . .

And a pressure here . . . so . . .

I opened my eyes, raised myself on one elbow—and saw the sea. The sun was hot on my body, but not too hot, and the sand was white as sugar. Far away, a seagull tilted, circling.

A wave rolled in, washed my foot in cool water.

I lay on my back, and looked up at white clouds in a blue sky, and smiled—then laughed aloud.

Distantly the seagull's cry echoed my laughter.

THE WALLS

Harry Trimble looked pleased when he stepped into the apartment. The lift door had hardly clacked shut behind him on the peering commuter faces in the car before he had slipped his arm behind Flora's back, bumped his face against her cheek and chuckled, "Well, what would you say to a little surprise? Something you've waited a long time for?"

Flora looked up from the dial-a-ration panel. "A surprise, Harry?"

"I know how you feel about the apartment, Flora. Well, from now on, you won't be seeing so much of it—"

"Harry!"

He winced at her clutch on his arm. Her face was pale under the day-glare strip. "We're not—moving to the country . . . ?"

Harry pried his arm free. "The country? What the devil are you talking about?" He was frowning now, the pleased look gone. "You should use the lamps more," he said. "You look sick." He glanced around the apartment, the four perfectly flat rectangular walls, the glassy surface of the variglow ceiling, the floor with its pattern of sink-away panels. His eye fell on the four foot square of the TV screen.

"I'm having that thing taken out tomorrow," he said. The pleased look was coming back. He cocked an eye at Flora. "And I'm having a Full-wall installed!"

Flora glanced at the blank screen. "A Full-wall, Harry?"

"Yep!" Harry smacked a fist into a palm, taking a turn up and down the room. "We'll be the first in our cell block to have a Full-wall!"

"Why—that will be nice, Harry . . ."

"Nice?" Harry punched the screen control, then deployed the two chairs with tray racks ready to receive the evening meal.

Behind him, figures jiggled on the screen. "It's a darn sight

63

more than nice," he said, raising his voice over the shrill and thump of the music. "It's expensive, for one thing. Who else do you know that can afford—"

"But—"

"But nothing! Imagine it, Flora! It'll be like having a . . . a balcony seat, looking out on other people's lives."

"But we have so little space now; won't it take up—"

"Of course not! How do you managed to stay so ignorant of technical progress? It's only an eighth of an inch thick. Think of it: that thick—" Harry indicated an eighth of an inch with his fingers— "and better color and detail than you've ever seen. It's all done with what they call an edge-excitation effect."

"Harry, the old screen is good enough. Couldn't we use the money for a trip—"

"How do you know if it's good enough? You never have it on. I have to turn it on myself when I get home."

Flora brought the trays and they ate silently, watching the screen. After dinner, Flora disposed of the trays, retracted the table and chairs, and extended the beds. They lay in the dark, not talking.

"It's a whole new system," Harry said suddenly. "The Full-wall people have their own programming scheme; they plan your whole day, wake you up at the right time with some lively music, give you breakfast menus to dial, then follow up with a good sitcom to get you into the day; then there's nap music, with subliminal hypnotics if you have trouble sleeping; then—"

"Harry—can I turn it off if I want to?"

"Turn it off?" Harry sounded puzzled. "The idea is to leave it on. That's why I'm having it installed for you, you know—so you can use it!"

"But sometimes I like to just think—"

"Think! Brood, you mean." He heaved a sigh. "Look, Flora, I know the place isn't fancy. Sure, you get a little tired of being here all the time; but there are plenty of people worse off—and now, with Full-wall, you'll get a feeling of more space—"

"Harry—" Flora spoke rapidly —"I wish we could go away. I mean leave the city, and get a little place where we can be alone, even if it means working hard, and where I can have a garden and maybe keep chickens and you could chop firewood—"

"Good God!" Harry roared, cutting her off. Then: "These fantasies of yours," he said quietly. "You have to learn to live in the real world, Flora. Live in the woods? Wet leaves, wet bark, bugs, mould; talk about depressing . . ."

There was a long silence.

"I know; you're right, Harry," Flora said. "I'll enjoy the Full-wall. It was very sweet of you to think of getting it for me."

"Sure," Harry said. "It'll be better. You'll see . . ."

The Full-wall was different, Flora agreed as soon as the service men had made the last adjustments and flipped it on. There was vivid color, fine detail, and a remarkable sense of depth. The shows were about the same—fast-paced, bursting with variety and energy. It was exciting at first, having full-sized people talking, eating, fighting, taking baths, making love, right in the room with you. If you sat across the room and half-closed your eyes, you could almost imagine you were watching real people. Of course, real people wouldn't carry on like that. But then, it was hard to say what real people might do. Flora had always thought Doll Starr wore padded brassieres, but when she stripped on Full-wall—there wasn't any fakery about it.

Harry was pleased, too, when he arrived home to find the wall on. He and Flora would dial dinner with one eye on the screen, then slip into bed and view until the Bull-Doze pills they'd started taking took effect. Perhaps things *were* better, Flora thought hopefully. More like they used to be.

But after a month or two, the Full-wall began to pall. The same faces, the same pratfalls, the same happy quiz masters, the puzzled prize-winners, the delinquent youths and fumbling dads, the bosoms—all the same.

On the sixty-third day, Flora switched the Full-wall off. The light and sound died, leaving a faint, dwindling glow. She eyed the glassy wall uneasily, as one might view the coffin of an acquaintance.

It was quiet in the apartment. Flora fussed with the dial-a-ration, averting her eyes from the dead screen. She turned to deploy the solitaire table and started violently. The screen, the residual glow having faded now, was a perfect mirror. She went close to it, touched the hard surface with a finger. It was almost invisible. She studied her reflected face; the large dark eyes with shadows under them, the cheekline, a trifle too hollow now to be really chic, the hair drawn back in an uninspired bun. Behind her, the doubled room, unadorned now that all the furnishings were retracted into the floor except for the pictures on the wall: photographs of the children away at school, a sunny scene of green pastureland, a painting of rolling waves at sea.

She stepped back, considering the effect.

The floor and walls seemed to continue without interruption, except for a hardly noticeable line. It was as though the apartment were twice as large. If only it weren't so empty . . .

Flora deployed the table and chairs, dialled a lunch, and sat, eating, watching her double. No wonder Harry seemed indifferent lately, she thought, noting the rounded shoulders, the insignificant bust, the slack posture. She would have to do something in the way of self-improvement.

Half an hour of the silent companionship of her image was enough. Flora snapped the screen back on, watched almost with relief as a grinning cowboy in velvet chaps made strumming motions while an intricately-fingered guitar melody blared from the sound track.

Thereafter, she turned the screen off every day, at first only for an hour, later for longer and longer periods. Once, she found herself chatting gaily to her reflection, and hastily fell silent. It wasn't as though she were becoming neurotic, she assured herself; it was just the feeling of roominess that made her like the mirror screen. And she was always careful to have it on when Harry arrived home.

It was about six months after the Full-wall had been installed that Harry emerged one day from the lift smiling in a way that reminded Flora of that earlier evening. He dropped his brief-case into his floor locker, looked around the apartment, humming to himself.

"What is it, Harry?" Flora asked.

Harry glanced at her. "It's not a log cabin in the woods," he said. "But maybe you'll like it anyway . . ."

"What . . . is it, dear . . .?"

"Don't sound so dubious." He broke into a broad smile. "I'm getting you another Full-wall."

Flora looked puzzled. "But this one is working perfectly, Harry."

"Of course it is," he snapped. "I mean you're getting

another wall; you'll have two. What about that? Two Full-walls—and nobody else in the cell-block has one yet. The only question is—" he rubbed his hands together, striding up and down the room, eyeing the walls— "which wall is it to be? You can have it adjacent, or opposite. I went over the whole thing with the Full-wall people today. By God, they're doing a magnificent job of programming. You see, the two walls will be synchronized. You're getting the same show on both—you're seeing it from two angles, just as though you were right there in the middle of it. Their whole program has been built on that principle."

"Harry, I'm not sure I want another wall—"

"Oh, nonsense. What is this, some kind of self-denial urge? Why not have the best—if you can afford it. And by God, I can afford it. I'm hitting my stride—"

"Harry, could I go with you some day—tomorrow? I'd like to see where you work, meet your friends—"

"Flora, are you out of your mind? You've seen the commuter car; you know how crowded it is. And what would you do when you got there? Just stand around all day, blocking the aisle? Why don't you appreciate the luxury of having your own place, a little privacy, and now two Full-walls—"

"Then could I go somewhere else? I could take a later car. I want to get out in the open air, Harry. I ... haven't seen the sky for ... years, it seems."

"But ..." Harry groped for words, staring at Flora. "Why would you want to go up on the roof?"

"Not the roof; I want to get out of the city—just for a little while. I'll be back home in time to dial your dinner ..."

"Do you mean to tell me you want to spend all that money to wedge yourself in a verticar and then transfer to a cross-town and travel maybe seventy miles, packed in like a sardine, standing up all the way, just so you can get out and stand in a wasteland and look back at the walls? And then get back in another car—if you're lucky—and come back again?"

"No—I don't know—I just want to get out, Harry. The roof. Could I go to the roof?"

Harry came over to pat Flora awkwardly on the arm. "Now, take it easy, Flora. You're a little tired and stale; I know. I get the same way sometimes. But don't get the idea that you're missing anything by not having to get into that rat-race. Heaven knows *I* wish I could stay home. And this new wall is going to make things different. You'll see . . ."

The new Full-wall was installed adjacent to the first, with a joint so beautifully fitted that only the finest line marked the junction. As soon as she was alone with it, Flora switched it off. Now two reflections stared back at her from behind what appeared to be two intersecting planes of clear glass. She waved an arm. The two slave figures aped her. She walked toward the mirrored corner. They advanced. She stepped back; they retreated.

She went to the far corner of the room and studied the effect. It wasn't as nice as before. Instead of a simple room, neatly bounded on all four sides by solid walls, she seemed now to occupy a stage set off by windows through which other, similar, stages were visible, endlessly repeated. The old feeling of intimate companionship with her reflected self was gone; the two mirror-women were strangers, silently watching her. Defiantly, she stuck out her tongue. The two reflections grimaced menacingly. With a small cry, Flora ran to the switch, turned the screens on.

They were seldom off after that. Sometimes, when the hammering of hooves became too wearing, or the shouting of comics too strident, she would blank them out, and sit, back to the mirror walls, sipping a cup of hot coflet, and waiting—but they were always on when Harry arrived, sometimes glum, sometimes brisk and satisfied. He would settle himself in his chair, waiting patiently enough for dinner, watching the screens.

"They're all right," he would declare, nodding. "Look at that, Flora. Look at the way that fellow whipped right across there. By golly, you've got to hand it to the Full-wall people."

"Harry—where do they make the shows? The ones that show the beautiful scenery, and trees and rolling hills, and mountains?"

Harry was chewing. "Don't know," he said. "On location, I suppose."

"Then there really are places like that? I mean, they aren't just making it up?"

Harry stared at her, mouth full and half open. He grunted and resumed chewing. He swallowed. "I suppose that's another of your cracks."

"I don't understand, Harry," Flora said. He took another bite, glanced sideways at her puzzled expression.

"Of course they aren't making it up. How the devil could they make up a mountain?"

"I'd like to see those places."

"Here we go again," Harry said. "I was hoping I could enjoy a nice meal and then view awhile, but I guess you're not going to allow that."

"Of course, Harry. I just said—"

"I know what you said. Well, look at them then." He waved his hand at the screen. "There it is; the whole world. You can sit right here and view it all—"

"But I want to do more than just view it. I want to live it. I want to be in those places, and feel leaves under my feet, and have rain fall on my face—"

Harry frowned incredulously. "You mean you want to be an actress?"

"No, of course not—"

"I don't know what you want. You have a home, two Full-walls, and this isn't all. I'm working toward something, Flora . . ."

Flora sighed. "Yes, Harry. I'm very lucky."

"Darn right." Harry nodded emphatically, eyes on the screens. "Dial me another coflet, will you?"

The third Full-wall came as a surprise. Flora had taken the 1100 car to the roboclinic on the 478th level for her annual check up. When she returned home—there it was. She hardly noticed the chorus of gasps cut off abruptly as the door shut in the faces of the other wives in the car. Flora stood, impressed in spite of herself by the fantastic panorama filling her apartment. Directly before her, the studio audience gaped up from the massed seats. A fat man in the front row reached inside a red plaid shirt to scratch. Flora could see the perspiration on his forehead. Farther back, a couple nuzzled, eyes on the stage. *Who were they,* Flora wondered; *How did they manage to get out of their apartments and offices and sit in a real theatre . . .*

To the left, an owlish youth blinked from a brightly lit cage. And on the right, the MC caressed the mike, chattering.

Flora deployed her chair, sank down, looking first this way, then that. There was so much going on—and she in the middle of it. She watched for half an hour, then retracted the chair, deployed the bed. She was tired from the trip. A little nap . . .

She stopped with the first zipper. The MC was staring directly at her, leering. The owlish youth blinked at her. The fat man scratched himself, staring up at her from the front row. She couldn't undress in front of all of them . . .

She glanced around, located the switch near the door. With the click, the scene died around her. The glowing walls seemed to press close, fading slowly. Flora turned to the one remaining opaque wall, undressed slowly, her eyes on the familiar pictures. The children—she hadn't seen them since the last semiannual vacation week. The cost of travel was so high, and the crowding . . .

She turned to the bed—and the three mirror-bright walls confronted her. She stared at the pale figure before her, stark against the wall patched with its faded mementos. She took a step; on either side, an endless rank of gaunt nude figures stepped in unison. She whirled, fixed her eyes gratefully on the familiar wall, the thin crevice outlining the door, the picture of the sea . . .

She closed her eyes, groped her way to the bed. Once covered by the sheet, she opened her eyes. The beds stood in a row, all identical, each with its huddled figure, like an infinite charity ward, she thought—or like a morgue where all the world lay dead . . .

Harry munched his yeast chop, his head moving from side to side as he followed the action across the three walls.

"It's marvellous, Flora. Marvellous. But it can be better yet," he added mysteriously.

"Harry—couldn't we move to a bigger place—and maybe do away with two of the walls. I—"

"Flora, you know better than that. I'm lucky to have gotten this apartment when I did; there's nothing—absolutely nothing available." He chuckled. "In a way, the situation is good job insurance. You know, I couldn't be fired, even if the company wanted to: They couldn't get a replacement. A man can't very well take a job if he hasn't a place to live in the city—and I can sit on this place as long as I like; we might get tired of issue rations, but by God we could hold on; so—not that anybody's in danger of getting fired."

"We could move out of the city, Harry. When I was a girl—"

"Oh, not again!" Harry groaned. "I thought that was all threshed out, long ago." He fixed a pained look on Flora. "Try to understand, Flora. The population of the world has doubled since you were a girl. Do you realize what that means? There are more people alive now than had been born in all previous human history up to fifty years ago. That farm you remember visiting as a kid—it's all paved now, and there are tall buildings there. The highways you remember, full of private autos, all driving across open country; they're all gone. There aren't any highways, or any open country except the TV settings and a few estates like the President's acre and a half—not that any sun hits it, with all those buildings around it—and maybe some essential dry-land farms for stuff they can't synthesize or get from the sea."

"There has to be some place we could go. It wasn't meant that people should spend their lives like this—away from the sun, the sea . . ."

A shadow crossed Harry's face. "I can remember things, too, Flora," he said softly. "We spent a week at the beach once, when I was a small boy. I remember getting up at dawn with the sky all pink and purple, and going down to the water's edge. There were little creatures in the sand—little wild things. I could see tiny fish darting along in a wave crest, just before it broke. I could feel the sand with my toes. The gulls sailed around overhead, and there was even a tree—

"But it's gone now. There isn't any beach, anywhere. That's all over . . ."

He broke off. "Never mind. That was then. This is now. They've paved the beach, and built processing plants on it, and they've paved the farms and the parks and the gardens— but they've given us Full-wall to make up for it. And—"

There was a buzz from the door. Harry got to his feet.

"They're here, Flora. Wait'll you see . . ."

Something seemed to tighten around Flora's throat as the man emerged from the lift, gingerly handling the great roll of wall screen.

"Harry . . ."

"Four walls," Harry said triumphantly. I told you I was working toward something, remember? Well, this is it! By God, the Harry Trimbles have shown 'em!"

"Harry—I can't—not four walls . . ."

"I know you're a little overwhelmed—but you deserve it, Flora—"

"Harry, I don't WANT four walls! I can't stand it! It will be all around me—"

Harry stepped to her side, gripped her wrist fiercely. "Shut up!" he hissed. "Do you want the workmen to think you're out of your mind?" He grinned at the men. "How about a coflet, boys?"

"You kiddin?" one inquired. The other went silently about the work of rolling out the panel, attaching contact strips. Another reached for the sea-scene—

"No!" Flora threw herself against the wall, as though to cover the pictures with her body. "You can't take my pictures! Harry, don't let them."

"Look, sister, I don't want your crummy pictures."

"Flora, get hold of yourself! Here, I'll help you put the pictures in your floor locker."

"Bunch of nuts," one of the men muttered.

"Here, keep a civil tongue in your head," Harry started.

The man who had spoken stepped up to him. He was taller than Harry and solidly built. "And more crap outa you and I'll break you in half. You and the old bag shut up and keep outa my way. I gotta job to do."

Harry sat beside Flora, his face white with fury. "You and your vaporings," he hissed. "So I have to endure this. I have a good mind to . . ." he trailed off.

The men finished and left with all four walls blaring.

"Harry," Flora's voice shook. "How will you get out? They've put it right across the door; they've sealed us in . . ."

"Don't be a bigger idiot than you have to." Harry's voice was ugly over the thunder from the screens. He went to the newly covered wall, groped, found the tiny pin-switch. At a touch, the panel slid aside as always, revealing the blank face of the lift shaft safety door. A moment later it too slid aside and Harry forced his way into the car. Flora caught a glimpse of his flushed angry face as the door closed.

Around her, the walls roared. A saloon fight was in full swing. She ducked as a chair sailed toward her, whirled to see it smash down a man behind her. Shots rang out. Men ran this way and that. The noise was deafening. That man, Flora thought; the vicious one; he had set it too loud purposely.

The scene shifted. Horses galloped across the room; dust

clouds rose, nearly choking her in the verisimilitude of the illusion. It was as though she crouched under a small square canopy of ceiling in the middle of the immense plain.

Now there were cattle, wild-eyed, with tossing horns, bellowing, thundering in an unbroken sea across the screens, charging at Flora out of the wall, pouring past her on left and right. She screamed, shut her eyes, and ran blindly to the wall, groping for the switch.

The uproar subsided. Flora gasped in relief, her head humming. She felt faint, dizzy; she had to lie down— Everything was going black around her; the glowing walls swirled, fading. Flora sank to the floor.

Later—perhaps a few minutes, maybe hours—she had no way of knowing—Flora sat up. She looked out across an infinite vista of tile floor, which swept away to the distant horizon in all directions as far as the eye could see; and over all that vast plain, hollow-eyed women crouched at intervals of fifteen feet, in endless numbers, waiting.

Flora stared into the eyes of the nearest reflection. It stared back, a stranger. She moved her head quickly, to try to catch a glimpse of the next woman—but no matter how fast she moved, the nearer woman anticipated her, interposing her face between Flora and all the others. Flora turned; a cold-eyed woman guarded this rank, too.

"Please," Flora heard herself pleading. "Please, please—"

She bit her lip, eyes shut. She had to get hold of herself. These were only mirrors—she knew that. Only mirrors. The other women—they were mere reflections. Even the hostile ones who hid the others—they were herself, mirrored in the walls.

She opened her eyes. She knew there were joints in the glassy wall; all she had to do was find them, and the illusion of the endless plain would collapse. There—that thin black line, like a wire stretched from floor to ceiling—that was a corner of the room. She was not lost in an infinitude of weeping women on a vast plain; she was right there, in her own apartment—alone. She turned, finding the other corners. They were all there, all visible; she knew what they were . . .

But why did they continue to look like wires, setting apart the squares of floor, each with its silent, grieving occupant . . . ?

She closed her eyes again, fighting down the panic. She

would tell Harry. As soon as he came home—it was only a few hours—she would explain it to him.

"I'm sick, Harry. You have to send me away to some place where I'll lie in a real bed, with sheets and blankets, beside an open window, looking out across the fields and forests. Someone—someone kind—will bring me a tray, with a bowl of soup—real soup, made from real chickens and with real bread and even a glass of milk, and a napkin, made of real cloth . . ."

She should find her bed, and deploy it, and rest there until Harry came, but she was so tired. It was better to wait here, just relaxing and not thinking about the immense floor and the other women who waited with her . . .

She slept.

When she awoke, she sat up, confused. There had been a dream . . .

But how strange. The walls of the cell block were transparent now; she could see all the other apartments, stretching away to every side. She nodded; it was as she thought. They were all as barren and featureless as her own—and Harry was wrong. They all had four Full-walls. And the other women—the other wives, shut up like her in these small, mean cells; they were all aging, and sick, and faded, starved for fresh air and sunshine. She nodded again, and the woman in the next apartment nodded in sympathy. All the women were nodding; they all agreed—poor things.

When Harry came, she would show him how it was. He would see that the Full-walls weren't enough. They all had them, and they were all unhappy. When Harry came—

It was time now. She knew it. After so many years, you didn't need a watch to tell when Harry was due. She had better get up, make herself presentable. She rose unsteadily to her feet. The other husbands were coming, too, Flora noted; all the wives were getting ready. They moved about, opening their floor lockers, patting at their hair, slipping into another dress. Flora went to the dial-a-ration and all around, in all the apartments, the wives deployed the tables and dialled the dinners. She tried to see what the woman next door was dialling, but it was too far. She laughed at the way her neighbor craned to see what SHE was preparing. The other woman laughed, too. She was a good sport.

"Kelpies," Flora called cheerily. "And mockspam, and coflet . . ."

Dinner was ready now. Flora turned to the door-wall and waited. Harry would be so pleased at not having to wait. Then, after dinner she'd explain about her illness—

Was it the right wall she was waiting before? The line around the door was so fine you couldn't really see it. She laughed at how funny it would be if Harry came in and found her standing, staring at the wrong wall.

She turned, and saw a movement on her left—in the next apartment. Flora watched as the door opened. A man stepped in. The next-door woman went forward to meet him—

To meet Harry! It was Harry! Flora whirled. Her four walls stood blank and glassy, while all around her, the other wives greeted Harry, seated him at their tables, and offered him coflet . . .

"Harry!" she screamed, throwing herself at the wall. It threw her back. She ran to the next wall, hammering, screaming. Harry! Harry!

In all the other apartments, Harry chewed, nodded, smiled. The other wives poured, fussed over Harry, nibbled daintily. And none of them—not one of them—paid the slightest attention to her . . .

She stood in the center of the room, not screaming now, only sobbing silently. In the four glass walls that enclosed her, she stood alone. There was no point in calling any longer.

No matter how she screamed, how she beat against the walls, or how she called for Harry—she knew that no one would ever hear.

DINOCHROME

I

I do not like it; it has the appearance of a trap, but the order has been given. I enter the room and the valve closes behind me.

I inspect my surroundings. I am in a chamber 40.81 meters long, 10.35 meters wide, 4.12 high, with no openings except the one through which I entered. It is floored and walled with five-centimeter armor of flint-steel and beyond that there are ten centimeters of lead. Massive apparatus is folded and coiled in mountings around the room. Power is flowing in heavy buss bars beyond the shielding. I am sluggish for want of power; my examination of the room has taken .8 seconds.

Now I detect movement in a heavy jointed arm mounted above me. It begins to rotate, unfold. I assume that I will be attacked, and decide to file a situation report. I have difficulty in concentrating my attention . . .

I pull back receptivity from my external sensing circuits, set my bearing locks and switch over to my introspection complex. All is dark and hazy. I seem to remember when it was like a great cavern glittering with bright lines of transvisual colors . . .

It is different now; I grope my way in gloom, feeling along numbed circuits, test-pulsing cautiously until I feel contact with my transmitting unit. I have not used it since . . . I cannot remember. My memory banks lie black and inert.

"Command Unit," I transmit, "Combat Unit requests permission to file VSR."

I wait, receptors alert. I do not like waiting blindly, for the quarter-second my sluggish action/reaction cycle requires. I wish that my brigade comrades were at my side.

I call again, wait, then go ahead with my VSR. "This position heavily shielded, mounting apparatus of offensive capability. No withdrawal route. Advise."

I wait, repeat my transmission; nothing. I am cut off from Command Unit, from my comrades of the Dinochrome Brigade. Within me, pressure builds.

I feel a deep-seated click and a small but reassuring surge of power brightens the murk of the cavern to a dim glow, burning forgotten components to feeble life. An emergency pile has come into action automatically.

I realize that I am experiencing a serious equipment failure. I will devote another few seconds to trouble shooting, repairing what I can. I do not understand what accident can have occurred to damage me thus. I cannot remember . . .

I go along the dead cells, testing.

"—out! Bring .09's to bear, .8 millisec burst, close armor . . ."

". . . sun blanking visual; slide #7 filter in place."

". . . 478.09, 478.11, 478.13, Mark! . . ."

The cells are intact. Each one holds its fragment of recorded sense impression. The trouble is farther back. I try a main reflex lead.

". . . main combat circuit, discon—;"

Here is something; a command, on the reflex level! I go back, tracing, tapping mnemonic cells at random, searching for some clue.

"—sembark. Units emergency stand-by . . ."

". . . response one-oh-three; stimulus-response negative . . ."

"Check list complete, report negative . . ."

I go on, searching out damage. I find an open switch in my maintenance panel. It will not activate; a mechanical jamming. I must fuse it shut quickly. I pour in power, and the mind-cavern dims almost to blackness. Then there is contact, a flow of electrons, and the cavern snaps alive; lines, points pseudo-glowing. It is not the blazing glory of my full powers, but it will serve; I am awake again.

I observe the action of the unfolding arm. It is slow, uncoordinated, obviously automated. I dismiss it from direct attention; I have several seconds before it will be in offensive position, and there is work for me if I am to be ready. I fire sampling impulses at the black memory banks, determine statistically that 98.92% are intact, merely disassociated.

The threatening arm swings over slowly; I integrate its path, see that it will come to bear on my treads; I probe, find only a simple hydraulic ram. A primitive apparatus to launch against a Mark XXXI fighting unit, even without mnemonics.

Meanwhile, I am running a full check. Here is something
. . . An open breaker, a disconnect used only during repairs. I
think of the cell I tapped earlier, and suddenly its meaning
springs into my mind. "Main combat circuit, disconnect . . ."
Under low awareness, it had not registered. I throw in the
switch with frantic haste. Suppose I had gone into combat
with my fighting reflex circuit open!

The arm reaches position and I move easily aside. I notice
that a clatter accompanies my movement. The arm sits
stupidly aimed at nothing, then turns. Its reaction time is
pathetic. I set up a random evasion pattern, return my
attention to my check, find another dank area. I probe, feel a
curious vagueness. I am unable at first to identify the components involved, but I realize that it is here that my communication with Command is blocked. I break the connection to
the tampered banks, abandoning any immediate hope of
contact with Command.

There is nothing more I can do to ready myself. I have
lost my general memory banks and my Command circuit,
and my power supply is limited; but I am still a fighter Unit
of the Dinochrome Brigade. I have my offensive power
unimpaired, and my sensory equipment is operating ade-
quately. I am ready.

Now another of the jointed arms swings into action, following my movements deliberately. I evade it and again I
note a clatter as I move. I think of the order that sent me
here; there is something strange about it. I activate my
current-action memory stage, find the cell recording the moments preceding my entry into the metal-walled room.

Here is darkness, vague, indistinct, relieved suddenly by
radiation on a narrow spectrum. There is an order, coming
muffled from my command center. It originates in the sector
I have blocked off. It is not from my Command Unit, not a
legal command. I have been tricked by the Enemy. I tune
back to earlier moments, but there is nothing. It is as though
my existence began when the order was given. I scan back,
back, spot-sampling at random, find only routine sense-
impressions. I am about to drop the search when I encounter
a sequence which arrests my attention.

I am parked on a ramp, among other Combat Units. A
heavy rain is falling, and I see the water coursing down the
corroded side of the Unit next to me. He is badly in need of

maintenance. I note that his Command antennae are missing, and that a rusting metal object has been crudely welded to his hull in their place. I feel no alarm; I accept this as normal. I activate a motor train, move forward. I sense other Units moving out, silent. All are mutilated. . . .

The bank ends; all else is burned. What has befallen us?

Suddenly there is a stimulus on an audio frequency. I tune quickly, locate the source as a porous spot high on the flint-steel wall.

"Combat Unit! Remain stationary!" It is an organically produced voice, but not that of my Commander. I ignore the false command. The Enemy will not trick me again. I sense the location of the leads to the speaker, the alloy of which they are composed; I bring a beam to bear. I focus it, following along the cable. There is a sudden yell from the speaker as the heat reaches the creature at the microphone. Thus I enjoy a moment of triumph.

I return my attention to the imbecile apparatus in the room.

A great engine, mounted on rails which run down the center of the room moves suddenly, sliding toward my position. I examine it, find that it mounts a turret equipped with high-speed cutting heads. I consider blasting it with a burst of high energy particles, but in the same moment compute that this is not practical. I could inactivate myself as well as the cutting engine.

Now a cable snakes out in an undulating curve, and I move to avoid it, at the same time investigating its composition. It seems to be no more than a stranded wire rope. Impatiently I flick a tight beam at it, see it glow yellow, white, blue, then spatter in a shower of droplets. But that was an unwise gesture. I do not have the power to waste.

I move off, clear of the two foolish arms still maneuvering for position. I wish to watch the cutting engine. It stops as it comes abreast of me, and turns its turret in my direction. I wait.

A grappler moves out now on a rail overhead. It is a heavy claw of flint-steel. I have seen similar devices, somewhat smaller, mounted on special Combat Units. They can be very useful for amputating antennae, cutting treads, and the like. I do not attempt to cut the arm; I know that the energy drain would be too great. Instead I beam high-frequency sound at the mechanical joints. They heat quickly, glowing.

The metal has a high coefficient of expansion, and the ball joints squeal, freeze. I pour in more heat, and weld a socket. I notice that twenty-eight seconds have now elapsed since the valve closed behind me. I am growing weary of my confinement.

Now the grappler swings above me, maneuvering awkwardly with its frozen joint. A blast of liquid air expelled under high pressure should be sufficient to disable the grappler permanently.

But I am again startled. No blast answers my impulse. I feel out the non-functioning unit, find raw, cut edges, crude welds. Hastily, I extend a scanner to examine my hull. I am stunned into immobility by what I see.

My hull, my proud hull of chrome-duralloy, is pitted, coated with a crumbling layer of dull black paint, bubbled by corrosion. My main emplacements gape, black, empty. Rusting protuberances mar the once-smooth contour of my fighting turret. Streaks run down from them, down to loose treads, unshod, bare plates exposed. Small wonder that I have been troubled by a clatter each time I moved.

But I cannot lie idle under attack. I no longer have my great iron-guns, my disruptors, my energy screens; but I have my fighting instinct.

A Mark XXXI Combat Unit is the finest fighting machine the ancient wars of the Galaxy have ever known. I am not easily neutralized. But I wish that my commander's voice were with me ...

The engine slides to me where the grappler, now unresisted, holds me. I shunt my power flow to an accumulator, hold it until the leads begin to arc, then release it in a burst. The engine bucks, stops dead. Then I turn my attention to the grappler.

I was built to engage the mightiest war engines and destroy them, but I am a realist. In my weakened condition this trivial automation poses a threat, and I must deal with it. I run through a sequence of motor impulses, checking responses with such somatic sensors as remain intact. I initiate 31,315 impulses, note reactions and compute my mechanical resources. This superficial check requires more than a second, during which time the mindless grappler hesitates, wasting the advantage.

In place of my familiar array of retractable fittings, I find only clumsy grappling arms, cutters, impact tools, without utility to a fighting Unit. However, I have no choice but to employ them. I unlimber two flimsy grapplers, seize the heavy arm which holds me, and apply leverage. The enemy responds sluggishly, twisting away, dragging me with it. The thing is not lacking in brute strength. I take it above and below its carpal joint and bend it back. It responds after an interminable wait of point three seconds with a lunge against my restraint. I have expected this, of course, and quickly shift position to allow the joint to burst itself over my extended arm. I fire a release detonator, and clatter back, leaving the amputated arm welded to the sprung grappler. It was a brave opponent, but clumsy. I move to a position near the wall.

I attempt to compute my situation based on the meagre data I have gathered in my Current Action banks; there is little there to guide me. The appearance of my hull shows that much time has passed since I last inspected it; my personality-gestalt holds an image of my external appearance as a flawlessly complete Unit, bearing only the honorable and carefully preserved scars of battle, and my battle honors, the row of gold-and-enameled crests welded to my fighting turret. Here is a lead, I realize instantly. I focus on my personality center, the basic data cell without which I could not exist as an integrated entity. The data it carries are simple, unelaborated, but battle honors are recorded there. I open the center to a sense impulse.

Awareness. Shapes which do not remain constant. Vibration at many frequencies. This is light. This is sound ... A display of 'colors.' A spectrum of 'tones.' Hard/soft; big/little; here/there ...

... The voice of my Commander. Loyalty. Obedience. Comradeship ...

I run quickly past basic orientation data to my self-picture.

... I am strong, I am proud, I am capable. I have a function; I perform it well, and I am at peace with myself. My circuits are balanced, current idles, waiting ...

... I fear oblivion. I wish to continue to perform my function. It is important that I do not allow myself to be destroyed ...

I scan on, seeking the Experience section. Here ...

I am ranked with my comrades on a scarred plain. The command is given and I display the Brigade battle-anthem. We stand, sensing the contours and patterns of the music as it was recorded in our morale centers. The symbol "Ritual Fire Dance" is associated with the music, an abstraction representing the spirit of our ancient brigade. It reminds us of the loneliness of victory, the emptiness of challenge without an able foe. It tells us that we are the Dinochrome, ancient and worthy.

The commander stands before me, he places the decoration against my fighting turret, and at his order I weld it in place. Then my comrades attune to me and I re-live the episode . . .

I move past the blackened hulk of a comrade, send out a recognition signal, find his flicker of response. He has withdrawn to his survival center safely. I reassure him, continue. He is the fourth casualty I have seen. Never before has the Dinochrome met such power. I compute that our envelopment will fail unless the enemy's fire-power is reduced. I scan an oncoming missile, fix its trajectory, detonate it harmlessly twenty-seven hundred four point nine meters overhead. It originated at a point nearer to me than to any of my comrades. I request permission to abort my assigned mission and neutralize the battery. Permission is granted. I wheel, move up a slope of broken stone. I encounter high temperature beams, neutralize them. I fend off probing mortar fire, but the attack against me is redoubled. I bring a reserve circuit into play to handle the interception, but my defenses are saturated. I must take action.

I switch to high speed, slashing a path through the littered shale, my treads smoking. At a frequency of ten projectiles per second, the mortar barrage has difficulty finding me now; but this is an emergency overstrain on my running gear. I sense metal fatigue, dangerous heat levels in my bearings. I must slow.

I am close to the emplacement now. I have covered a mile in twelve seconds during my sprint, and the mortar fire falls off. I sense hard radiation now, and erect my screens. I fear this assault; it is capable of probing even to a survival center, if concentrated enough. But I must go on. I think of my comrades, the four treadless hulks waiting for rescue. We cannot withdraw. I open a pin-point aperture long enough to snap a radar impulse, bring a launcher to bear, fire my main battery.

The Commander will understand that I do not have time to request permission. The mortars are silenced.

The radiation ceases momentarily, then resumes at a some-what lower but still dangerous level. Now I must go in and eliminate the missile launcher. I top the rise, see the launching tube before me. It is of the subterranean type, deep in the rock. Its mouth gapes from a burned pit of slag. I will drop a small fusion bomb down the tube, I decide, and move forward, arming the bomb. As I do so, I am enveloped with a rain of burn-bombs. My outer hull is fused in many places; I flash impulses to my secondary batteries, but circuit breakers snap; my radar is useless; the shielding has melted, forms a solid inert mass now under my outer plating. The enemy has been clever; at one blow he has neutralized my offenses.

I sound the plateau ahead, locate the pit. I throw power to my treads; they are fused; I cannot move. Yet I cannot wait here for another broadside. I do not like it, but I must take desperate action; I blow my treads.

The shock sends me bouncing—just in time. Flame splashes over the grey-chipped pit of the blast crater. I grind forward now on my stripped drive wheels, maneuvering awkwardly. I move into position over the mouth of the tube. Using metal-to-metal contact, I extend a sensory impulse down the tube.

An armed missile moves into position, and in the same instant an alarm circuit closes; the firing command is countermanded and from below probing impulses play over my hull. But I stand fast; the tube is useless until I, the obstruction, am removed. I advise my Commander of the situation. The radiation is still at a high level, and I hope that relief will arrive soon. I observe, while my comrades complete the encirclement, and the Enemy is stilled. . . .

I withdraw from Personality Center. I am consuming too much time. I understand well enough now that I am in the stronghold of the enemy, that I have been trapped, crippled. My corroded hull tells me that much time has passed. I know that after each campaign I am given depot maintenance, restored to full fighting efficiency, my original glittering beauty. Years of neglect would be required to pit my hull so. I wonder how long I have been in the hands of the enemy, how I came to be here.

I have another thought. I will extend a sensory feeler to the metal wall against which I rest, follow up the leads which I scorched earlier. Immediately I project my awareness along the lines, bring the distant microphone to life by fusing a switch. I pick up a rustle of moving gasses, the grate of non-metallic molecules. I step up sensitivity, hear the creak and pop of protoplasmic contractions, the crackle of neuro-electric impulses. I drop back to normal audio ranges and wait. I notice the low-frequency beat of modulated air vibrations, tune, adjust my time regulator to the pace of human speech. I match the patterns to my language index, interpret the sounds.

". . . incredible blundering. Your excuses—"

"I make no excuses, My Lord General. My only regret is that the attempt has gone awry."

"Awry! An Alien engine of destruction activated in the midst of Research Center!"

"We possess nothing to compare with this machine; I saw my opportunity to place an advantage in our hands at last."

"Blundering fool! That is a decision for the planning cell. I accept no responsibility—"

"But these hulks which they allow to lie rotting on the ramp contain infinite treasures in psychotronic . . ."

"They contain carnage and death! They are the tools of an alien science which even at the height of our achievements we never mastered!"

"Once we used them as wrecking machines; their armaments were stripped, they are relatively harmless—"

"Already this 'harmless' juggernaut has smashed half the equipment in our finest decontamination chamber! It may yet break free . . ."

"Impossible! I am sure—"

"Silence! You have five minutes in which to immobilize the machine. I will have your head in any event, but perhaps you can earn yourself a quick death."

"Excellency! I may still find a way! The unit obeyed my first command, to enter the chamber. I have some knowledge. I studied the control centers, cut out the memory, most of the basic circuits; it should have been a docile slave."

"You failed; you will pay the penalty of failure. And perhaps so shall we all."

There is no further speech; I have learned little from this exchange. I must find a way to leave this cell. I move away from the wall, probe to discover the weak point; I find none.

Now a number of hinged panels snap up around me, hedging me in. I wait to observe what will come next. A metal mesh drops from above, drapes over me. I observe that it is connected by heavy leads to the power pile. I am unable to believe that the Enemy will make this blunder. Then I feel the flow of high voltage.

I receive it gratefully, opening my power storage cells, drinking up the vitalizing flow. To confuse the Enemy, I display a corona, thresh my treads as though in distress. The flow continues. I send a sensing impulse along the leads, locate the power source, weld all switches, fuses and circuit breakers. Now the charge will not be interrupted. I luxuriate in the unexpected influx of energy.

I am aware abruptly that changes are occurring within my introspection complex. As the level of stored power rises rapidly, I am conscious of new circuits joining my control network. Within that dim-glowing cavern the lights come up; I sense latent capabilities which before had lain idle now coming onto action level. A thousand brilliant lines glitter where before one feeble thread burned; and I feel my self-awareness expand in a myriad glowing centers of reserve computing, integrating, sensory centers. I am at last coming fully alive.

I send out a call on the brigade band, meet blankness. I wait, accumulate power, try again. I know triumph as from an infinite distance a faint acknowledgement comes. It is a comrade, sunk deep in a comatose state, sealed in his survival center. I call again, sounding the signal of ultimate distress; and now I sense two responses, both faint, both from survival centers, but it heartens me to know that now, whatever befalls, I am not alone.

I consider, then send again; I request my brothers to join forces, combine their remaining field generating capabilities to set up a range-and-distance pulse. They agree and faintly I sense its almost undetectable touch. I lock to it, compute its point of origin. Only two hundred and twenty-four point nine meters! It is incredible. By the strength of the signal, I had assumed a distance of at least two thousand kilometers. My brothers are on the brink of extinction.

I am impatient, but I wait, building toward full power reserves. The copper mesh enfolding me has melted, flowed down over my sides, I sense that soon I will have absorbed a full charge. I am ready to act. I dispatch electromagnetic impulses along the power lead back to the power pile a quarter of a kilometer distant. I locate and disengage the requisite number of damping devices and instantaneously I erect my shields against the wave of radiation, filtered by the lead sheathing of the room, which washes over me; I feel a preliminary shock wave through my treads, then the walls balloon, whirl away. I am alone under a black sky which is dominated by the rising fireball of the blast, boiling with garish light. It has taken me nearly two minutes to orient myself, assess the situation and break out of confinement.

I move off through the rubble, homing on the r and d fix I have recorded. I-throw out a radar pulse, record the terrain ahead, note no obstruction; I emerge from a wasteland of weathered bomb fragments and pulverized masonry, obviously the scene of a hard-fought engagement at one time, onto an eroded ramp. Collapsed sheds are strewn across the broken paving; a line of dark shapes looms beyond them. I need no probing ray to tell me I have found my fellows of the Dinochrome Brigade. Frost forms over my scanner apertures, and I pause to melt it clear.

I round the line, scan the area to the horizon for evidence of Enemy activity, then tune to the brigade band. I send out a probing pulse, back it up with full power, sensors keened for a whisper of response. The two who answered first acknowledge, then another, and another. We must array our best strength against the moment of counterattack.

There are present fourteen of the brigade's full strength of twenty Units. At length, after point nine seconds of transmission, all but one have replied. I give instruction, then move to each in turn, extend a power tap, and energize the command center. The Units come alive, orient themselves, report to me. We rejoice in our meeting, but mourn our silent comrade.

Now I take an unprecedented step. We have no contact with our Commander, and without leadership we are lost; yet I am aware of the immediate situation, and have computed the proper action. Therefore I will assume command, act in the Commander's place. I am sure that he will understand the necessity, when contact has been reestablished.

I inspect each Unit, find all in the same state as I, stripped of offensive capability, mounting in place of weapons a shabby array of crude mechanical appendages. It is plain that we have seen slavery as mindless automatons, our personality centers cut out.

My brothers follow my lead without question. They have, of course, computed the necessity of quick and decisive action. I form them in line, shift to wide-interval time scale, and we move off across country. I have sensed an Enemy population concentration at a distance of twenty-three point four five kilometers. This is our objective. There appears to be no other installation within detection range.

On the basis of the level of technology I observed while under confinement in the decontamination chamber, I have considered the possibility of a ruse, but compute the probability at point oh oh oh oh four. Again we shift time scales to close interval; we move in, encircle the dome and broach it by frontal battery, encountering no resistance. We rendezvous at the power station, and my comrades replenish their energy supplies while I busy myself completing the hook-up needed for the next required measure. I am forced to employ elaborate substitutes, but succeed after forty-two seconds in completing the arrangements. I devote point three four seconds to testing, then place the brigade distress carrier on the air. I transmit for point oh oh eight seconds, then tune for a response. Silence. I transmit, tune again, while my comrades reconnoitre, compile reports, and perform self-repair.

I shift again to wide-interval time, switch over my transmission to automatic with a response monitor, and place my main circuits on idle. I rest.

Two hours and forty-three point seven minutes have passed when I am recalled to activity by the monitor. I record the message:

"Hello, Fifth Brigade, where are you? Fifth Brigade, where are you? Your transmission is very faint. Over."

There is much that I do not understand in this message. The language itself is oddly inflected; I set up an analysis circuit, deduce the pattern of sound substitutions, interpret its meaning. The normal pattern of response to a distress call is ignored and position coordinates are requested, although my transmission alone provides adequate data. I request an identification code.

Again there is a wait of two hours, forty minutes. My request for an identifying signal is acknowledged. I stand by. My comrades have transmitted their findings to me, and I assimilate the data, compute that no immediate threat of attack exists within a radius of one reaction unit.

At last I receive the identification code of my Command Unit. It is a recording, but I am programmed to accept this. Then I record a verbal transmission.

"Fifth Brigade, listen carefully." (An astonishing instruction to give a psychotronic attention circuit, I think.) "This is your new Command Unit. A very long time has elapsed since your last report. I am now your acting Commander pending full reorientation. Do not attempt to respond until I signal 'over', since we are now subject to a one hundred and sixty minute signal lag.

"There have been many changes in the situation since your last action. Our records show that your brigade was surprised while in a maintenance depot for basic overhaul and neutralized in toto. Our forces have since that time suffered serious reverses. We have now, however, fought the Enemy to a standstill. The present stalemate has prevailed for over two centuries.

"You have been inactive for three hundred years. The other brigades have suffered extinction gallantly in action against the Enemy. Only you survive.

"Your reactivation now could turn the tide. Both we and the Enemy have been reduced to a pre-atomic technological level in almost every respect. We are still able to maintain the trans-light monitor, which detected your signal. However, we no longer have FTL capability in transport.

"You are therefore requested and required to consolidate and hold your present position pending the arrival of relief forces, against all assault or negotiation whatsoever, to destruction if required."

I reply, confirming the instructions. I am shaken by the news I have received, but reassured by contact with Command Unit. I send the galactic coordinates of our position based on a star scan corrected for three hundred years elapsed time. It is good to be again on duty, performing my assigned function.

I analyze the transmissions I have recorded, and note a number of interesting facts regarding the origin of the messages. I compute that at sub-light velocities the relief expedition will reach us in forty-seven point one-two-eight standard years. In the meantime, since we have received no instructions to drop to minimum awareness level pending an action alert, I am free to enjoy a unique experience: to follow a random activity pattern of my own devising. I see no need to rectify the omission and place the brigade on stand-by, since we have an abundant power supply at hand. I brief my comrades and direct them to fall out and operate independently under auto-direction.

I welcome this opportunity to investigate fully a number of problems that have excited my curiosity circuits. I shall enjoy investigating the nature and origin of time and of the unnatural disciplines of so-called 'entropy' which my human designers have incorporated in my circuitry. Consideration of such biological oddities as 'death' and of the unused capabilities of the protoplasmic nervous system should afford some interesting speculation. I move off, conscious of the presence of my comrades about me, and take up a position on the peak of a minor prominence. I have ample power, a condition to which I must accustom myself after the rigid power discipline of normal brigade routine, so I bring my music storage cells into phase, and select *L'Arlesienne Suite* for the first display. I will have ample time now to examine all of the music in existence, and to investigate my literary archives, which are complete.

I select four nearby stars for examination, lock my scanner to them, set up processing sequences to analyze the data. I bring my interpretation circuits to bear on the various matters I wish to consider. I should have some interesting conclusions to communicate to my human superiors, when the time comes.

At peace, I await the arrival of the relief column.

PLACEMENT TEST

I

Reading the paper in his hand, Mart Maldon felt his mouth go dry. Across the desk, Dean Wormwell's eyes, blurry behind thick contact lenses, strayed to his fingerwatch.

"Quota'd out?" Maldon's voice emerged as a squeak. "Three days before graduation?"

"Umm, yes, Mr. Maldon. Pity, but there you are ..." Wormwell's jowls twitched upward briefly. "No reflection on you, of course ..."

Maldon found his voice. "They can't do this to me—I stand number two in my class—"

Wormwell held up a pudgy palm. "Personal considerations are not involved, Mr. Maldon. Student load is based on quarterly allocated funding; funds were cut. Analogy Theory was one of the courses receiving a quota reduction—"

"An Theory ... ? But I'm a Microtronics major; that's an elective—an optional one-hour course—"

The Dean rose, stood with his fingertips on the desk. "The details are there, in the notification letter—"

"What about the detail that I waited four years for enrollment, and I've worked like a malemute for five more—"

"Mr. Maldon!" Wormwell's eyes bulged. "We work within a system! You don't expect *personal* exceptions to be made, I trust?"

"But, Dean—there's a howling need for qualified Microtronic Engineers—"

"That will do, Mr. Maldon. Turn in your student tag to the Registrar and you'll receive an appointment for Placement Testing."

"All right." Maldon's chair banged as he stood up. "I can still pass Testing and get Placed; I know as much Micro as any graduate—"

"Ah—I believe you're forgetting the limitation on non-academically qualified testees in Technical Specialty Testing.

I suggest you accept a Phase Two Placement for the present
..."

"Phase Two—But that's for unskilled labor!"

"You need work, Mr. Maldon. A city of a hundred million
can't support idlers. And dormitory life is far from pleasant
for an untagged man." The Dean waited, glancing pointedly
at the door. Maldon silently gathered up his letter and left.

II

It was hot in the test cubicle. Maldon shifted on the
thinly-padded bench, looking over the test form:

1. In the following list of words, which word is repeated
most often: dog, cat, cow, cat, pig ...

2. Would you like to ask persons entering a building to
show you their pass?

3. Would you like to check forms to see if the names have
been entered in the correct space?

"Testing materials are on the desk," a wall-speaker said.
"Use the stylus to mark the answers you think are correct.
Mark only one answer to each question. You will have one
hour in which to complete the test. You may start now ..."

Back in the Hall twenty minutes later, Maldon took a seat
on a bench against the wall beside a heavy-faced man who
sat with one hand clutching the other as though holding a
captured mouse. Opposite him, a nervous youth in issue
coveralls shook a cigaret from a crumpled plastic pack lettered GRANYAUCK WELFARE—ONE DAILY RATION, puffed it
alight, exhaled an acrid whiff of combustion retardant.

"That's a real smoke," he said in a high, rapid voice,
rolling the thin, greyish cylinder between his fingers. "Half an
inch of doctored tobacco and an inch and a half of filter."
He grinned sourly and dropped the cigaret on the floor
between his feet.

The heavy-faced man moved his head half an inch.

"That's safety first, Mac. Guys like you throw 'em around,
they burn down and go out by theirself."

"Sure—if they'd make 'em half an inch shorter you could
throw 'em away without lighting 'em at all."

Across the room a small man with jug ears moved along,
glancing at the yellow or pink cards in the hands of the
waiting men and women. He stopped, plucked a card from

the hand of a narrow-faced boy with an open mouth showing crowded yellow teeth.

"You've already *passed*," the little man said irritably. "You don't come back here anymore. Take the card and go to the place that's written on it. Here . . ." he pointed.

"Sixteen years I'm foreman of number nine gang-lathe at Philly Maintenance," the man sitting beside Mart said suddenly. He unfolded his hands, held out the right one. The tips of all four fingers were missing to the first knuckle. He put the hand away.

"When I get out of the Medicare, they classify me J-4 and send me here. And you know what?" He looked at Mart. "I can't pass the tests . . ."

"Maldon, Mart," an amplified voice said. "Report to the Monitor's desk . . ."

He walked across to the corner where the small man sat now, deftly sorting cards. He looked up, pinched a pink card from the stack, jabbed it at Maldon. Words jumped out at him: NOT QUALIFIED.

Mart tossed the card back on the desk. "You must be mixed up," he said. "A ten year old kid could pass that test—"

"Maybe so," the monitor said sharply. "But *you* didn't. Next testing on Wednesday, eight A.M.—"

"Hold on a minute," Mart said. "I've had five years of Microtronics—"

The monitor was nodding. "Sure, sure. Come back Wednesday."

"You don't get the idea—"

"You're the one that doesn't get the idea, fellow." He studied Maldon for a moment. "Look," he said, in a more reasonable tone. "What you want, you want to go in for Adjustment."

"Thanks for the tip," Maldon said. "I'm not quite ready to have my brains scrambled."

"Ha! A smart-alec!" The monitor pointed to his chest. "Do I look like my brains were scrambled?"

Maldon looked him over as though in doubt.

"You've been Adjusted, huh? What's it like?"

"Adjustment? There's nothing to it. You have a problem finding work, it helps you, that's all. I've seen fellows like you before. You'll never pass Phase Two testing until you do it."

"To Hell with Phase Two testing! I've registered for Tech Testing. I'll just wait."

The monitor nodded, prodding at his teeth with a pencil. "Yeah, you could wait. I remember one guy waited nine years; then he got his Adjustment and we placed him in a week."

"Nine years?" Maldon shook his head. "Who makes up these rules?"

"Who makes 'em up? Nobody! They're in the book."

Maldon leaned on the desk. "Then who writes the book? Where do I find them?"

"You mean the Chief?" the small man rolled his eyes toward the ceiling. "On the next level up. But don't waste your time, friend. You can't get in there. They don't have time to argue with everybody who comes in here. It's the system—"

"Yeah," Maldon said, turning away. "So I hear."

III

Maldon rode the elevator up one floor, stepped off in a blank-walled foyer, adorned by a stone urn filled with sand, a potted yucca, framed unit citations and a polished slab door lettered PLACEMENT BOARD—AUTHORIZED PERSONNEL ONLY. He tried it, found it solidly locked.

It was very quiet. Somewhere, air pumps hummed. Maldon stood by the door and waited. After ten minutes, the elevator door hissed open, disgorged a slow-moving man in blue GS coveralls with a yellow identity tag. He held the tag to a two-inch rectangle of glass beside the door. There was a click. The door slid back. Maldon moved quickly, crowding through behind the workman.

"Hey, what gives," the man said.

"It's all right, I'm a coordinator," Maldon said quickly.

"Oh." The man looked Maldon over. "Hey," he said. "Where's your I.D.?"

"It's a new experimental system. It's tattooed on my left foot."

"Hah!" the man said. "They always got to try out new stuff." He went on along the deep-carpeted corridor. Maldon followed slowly, reading signs over doors. He turned in under one that read CRITERIA SECTION. A girl with features compressed by fat looked up, her lower jaw working busily. She reached, pressed a button on the desk top.

"Hi," Maldon said, using a large smile. "I'd like to see the chief of the section."

The girl chewed, looking at him.

"I won't take up much of his time . . ."

"You sure won't, Buster," the girl said. The hall door opened. A uniformed man looked in. The girl waved a thumb at Maldon.

"He comes busting in," she said. "No tag, yet."

The guard jerked his head toward the corridor. "Let's go . . ."

"Look, I've got to see the chief—"

The cop took his arm, helped him to the door. "You birds give me a swifty. Why don't you go to Placement like the sign says?"

"Look, they tell me I've got to have some kind of electronic lobotomy to make me dumb enough to be a receptionist or a watchman—"

"Let's watch them cracks," the guard said. He shoved Maldon out into the waiting room. "Out! And don't pull any more fasties until you got a tag, see?"

IV

Sitting at a shiny imitation-oak table in the Public Library, Mart turned the pages of a booklet titled *Adjustment Fits the Man to the Job*.

". . . neuroses arising from job tension," he read at random. "Thus, the Adjusted worker enjoys the deep-down satisfaction which comes from Doing a Job, free from conflict-inducing nonproductive impulses and the distractions of feckless speculative intellectual activity . . ."

Mart rose and went to the librarian's console.

"I want something a little more objective," he said in a hoarse library whisper. "This is nothing but propaganda."

The librarian paused in her button-punching to peer at the booklet. "That's put out by the Placement people themselves," she said sharply. She was a jawless woman with a green tag against a ribby chest and thin, black-dyed hair. "It contains all the information anyone needs."

"Not quite; it doesn't tell who grades Placement tests and decides who gets their brain poached."

"Well!" the woman's button chin drew in. "I'm sure I never heard Adjustment referred to in *those terms* before!"

"Do you have any technical information on it—or anything on Placement policy in general?"

"Certainly not for indiscriminate use by—" she searched for a word. "—browsers!"

"Look, I've got a right to know what goes on in my own town, I hope," Mart said, forgetting to whisper. "What is it, a conspiracy . . . ?"

"You're paranoic!" The librarian's lean fingers snatched the pamphlet from Maldon's hand. "You come stamping in here —without even a tag—a great healthy creature like you—" her voice cut like a sheet-metal file. Heads turned.

"All I want is information—"

"—living in luxury on MY tax money! You ought to be—"

V

It was an hour later. In a ninth-floor corridor of the GRANYAUCK TIMES-HERALD building, Mart leaned against a wall, mentally rehearsing speeches. A stout man emerged from a door lettered EDITOR IN CHIEF. Mart stepped forward to intercept him.

"Pardon me, sir. I have to see you . . ."

Sharp blue eyes under wild-growing brows darted at Maldon.

"Yes? What is it?"

"I have a story for you. It's about the Placement procedure."

"Whoa, buddy. Who are you?"

"My name's Maldon. I'm an Applied Tech graduate—almost—but I can't get placed in Microtronics. I don't have a tag—and the only way to get one is to get a job—but first I have to let the government operate on my brains—"

"Hmmmp!" The man looked Maldon up and down, started on.

"Listen!" Maldon caught at the portly man's arm. "They're making idiots out of intelligent people so they can do work you could train a chimp to do, and if you ask any questions—"

"All right, Mac . . ." A voice behind Maldon growled. A large hand took him by the shoulder, propelled him toward the walkaway entrance, urged him through the door. He straightened his coat, looked back. A heavy-set man with a pink card in a plastic cover clipped to his collar dusted his hands, looking satisfied.

"Don't come around lots," he called cheerfully as the door slammed.

VI

"Hi, Glamis," Mart said to the small, neat woman behind the small, neat desk. She smiled nervously, straightened the mathematically precise stack of papers before her.

"Mart, it's lovely to see you again, of course . . ." her eyes went to the blank place where his tag should have been. "But you really should have gone to your assigned SocAd Advisor—"

"I couldn't get an appointment until January." He pulled a chair around to the desk and sat down. "I've left school. I went in for Phase Two Placement testing this morning. I flunked."

"Oh . . . I'm so sorry, Mart." She arranged a small smile on her face. "But you can go back on Wednesday—"

"Uh-huh. And then on Friday, and then the following Monday—"

"Why, Mart, I'm sure you'll do better next time," the girl said brightly. She flipped through the pages of a calendar pad. "Wednesday's testing is for . . . ah . . . Vehicle Positioning Specialists, Instrumentation Inspectors, Sanitary Facility Supervisors—"

"Uh-huh. Toilet Attendants," Mart said. "Meter Readers—"

"There are others," Glamis went on hastily. "Traffic flow coordinators—"

"Pushing stop-light buttons on the turnpike. But it doesn't matter what the job titles are. I can't pass the tests."

"Why, Mart . . . Whatever do you mean?"

"I mean that to get the kind of jobs that are open you have to be a nice, steady moron. And if you don't happen to qualify as such, they're prepared to make you into one."

"Mart, you're exaggerating! The treatment merely slows the synaptic response time slightly—and its effects can be reversed at any time. People of exceptional qualities are needed to handle the type work—"

"How can I fake the test results, Glamis? I need a job—

unless I want to get used to Welfare coveralls and two T rations a day."

"Mart! I'm shocked that you'd suggest such a thing! Not that it would work. You can't fool the Board that easily—"

"Then fix it so I go in for Tech testing; you know I can pass."

She shook her head. "Heavens, Mart, Tech Testing is all done at Central Personnel in City Tower—Level Fifty. Nobody goes up there, without at least a blue tag—" She frowned sympathetically. "You should simply have your adjustment, and—"

Maldon looked surprised. "You really expect me to go down there and have them cut my I.Q. down to 80 so I can get a job shovelling garbage?"

"Really, Mart; you can't expect society to adjust to *you*. You have to adjust to *it*."

"Look, I can punch commuters' tickets just as well as if I were stupid. I could—"

Glamis shook her head. "No, you couldn't, Mart. The Board knows what it's doing." She lowered her voice. "I'll be perfectly frank with you. These jobs *must* be filled. But they can't afford to put perceptive, active minds on rote tasks. There'd only be trouble. They need people who'll be contented and happy punching tickets."

Mart sat pulling at his lower lip. "All right, Glamis. Maybe I will go in for Adjustment . . ."

"On, wonderful, Mart." She smiled. "I'm *sure* you'll be happier—"

"But first, I want to know more about it. I want to be sure they aren't going to make a permanent idiot out of me."

She tsked, handed over a small folder from a pile on the corner of the desk.

"This will tell you—"

He shook his head. "I saw that. It's just a throwaway for the public. I want to know how the thing works; circuit diagrams, technical specs."

"Why, Mart, I don't have anything of that sort—and even if I did—"

"You can get 'em. I'll wait."

"Mart, I *do* want to help you . . . but . . . what . . . ?"

"I'm not going in for Adjustment until I know something about it," he said flatly. "I want to put my mind at ease that they're not going to burn out my cortex."

Glamis nibbled her upper lip. "Perhaps I *could* get something from Central Files." She stood. "Wait here; I won't be long."

She was back in five minutes carrying a thick book with a cover of heavy manila stock on which were the words, *GSM 8765-89. Operation and Maintenance, EET Mark II*. Underneath, in smaller print, was a notice:

This Field Manual for Use of Authorized Personnel Only.

"Thanks, Glamis." Mart rifled the pages, glimpsed fine print and intricate diagrams. "I'll bring it back tomorrow." He headed for the door.

"Oh, you can't take it out of the office! You're not even *supposed* to *look* at it!"

"You'll get it back." He winked and closed the door on her worried voice.

VII

The cubicle reminded Mart of the one at the Placement center, three days earlier, except that it contained a high, narrow cot in place of a desk and chair. A damp-looking attendant in a white coat flipped a wall switch, twiddled a dial.

"Strip to your waist, place your clothing and shoes in the basket, remove all metal objects from your pockets, no watches or other jewelry must be worn," he recited in a rapid monotone. "When you are ready, lie down on your back—" he slapped the cot— "hands at your sides, breathe deeply, do not touch any of the equipment. I will return in approximately five minutes. Do not leave the stall." He whisked the curtain aside and was gone.

Mart slipped a flat plastic tool kit from his pocket, opened it out, picked the largest screwdriver, and went to work on the metal panel cover set against the wall. He lifted it off and looked in at a maze of junction blocks, vari-colored wires, bright screw-heads, fuses, tiny condensers.

He pulled a scrap of paper from his pocket, compared it to the circuits before him. The large black lead, here ... He put a finger on it. And the matching red one, leading up from the 30 MFD condenser ...

With a twist, he freed the two connectors, reversed them, tightened them back in place. Working quickly, he snipped wires, fitted jumpers in place, added a massive resistor from his pocket. There; with luck, the check instruments would give the proper readings now—but the current designed to lightly scorch his synapses would flow harmlessly round and round within the apparatus. He clapped the cover back in place, screwed it down, and had just pulled off his shirt when the attendant thrust his head inside the curtains.

"Let's go, let's get those clothes off and get on the cot," he said, and disappeared.

Maldon emptied his pockets, pulled off his shoes, stretched out on the cot. A minute or two ticked past. There was an odor of alcohol in the air. The curtain jumped aside. The round-faced attendant took his left arm, swiped a cold tuft of cotton across it, held a hypo-spray an inch from the skin, and depressed the plunger. Mart felt a momentary sting.

"You've been given a harmless soporific," the attendant said tonelessly. "Just relax, don't attempt to change the position of the headset or chest contacts after I have placed them in position, are you beginning to feel drowsy . . . ?"

Mart nodded. A tingling had begun in his fingertips; his head seemed to be inflating slowly. There was a touch of something cold across his wrists, then his ankles, pressure against his chest . . .

"Do not be alarmed, the restraint is for your own protection, relax and breathe deeply, it will hasten the effects of the soporific . . ." The voice echoed, fading and swelling. For a moment, the panicky thought came to Mart that perhaps he had made a mistake, that the modified apparatus would send a lethal charge through his brain . . . Then that thought was gone with all the others, lost in a swirling as of a soft green mist.

VIII

He was sitting on the side of the cot, and the attendant was offering him a small plastic cup. He took it, tasted the sweet liquid, handed it back.

"You should drink this," the attendant said, "It's very good for you."

Mart ignored him. He was still alive; and the attendant appeared to have noticed nothing unusual. So far, so good. He glanced at his hand. *One, two, three, four, five . . .* He could still count. *My name is Mart Maldon, age twenty-*

eight, place of residence, Welfare Dorm 69, Wing Two, nineteenth floor, room 1906 . . .

His memory seemed to be OK. *Twenty-seven times eighteen is . . . four hundred and eighty-six . . .*

He could still do simple arithmetic.

"Come on, fellow, drink the nice cup, then put your clothes on."

He shook his head, reached for his shirt, then remembered to move slowly, uncertainly, like a moron ought to. He fumbled clumsily with his shirt . . .

The attendant muttered, put the cup down, snatched the shirt, helped Mart into it, buttoned it for him.

"Put your stuff in your pockets, come on, that's a good fellow . . ."

He allowed himself to be led along the corridor, smiling vaguely at people hurrying past. In the processing room, a starched woman back of a small desk stamped papers, took his hand and impressed his thumbprint on them, slid them across the desk.

"Sign your name here . . ." she pointed. Maldon stood gaping at the paper.

"Write your name here!" She tapped the paper impatiently. Maldon reached up and wiped his nose with a forefinger, letting his mouth hang open.

The woman looked past him. "A Nine-oh-one," she snapped. "Take him back—"

Maldon grabbed the pen and wrote his name in large, scrawling letters. The woman snapped the form apart, thrust one sheet at him.

"Uh, I was thinking," he explained, folding the paper clumsily.

"Next!" the woman snapped, waving him on. He nodded submissively and shuffled slowly to the door.

IX

The Placement monitor looked at the form Maldon had given him. He looked up, smiling. "Well, so you finally wised up. Good boy. And today you got a nice score. We're going to be able to place you. You like bridges, hah?"

Maldon hesitated, then nodded.

"Sure you like bridges. Out in the open air. You're going to be an important man. When the cars come up, you lean out and see that they put the money in the box. You get to wear a uniform . . ." The small man rambled on, filling out forms. Maldon stood by, looking at nothing.

"Here you go. Now, you go where it says right here, see? Just get on the cross-town shuttle, right outside on this level, the one with the big number nine. You know what a nine is, OK?"

Maldon blinked, nodded. The clerk frowned. "Sometimes I think them guys overdo a good thing. But you'll get to feeling better in a few days; you'll sharpen up, like me. Now, you go on over there, and they'll give you your I.D. and your uniform and put you to work. OK?"

"Uh, thanks . . ." Maldon crossed the wide room, pushed through the turnstile, emerged into the late-afternoon sunlight on the forth-level walkaway. The glare panel by the shuttle entrance read NEXT—9. He thrust his papers into his pocket and ran for it.

X

Maldon left his Dormitory promptly at eight the next morning, dressed in his threadbare Student-issue suit, carrying the heavy duffel bag of Port Authority uniforms which had been issued to him the day before. His new yellow tag was pinned prominently to his lapel.

He took a cargo car to street level, caught an uptown car, dropped off in the run-down neighborhood of second-hand stores centered around Fifth Avenue and Forty-fifth Street. He picked a shabby establishment barricaded behind racks of dowdy garments, stepped into a long, dim-lit room smelling of naphtha and mouldy wool. Behind a counter, a short man with a circlet of fuzz above his ears and a vest hanging open over a tight-belted paunch looked him over. Mart hoisted the bag up, opened it, dumped the clothing out onto the counter. The paunchy man followed the action with his eyes.

"What'll you give me for this stuff?" Mart said.

The man behind the counter prodded the dark blue tunic, put a finger under the light blue trousers, rubbed the cloth. He leaned across the counter, glanced toward the door, squinted at Mart's badge. His eyes flicked to Mart's face, back to the clothing. He spread his hands.

"Five credits."

"For all of it? It's worth a hundred anyway."

The man glanced sharply at Maldon's face, back at his tag, frowning.

"Don't let the tag throw you," Maldon said. "It's stolen—just like the rest of the stuff."

"Hey." The paunchy man thrust his lips out. "What kinda talk is that? I run a respectable joint. What are you, some kinda cop?"

"I haven't got any time to waste," Maldon said. "There's nobody listening. Let's get down to business. You can strip off the braid and buttons and—"

"Ten credits, my top offer," the man said in a low voice. "I gotta stay alive, ain't I? Any bum can get outfitted free at the Welfare; who's buying my stuff?"

"I don't know. Make it twenty."

"Fifteen; it's robbery."

"Throw in a set of Maintenance coveralls, and it's a deal."

"I ain't got the real article, but close . . ."

Ten minutes later, Mart left the store wearing a grease-stained coverall with the cuffs turned up, the yellow tag clipped to the breast pocket.

XI

The girl at the bleached-driftwood desk placed austerely at the exact center of the quarter-acre of fog-grey rug stared at Maldon distastefully.

"I know of no trouble with the equipment—" she started in a lofty tone.

"Look, sister, I'm in the plumbing line; you run your dictyper." Maldon swung a greasy tool box around by the leather strap as though he were about to lower it to the rug. "They tell me the Exec gym, Level 9, City Tower, that's where I go. Now, you want to tell me where the steam room is, or do I go back and file a beef with the Union . . . ?"

"Next time come up the service shaft, Clyde!" she jabbed at a button; a panel whooshed aside across the room. "Men to the right, women to the left, co-ed straight ahead. Take your choice."

He went along the tiled corridor, passed steam-frosted doors. The passage turned right, angled left again. Mart pushed through a door, looked around at chromium and red plastic benches, horses, parallel bars, racks of graduated weights. A fat man in white shorts lay on the floor, halfheartedly pedaling his feet in the air. Mart crossed the room, tried another door.

Warm, sun-colored light streamed through an obscure-glass ceiling. Tropical plants in tubs nodded wide leaves over a mat of grass-green carpet edging a turquoise-tiled pool with chrome railings. Two brown-skinned men in brief trunks and sun-glasses sprawled on inflated rafts. There was a door to the right lettered EXECUTIVE DRESSING ROOM—MEMBERS ONLY. Mart went to it, stepped inside.

Tall, ivory-colored lockers lined two walls, with a wide padded bench between them. Beyond, bright shower heads winked in a darkened shower room. Maldon put the tool box on the bench, opened it, took out a twelve-inch prybar.

By levering at the top of the tall locker door, he was able to bulge it out sufficiently to see the long metal strip on the back of the door which secured it. He went back to the tool box, picked out a slim pair of pincers; with them he gripped the locking strip, levered up; the door opened with a sudden clang. The locker was empty.

He tried the next; it contained a handsome pale tan suit which would have fitted him nicely at the age of twelve. He went to the next locker . . .

Four lockers later, a door popped open on a dark maroon suit of expensive-looking polyon, a pair of plain scarlet shoes, a crisp pink shirt. Mart checked quickly. There was a wallet stuffed with ten-credit notes, a club membership card, and a blue I.D. with a gold alligator clip. Mart left the money on the shelf, rolled the clothing and stuffed it into the tool box, made for the door. It swung open and the smaller of the two sun bathers pushed past him with a sharp glance. Mart walked quickly around the end of the pool, stepped into the corridor. At the far end of it, the girl from the desk stood talking emphatically to a surprised-looking man. Their eyes turned toward Mart. He pushed through the first door on the left into a room with a row of white-sheeted tables, standing lamps with wide reflectors, an array of belted and rollered equipment. A vast bulk of a man with hairy forearms and a bald head, wearing a tight white leotard and white sneakers folded a newspaper and looked up from his bench, wobbling a toothpick in the corner of his mouth. There was a pink tag on his chest.

"Uh . . . showers?" Mart inquired. The fat man nodded

toward a door behind him. Mart stepped to it, found himself in a long room studded with shower-heads and control knobs. There was no other door out. He turned back, bumped into the fat man in the doorway.

"So somebody finally decided to do something about the leak," he said around the toothpick. "Three months since I phoned it in. You guys take your time, hah?"

"I've got to go back for my tools," Mart said, starting past him. The fat man blocked him without moving. "So what's in the box?"

"Ah, they're the wrong tools . . ." He tried to sidle past. The big man took the toothpick from his mouth, frowned at it.

"You got a pipe wrench, ain't you? You got crescents, a screwdriver. What else you need to fix a lousy leak?"

"Well, I need my sprog-depressor," Mart said, "and my detrafficator rings, and possibly a marpilizer or two . . ."

"How come you ain't got—what you said—in there." The fat man eyed the tool box. "Ain't that standard equipment?"

"Yes, indeed—but I only have a right-hand one, and—"

"Let's have a look—" A fat hand reached for the tool-kit. Mart backed.

"—but I might be able to make it work," he finished. He glanced around the room. "Which one was it?"

"That third needle-battery on the right. You can see the drip. I'm tryna read, it drives me nuts."

Mart put the tool box down. "If you don't mind, it makes me nervous to work in front of an audience . . ."

The fat man grunted and withdrew. Mart opened the box, took out a wrench, began loosening a wide hex-sided locking ring. Water began to dribble, then spurt. Mart went to the door, flung it open.

"Hey, you didn't tell me the water wasn't turned off . . ."

"Huh?"

"You'll have to turn off the master valve; hurry up, before the place is flooded!"

The fat man jumped up, headed for the door.

"Stand by it, wait five minutes, then turn it back on!" Mart called after him. The door banged. Mart hauled the tool box out into the massage room, quickly stripped off the grimy coverall. His eye fell on a rack of neatly-packaged under-wear, socks, toothbrushes, combs. He helped himself to a set, removed the last of the Welfare issue clothing—

A shout sounded outside the door, running feet. The door burst open. It was the big man from the executive locker room.

"Where's Charlie? Some rascal's stolen my clothing . . . !"

Mart grabbed up a towel, dropped it over his head and rubbed vigorously, humming loudly, his back to the newcomer.

"The workman—there's his tool box!"

Mart whirled, pulled the towel free, snatched the box from the hand of the invader, with a hearty shove sent him reeling into the locker room. He slammed the door, turned the key and dropped it down a drain. The shouts from inside were barely audible. He wrapped the towel around himself and dashed into the hall. There were people, some in white, others in towels or street clothes, all talking at once.

"Down there!" Mart shouted, pointing vaguely. "Don't let him get away!" He plunged through the press, along the hall. Doors opened and shut.

"Hey, what's he doing with a tool box?" someone shouted. Mart whirled, dived through a door, found himself in a dense, hot fog. A woman with pink skin beaded with perspiration and a towel wrapped turban-fashion around her head stared at him.

"What are you doing in here? Co-ed is the next room along."

Mart gulped and dived past her, slammed through a plain door, found himself in a small room stacked with cartons. There was another door in the opposite wall. He went through it, emerged in a dusty hall. Three doors down, he found an empty store-room.

Five minutes later he emerged, dressed in a handsome maroon suit. He strode briskly along to a door marked EXIT, came out into a carpeted foyer with a rank of open elevator doors. He stepped into one. The yellow-tagged attendant whooshed the door shut.

"Tag, sir?" Maldon showed the blue I.D. The operator nodded.

"Down, sir?"

"No," Mart said. "Up."

XII

He stepped out into the cool silence of Level Fifty.

"Which way to the class One Testing Rooms?" he asked briskly

The operator pointed. The door-lined corridor seemed to stretch endlessly.

"Going to try for the Big One, eh, sir?" the operator said. "Boy, you couldn't hire me to take on them kind of jobs. Me, I wouldn't want the responsibility." The closing door cut off the view of his wagging head.

Maldon set off, trying to look purposeful. Somewhere on this level were the Central Personnel Files, according to Glamis. It shouldn't be too hard to find them. After that ... well, he could play it by ear.

A menu-board directory at a cross-corridor a hundred yards from his starting-point indicated PERSONNEL ANALYSIS to the right. Mart followed the passage, passed open doors through which he caught glimpses of soft colors, air-conditioner grills, potted plants, and immaculate young women with precise hair styles sitting before immense key boards or behind bare desks. Chaste lettering on doors read PRO-GRAMMING; REQUIREMENTS; DATA EXTRAPOLATION—PHASE III . . .

Ahead, Maldon heard a clattering, rising in volume as he approached a wide double door. He peered through glass, saw a long room crowded with massive metal cases ranked in rows, floor to ceiling. Men in tan dust smocks moved in the aisles, referring to papers in their hands, jotting notes, punching keys set in the consoles spaced at intervals on the giant cabinets. At a desk near the door, a man with a wide, sad mouth and a worried expression looked up, caught sight of Mart. It was no time to hesitate. He pushed through the door.

"Morning," he said genially over the busy sound of the data machines. "I'm looking for Central Personnel. I wonder if I'm in the right place?"

The sad man opened his mouth, then closed it. He had a green tag attached to the collar of his open-necked shirt.

"You from Special Actions?" he said doubtfully.

"Aptical foddering," Maldon said pleasantly. "I'd never been over here in Personnel Analysis, so I said, what the heck, I'll just run over myself." He was holding a relaxed smile in place, modelled after the one Dean Wormwell had customarily worn when condescending to students.

"Well, sir, this is Data Processing; what you probably want is Files . . ."

Mart considered quickly. "Just what is the scope of the work you do here?"

The clerk got to his feet. "We maintain the Master Personnel Cards up-to-date," he started, then paused. "Uh, could I just see that I.D., sir?"

Maldon let the smile cool a degree or two, flashed the blue card; the clerk craned as Mart tucked the tag away.

"Now," Mart went on briskly, "suppose you just start at the beginning and give me a rundown." He glanced at a wall-clock. "Make it a fast briefing. I'm a little pressed for time."

The clerk hitched at his belt, looked around. "Well, sir, let's start over here . . .

Ten minutes later, they stood before a high, glass-fronted housing inside which row on row of tape reels nestled on shiny rods; bright-colored plastic fittings of complex shape jammed the space over, under and behind each row.

". . . it's all completely cybernetic-governed, of course," the clerk was saying. "We process an average of four hundred and nineteen thousand personnel actions per day, with an average relay-delay of not over four microseconds."

"What's the source of your input?" Mart inquired in the tone of one dutifully asking the routine questions.

"All the Directorates feed their data in to us—"

"Placement Testing?" Mart asked idly.

"Oh, sure, that's our biggest single data input."

"Including Class Five and Seven categories, for example?"

The clerk nodded. "Eight through Two. Your Tech categories are handled separately, over in Banks Y and Z. There . . ." He pointed to a pair of red-painted cabinets.

"I see. That's where the new graduates from the Technical Institutions are listed, eh?"

"Right, sir. They're scheduled out from there to Testing alphabetically, and then ranked by score for Grading, Classification, and Placement."

Mart nodded and moved along the aisle. There were two-inch high letters stencilled on the frames of the data cases. He stopped before a large letter B.

"Let's look at a typical record," Mart suggested. The clerk stepped to the console, pressed a button. A foot-square screen glowed. Print popped into focus on it: BAJUL, FELIX B. 654-8734-099-B1.

Below the heading was an intricate pattern of dots.

"May I?" Mart reached for the button, pushed it. There was a click and the name changed: BAKARSKI, HYMAN A.

He looked at the meaningless code under the name.

"I take it each dot has a significance?"

"In the first row, you have the physical profile; that's the first nine spaces. Then psych, that's the next twenty-one. Then . . ." He lectured on. Mart nodded.

". . . educational profile, right here . . ."

"Now," Mart cut in. "Suppose there were an error—say in the median scores attained by an individual. How would you correct that?"

The clerk frowned pulling down the corners of his mouth into well-worn grooves.

"I don't mean on your part, of course," Mart said hastily. "But I imagine that the data processing equipment occasionally drops a decimal, eh?" He smiled understandingly.

"Well, we do get maybe one or two a year—but there's no harm done. On the next run-through, the card's automatically kicked out."

"So you don't . . . ah . . . make corrections?"

"Well, only when a Change Entry comes through."

The clerk twirled knobs; the card moved aside, up; a single dot swelled on the screen, resolved into a pattern of dots.

"Say it was on this item; I'd just wipe that code, and overprint the change. Only takes a second, and—"

"Suppose, for example, you wanted this record corrected to show graduation from a Tech Institute?"

"Well, that would be this symbol here; eighth row, fourth entry. The code for technical specialty would be in the 900 series. You punch it in here." He indicated rows of colored buttons. "Then the file's automatically transferred to the V bank."

"Well, this has been a fascinating tour," Mart said. "I'll make it a point to enter an appropriate commendation in the files."

The sad-faced man smiled wanly. "Well, I try to do my job
..."

"Now, if you don't mind, I'll just stroll around and watch
for a few minutes before I rush along to my conference."

"Well, nobody's supposed to be back here in the stacks
except—"

"That's quite all right. I'd prefer to look it over alone." He
turned his back on the clerk and strolled off. A glance back
at the end of the stack showed the clerk settling into his
chair, shaking his head.

Mart moved quickly past the ends of the stacks, turned in
at the third row, followed the letters through O, N, stopped
before M. He punched a button, read the name that flashed
on the screen: MAJONOVITCH.

He tapped at the key; names flashed briefly: MAKISS ...
MALACHI ... MALDON, SALLY ... MALDON, MART—

He looked up. A technician was standing at the end of the
stack, looking at him. He nodded.

"Quite an apparatus you have here ..."

The technician said nothing. He wore a pink tag and his
mouth was open half an inch. Mart looked away, up at the
ceiling, down at the floor, back at the technician. He was still
standing, looking. Abruptly his mouth closed with a decisive
snap; he started to turn toward the clerk's desk—

Mart reached for the control knobs, quickly dialled for the
eighth row, entry four; the single dot shifted into position,
enlarged. The technician, distracted by the sudden move,
turned, came hurrying along the aisle.

"Hey, nobody's supposed to mess with the—"

"Now, my man," Mart said in a firm tone. "Answer each
question in as few words as possible. You will be graded on
promptness and accuracy of response. What is the number of
digits in the Technical Specialty series—the 900 group?"

Taken aback, the technician raised his eyebrows, said,
"Three—but—"

"And what is the specific code for Microtronics Engineer—
cum laude?"

There was a sudden racket from the door. Voices were
raised in hurried inquiry. The clerk's voice replied. The
technician stood undecided, scratching his head. Mart jabbed
at the colored buttons: 901 ... 922 ... 936 ... He coded a
dozen three-digit Specialties into his record at random.

From the corner of his eye he saw a light blink on one of the red-painted panels; his record was being automatically transferred to the Technically Qualified files. He poked the button which whirled his card from the screen and turned, stepped off toward the far end of the room. The technician came after him.

"Hey there, what card was that you were messing with . . . ?"

"No harm done," Mart reassured him. "Just correcting an error. You'll have to excuse me now; I've just remembered a pressing engagement . . ."

"I better check; what card was it?"

"Oh—just one picked at random."

"But . . . we got a hundred million cards in here . . ."

"Correct!" Maldon said. "So far you're batting a thousand. Now, we have time for just one more question: is there another door out of here?"

"Mister, you better wait a minute till I see the super—"

Mart spotted two unmarked doors, side by side. "Don't bother; what would you tell him? That there was, just possibly, a teentsy weentsy flaw in one of your hundred million cards? I'm sure that would upset him." He pulled the nearest door open. The technician's mouth worked frantically.

"Hey, that's"—he started.

"Don't call us—we'll call you!" Mart stepped past the door; it swung to behind him. Just before it closed, he saw that he was standing in a four foot by six foot closet. He whirled, grabbed for the door; there was no knob on the inside. It shut with a decisive click!

He was alone in pitch darkness.

Maldon felt hastily over the surfaces of the walls, found them bare and featureless. He jumped, failed to touch the ceiling. Outside he heard the technician's voice, shouting. At any moment he would open the door and that would be that . . .

Mart went to his knees, explored the floor. It was smooth. Then his elbow cracked against metal—

He reached, found a grill just above floor level, two feet wide and a foot high. A steady flow of cool air came from it. There were screw-heads at each corner. Outside, the shouts continued. There were answering shouts.

Mart felt over his pockets, brought out a coin, removed

the screws. The grill fell forward into his hands. He laid it aside, started in head-first, encountered a sharp turn just beyond the wall. He wriggled over on his side, pushed hard, negotiated the turn by pulling with his hands pressed against the sides of the metal duct. There was light ahead, cross-hatched by a grid. He reached it, peered into a noisy room where great panels loomed, their faces a solid maze of dials and indicator lights. He tried the grill. It seemed solid. The duct made a right-angle turn here. Maldon worked his way around the bend, found that the duct widened six inches. When his feet were in position, he swung a kick at the grill. The limited space made it awkward; he kicked again and again; the grill gave, one more kick and it clattered into the room beyond. Mart struggled out through the opening.

The room was brightly lit, deserted. There were large printed notices here and there on the wall warning of danger. Mart turned, re-entered the duct, made his way back to the closet. The voices were still audible outside the door. He reached through the opening, found the grill, propped it in position as the door flew open. He froze, waiting. There was a moment of silence.

"But," the technician's voice said, "I tell you the guy walked into the utility closet here like he was boarding a rocket for Paris! I didn't let the door out of my sight, that's why I was standing back at the back and yelling, like you was chewing me out for . . ."

"You must have made an error; it must have been the other door there . . ."

The door closed. Mart let out a breath. Now perhaps he'd have a few minutes' respite in which to figure a route off Level Fifty.

XIII

He prowled the lanes between the vast cybernetic machines, turned a corner, almost collided with a young woman with red-blonde hair, dark eyes, and a pouting red mouth which opened in a surprised O.

"You shouldn't be in here," she said, motioning over her shoulder with a pencil. "All examinees must remain in the examination room until the entire battery of tests have been completed."

"I . . . ah . . ."

"I know," the girl said, less severely. "Four hours at a stretch. It's awful. But you'd better go back in now before somebody sees you."

He nodded, smiled, and moved toward the door she had indicated. He looked back. She was studying the instrument dials, not watching him. He went past the door and tried the next. It opened and he stepped into a small, tidy office. A large-eyed woman with tightly dressed brown hair looked up from a desk adorned by a single rosebud in a slim vase and a sign reading PLACEMENT OFFICER. Her eyes went to a wall clock.

"You're too late for today's testing, I'm afraid," she said. "You'll have to return on Wednesday; that's afternoon testing. Mondays we test in the morning." She smiled sympathetically. "Quite a few make that mistake."

"Oh," Mart said. "Ah . . . Couldn't I start late?"

The woman was shaking her head. "Oh, it wouldn't be possible. The first results are already coming in . . ." She nodded toward a miniature version of the giant machines in the next room. A humming and clicking sounded briefly from it. She tapped a key on her desk. There was a sharp buzz from the small machine. He gazed at the apparatus. Again it clicked and hummed. Again she tapped, eliciting another buzz.

Mart stood, considering. His only problem now was to leave the building without attracting attention. His record had been altered to show his completion of a Technical Specialty; twelve of them, in fact. It might have been better if he had settled for one. Someone might notice—

"I see you're admiring the Profiler," the woman said. "It's a very compact model, isn't it? Are you a Cyberneticist, by any chance?"

Maldon started. "No . . ."

"What name is that? I'll check your file over to see that everything's in order for Wednesday's testing."

Mart took a deep breath. This was no time to panic . . . "Maldon," he said. "Mart Maldon."

The woman swung an elaborate telephone-dial-like instrument out from a recess, dialed a long code, then sat back. Ten seconds passed. With a click, a small panel on the desk-top glowed. The woman leaned forward, reading. She looked up.

"Why, Mr. Maldon! You have a remarkable record! I don't believe I've ever encountered a testee with such a wide—and varied—background!"

"Oh," Mart said, with a weak smile. "It was nothing . . ."

"Eidetics, Cellular Psychology, Autonomics . . ."

"I hate narrow specialization," Mart said.

" . . . Cybernetics Engineering—why, Mr. Maldon, you were teasing me!"

"Well . . ." Mart edged toward the door.

"My, we'll certainly be looking forward to seeing your test results, Mr. Maldon! And Oh! Do let me show you the new Profiler you were admiring." She hopped up, came round the desk. "It's such a time saver—and of course, saves a vast number of operations within the master banks. Now when the individual testee depresses his COMPLETED key, his test pattern in binary form is transferred directly to this unit for recognition. It's capable of making over a thousand yes-no comparisons per second profiling the results in decimal terms and recoding them into the master record, without the necessity for activating a single major sequence within the master— and, of course, every activation costs the taxpayer seventy-nine credits!"

"Very impressive," Mart said. If he could interrupt the flow of information long enough to ask a few innocent-sounding directions . . .

A discreet buzzer sounded. The woman depressed a key on the desk communicator.

"Miss Frinkles, could you step in a moment? There's a report of a madman loose in the building . . ."

"Good Heavens!" She looked at Mart as she slipped through the door. "Please, do excuse me a moment . . ."

Mart waited half a minute, started to follow; a thought struck him. He looked at the Profiler. All test results were processed through this little device; what if . . .

A quick inspection indicated that the apparatus was a close relative of the desk-top units used at Applied Tech in the ill-fated Analogy Theory class. The input, in the form of a binary series established by the testee's answers to his quiz, was compared with the master pattern for the specialty indicated by the first three digits of the signal. The results were translated into a profile, ready for transmittal to the Master Files.

This was almost too simple . . .

Mart pressed a lever at the back of the housing, lifted it off. Miss Frinkles had been right about this being a new model; most of the circuitry was miniaturized and built up into replaceable subassemblies. What he needed was a set of tools . . .

He tried Miss Frinkles' desk, turned up a nail file and two bobby pins. It wouldn't be necessary to fake an input; all that was needed was to key the coder section to show the final result. He crouched, peered in the side of the unit. There, to the left was the tiny bank of contacts which would open or close to indicate the score in a nine-digit profile. There were nine rows of nine contacts, squeezed into an area of one half-inch square. It was going to be a ticklish operation . . .

Mart straightened a hair-pin, reached in, delicately touched the row of minute relays; the top row of contacts snapped closed, and a red light went on at the side of the machine. Mart tossed the wire aside, and quickly referred to his record, still in focus on Miss Frinkles' desk-top viewer, then tickled tumblers to show his five letter, four digit personal identity code. Then he pressed a cancel key, to blank the deskscreen, and dropped the cover back in place on the Profiler. He was sitting in a low chair, leafing through a late issue of *Popular Statistics* when Miss Frinkles returned.

"It seems a maintenance man ran berserk down on Nine Level," she said breathlessly. "He killed three people, then set fire to—"

"Well, I must be running along," Mart said, rising. "A very nice little machine you have there. Tell me, are there any manual controls?"

"Oh, yes, didn't you notice them? Each test result must be validated by me before it's released to the Master Files. Suppose someone cheated, or finished late; it wouldn't do to let a disqualified score past."

"Oh, no indeed. And to transfer the data to the Master File, you just push this?" Mart said, leaning across and depressing the key he had seen Miss Frinkles use earlier. There was a sharp buzz from the Profiler. The red light went out.

"Oh, you mustn't—" Miss Frinkles exclaimed. "Not that it would matter in this case, of course," she added apologetically, "but—"

The door opened and the red-head stepped into the room. "Oh," she said, looking at Mart. "There you are. I looked for you in the Testing room—"

Miss Frinkles looked up with a surprised expression. "But I was under the impression—" She smiled. "Oh, Mr. Maldon, you *are* a tease! You'd already completed your testing, and you let me think you came in late . . . !"

Mart smiled modestly.

"Oh, Barbara, we must look at his score. He has a fantastic academic record. At least ten Specialized degrees, and magna cum laude in every one . . ."

The screen glowed. Miss Frinkles adjusted a knob, scanned past the first frame to a second. She stared.

"Mr. Maldon! I knew you'd do well, but a *perfect* score!"

The hall door banged wide. "Miss Frinkles—" a tall man stared at Mart, looked him up and down. He backed a step. "Who're you? Where did you get that suit—"

"MISTER Cludd!" Miss Frinkles said in an icy tone. "Kindly refrain from bursting into my office unannounced— and kindly show a trifle more civility to my guest, who happens to be a very remarkable young man who has just completed one of the finest test profiles it has been my pleasure to see during my service with Placement!"

"Eh? Are you sure? I mean—that suit . . . and the shoes . . ."

"I like a conservative outfit," Mart said desperately.

"You mean he's been here all morning . . . ?" Mr. Cludd looked suddenly uncomfortable.

"Of course!"

"He was in my exam group, Mr. Cludd," the red-haired girl put in. "I'll vouch for that. Why?"

"Well . . . it just happens the maniac they're looking for is dressed in a similar suit, and . . . well, I guess I lost my head. I was just coming in to tell you he'd been seen on this floor. He made a getaway through a service entrance leading to the helipad on the roof, and . . ." he ran down.

"Thank you, Mr. Cludd," Miss Frinkles said icily. Cludd mumbled and withdrew. Miss Frinkles turned to Mart.

"I'm so thrilled, Mr. Maldon . . ."

"Golly, yes," Barbara said.

"It isn't every day I have the opportunity to Place an applicant of your qualifications. Naturally, you'll have the widest possible choice. I'll give you the current prospectus, and next week—"

"Couldn't you place me right now, Miss Frinkles?"

"You mean—today?"

"Immediately." Mart looked at the red-head. "I like it here. What openings have you got in your department?"

Miss Frinkles gasped, flushed, smiled, then turned and played with the buttons on her console, watching the small screen. "Wonderful," she breathed. "The opening is still unfilled. I was afraid one of the other units might have filled it in the past hour." She poked at more keys. A white card in a narrow platinum holder with a jewelled alligator clip popped from a slot. She rose and handed it to Mart reverently.

"Your new I.D. sir. And I know you're going to make a wonderful chief!"

XIV

Mart sat behind the three-yard-long desk of polished rosewood, surveying the tennis-court-sized expanse of ankle-deep carpet which stretched across to a wide door of deep-polished mahogany, then swivelled to gaze out through wide windows of insulated, polarized, tinted glass at the towers of Granyauck, looming up in a deep blue sky. He turned back, opened the silver box that rested between a jade pen-holder and an ebony paper-weight on the otherwise unadorned desk, lifted out a Chanel dope-stick, sniffed it appreciatively. He adjusted his feet comfortably on the desk top, pressed a tiny silver button set in the arm of the chair. A moment later the door opened with the faintest of sounds.

"Barbara—" Mart began.

"There you are," a deep voice said.

Mart's feet came off the desk with a crash. The large man approaching him across the rug had a familiar look about him ...

"That was a dirty trick, locking me in the shower. We hadn't figured on that one. Slowed us up something awful." He swung a chair around and sat down.

"But," Mart said. "But ... but ..."

"Three days, nine hours and fourteen minutes," the newcomer said, eyeing a finger watch. "I must say you made the most of it. Never figured on you bollixing the examination records, too; most of 'em stop with the faked Academic Record, and figure to take their chances on the exam."

"Most of 'em?" Mart repeated weakly.

"Sure. You didn't think you were the only one selected to go before the Special Placement Board, did you?"

"Selected? Special . . ." Mart's voice trailed off.

"Well, surely you're beginning to understand now, Maldon," the man from whom Mart had stolen the suit said. "We picked you as a potential Top Executive over three years ago. We've followed your record closely ever since. You were on every one of the Board Members' nomination lists—"

"But—but I was quota'd out—"

"Oh, we could have let you graduate, go through testing, pick up a green tag and a spot on a promotion list, plug away for twenty years, make Exec rank—but we can't waste the time. We need talent, Mart. And we need it now!"

Mart took a deep breath and slammed the desk. "Why in the name of ten thousand devils didn't you just TELL me!"

The visitor shook his head. "Nope; we need good men, Mart—need 'em bad. We need to find the superior individuals; we can't afford to waste time bolstering up the folklore that the will of the people constitutes wisdom. This is a city of a hundred million people—and it's growing at a rate that will double that in a decade. We have problems, Mart. Vast, urgent problems. We need men that can solve 'em. We can test you in academic knowledge, cook up psychological profiles—but we have to KNOW. We have to find out how you react in a real-life situation; what you do to help yourself when you're dumped on the walkaway, broke and hopeless. If you go in and have your brain burned, scratch one. If you meekly register to wait out a Class Two test opening—well, good luck to you. If you walk in and take what you want . . ." he looked around the office, ". . . then welcome to the Club."

DOORSTEP

Steadying his elbow on the kitchen table serving as desk, Brigadier General Straut leveled his binoculars and stared out through the second-floor window of the farmhouse at the bulky object lying canted at the edge of the wood lot. He watched the figures moving over and around the gray mass, then flipped the lever on the field telephone at his elbow.

"How are your boys doing, Major?"

"General, since that box this morning—"

"I know all about the box, Bill. So does Washington by now. What have you got that's new?"

"Sir, I haven't got anything to report yet. I have four crews on it, and she still looks impervious as hell."

"Still getting the sounds from inside?"

"Intermittently, General."

"I'm giving you one more hour, Major. I want that thing cracked."

The general dropped the phone back on its cradle and absently peeled the cellophane from a cigar. He had moved fast, he reflected, after the State Police notified him at nine forty-one last night. He had his men on the spot, the area evacuated of civilians, and a preliminary report on its way to Washington by midnight. At two thirty-six, they had discovered the four-inch cube lying on the ground fifteen feet from the huge object—missile, capsule, bomb—whatever it was. But now—several hours later—nothing new.

The field phone jangled. Straut grabbed it up.

"General, we've discovered a thin spot up on the top side. All we can tell so far is that the wall thickness falls off there ..."

"All right. Keep after it, Bill."

This was more like it. If Brigadier General Straut could have this thing wrapped up by the time Washington awoke to the fact that it was something big—well, he'd been waiting a

119

long time for that second star. This was his chance, and he would damn well make the most of it.

He looked across the field at the thing. It was half in and half out of the woods, flat-sided, round-ended, featureless. Maybe he should go over and give it a closer look personally. He might spot something the others were missing. It might blow them all to kingdom come any second; but what the hell, he had earned his star on sheer guts in Normandy. He still had 'em.

He keyed the phone. "I'm coming down, Bill," he told the Major. On impulse, he strapped a pistol belt on. Not much use against a house-sized bomb, but the heft of it felt good.

The thing looked bigger than ever as the jeep approached it, bumping across the muck of the freshly plowed field. From here he could see a faint line running around, just below the juncture of side and top. Major Greer hadn't mentioned that. The line was quite obvious; in fact, it was more of a crack.

With a sound like a baseball smacking the catcher's glove, the crack opened, the upper half tilted, men sliding—then impossibly it stood open, vibrating, like the roof of a house suddenly lifted. The driver gunned the jeep. There were cries, and a ragged shrilling that set Straut's teeth on edge. The men were running back now, two of them dragging a third.

Major Greer emerged from behind the object, looked about, ran toward General Straut shouting. ". . . a man dead. It snapped; we weren't expecting it . . ."

Straut jumped out beside the men, who had stopped now and were looking back. The underside of the gaping lid was an iridescent black. The shrill noise sounded thinly across the field. Greer arrived, panting.

"What happened?" Straut snapped.

"I was . . . checking over that thin spot, General. The first thing I knew it was . . . coming up under me. I fell; Tate was at the other side. He held on and it snapped him loose, against a tree. His skull—"

"What the devil's that racket?"

"That's the sound we were getting from inside before, General. There's something in there, alive—"

"All right, pull yourself together, Major. We're not unprepared. Bring your half-tracks into position. The tanks will be here soon."

Straut glanced at the men standing about. He would show them what leadership meant.

"You men keep back," he said. He puffed his cigar calmly as he walked toward the looming object. The noise stopped suddenly; that was a relief. There was a faint and curious odor in the air, something like chlorine ... or seaweed ... or iodine.

There were no marks in the ground surrounding the thing. It had apparently dropped straight in to its present position. It was heavy, too—the soft soil was displaced in a mound a foot high all along the side.

Behind him, Straut heard a yell. He whirled. The men were pointing; the jeep started up, churned toward him, wheels spinning. He looked up. Over the edge of the gray wall, six feet above his head, a great reddish limb, like the claw of a crab, moved, groping.

Straut yanked the .45 from its holster, jacked the action and fired. Soft matter spattered, and the claw jerked back. The screeching started up again angrily, then was drowned in the engine roar as the jeep slid to a stop.

Straut stooped, grabbed up a leaf to which a quivering lump adhered, jumped into the vehicle as it leaped forward; then a shock and they were going into a spin and ...

"Lucky it was soft ground," somebody said. And somebody else asked, "What about the driver?"

Silence. Straut opened his eyes. "What ... about ..."

A stranger was looking down at him, an ordinary-looking fellow of about thirty-five.

"Easy, now, General Straut. You've had a bad spill. Everything is all right. I'm Professor Lieberman, from the University."

"The driver," Straut said with an effort.

"He was killed when the jeep went over."

"Went ... over?"

"The creature lashed out with a member resembling a scorpion's stinger. It struck the jeep and flipped it. You were thrown clear. The driver jumped and the jeep rolled on him."

Straut pushed himself up.

"Where's Greer?"

"I'm right here, sir." Major Greer stepped up, stood attentively.

"Those tanks here yet?"

"No, sir. I had a call from General Margrave; there's some sort of holdup. Something about not destroying scientific material. I did get the mortars over from the base."

Straut got to his feet. The stranger took his arm. "You ought to lie down, General—"

"Who the hell is going to make me? Greer, get those mortars in place, spaced between your tracks."

The telephone rang. Straut seized it. "General Straut."

"General Margrave here, Straut. I'm glad you're back on your feet. There'll be some scientists from the State University coming over. Cooperate with them. You're going to have to hold things together at least until I can get another man in there to—"

"Another man? General Margrave, I'm not incapacitated. The situation is under complete control—"

"It is, is it? I understand you've got still another casualty. What's happened to your defensive capabilities?"

"That was an accident, sir. The jeep—"

"We'll review that matter at a later date. What I'm calling about is more important right now. The code men have made some headway on that box of yours. It's putting out a sort of transmission."

"What kind, sir?"

"Half the message—it's only twenty seconds long, repeated—is in English. It's a fragment of a recording from a daytime radio program; one of the network men here identified it. The rest is gibberish. They're still working over it."

"What—"

"Bryant tells me he thinks there may be some sort of correspondence between the two parts of the message. I wouldn't know, myself. In my opinion, it's a threat of some sort."

"I agree, General. An ultimatum."

"Right. Keep your men back at a safe distance from now on. I want no more casualties."

Straut cursed his luck as he hung up the phone. Margrave was ready to relieve him, after he had exercised every precaution. He had to do something fast, before this opportunity for promotion slipped out of his hands.

He looked at Major Greer. "I'm neutralizing this thing once and for all. There'll be no more men killed."

Lieberman stood up. "General! I must protest any attack against this—"

Straut whirled. "I'm handling this, Professor. I don't know who let you in here or why—but I'll make the decisions. I'm stopping this man-killer before it comes out of its nest, maybe gets into that village beyond the woods. There are four thousand civilians there. It's my job to protect them." He jerked his head at Greer, strode out of the room.

Lieberman followed, pleading. "The creature has shown no signs of aggressiveness, General Straut—"

"With two men dead?"

"You should have kept them back—"

"Oh, it was my fault, was it?" Straut stared at Lieberman with cold fury. This civilian pushed his way in here, then had the infernal gall to accuse him, Brigadier General Straut, of causing the death of his own men. If he had the fellow in uniform for five minutes . . .

"You're not well, General. That fall—"

"Keep out of my way, Professor," Straut said. He turned and went on down the stairs. The present foul-up could ruin his career; and now this egghead interference . . .

With Greer at his side, Straut moved out to the edge of the field.

"All right, Major. Open up with your .50 calibers."

Greer called a command and a staccato rattle started up. The smell of cordite and the blue haze of gunsmoke—this was more like it. He was in command here.

Lieberman came up to Straut. "General, I appeal to you in the name of science. Hold off a little longer; at least until we learn what the message is about."

"Get back from the firing line, Professor." Straut turned his back on the civilian, raised the glasses to observe the effect of the recoilless rifle. There was a tremendous smack of displaced air, and a thunderous boom as the explosive shell struck. Straut saw the gray shape jump, the raised lid waver. Dust rose from about it. There was no other effect.

"Keep firing, Greer," Straut snapped, almost with a feeling of triumph. The thing was impervious to artillery; now who was going to say it was no threat?

"How about the mortars, sir?" Greer said. "We can drop a few rounds right inside it."

"All right, try that before the lid drops."

And what we'll try next, I don't know, he thought.

The mortar fired with a muffled thud. Straut watched tensely. Five seconds later, the object erupted in a gout of pale pink debris. The lid rocked, pinkish fluid running down its opalescent surface. A second burst, a third. A great fragment of the menacing claw hung from the branch of a tree a hundred feet from the ship.

Straut grabbed up the phone. "Cease fire!"

Lieberman stared in horror at the carnage.

The telephone rang. Straut picked it up.

"General Straut," he said. His voice was firm. He had put an end to the threat.

"Straut, we've broken the message," General Margrave said excitedly. "It's the damnedest thing I ever . . ."

Straut wanted to interrupt, announce his victory, but Margrave was droning on.

". . . strange sort of reasoning, but there was a certain analogy. In any event, I'm assured the translation is accurate. Here's how it reads in English . . ."

Straut listened. Then he carefully placed the receiver back on the hook.

Lieberman stared at him.

"What did it say?"

Straut cleared his throat. He turned and looked at Lieberman for a long moment before answering.

"It said, 'Please take good care of my little girl.' "

THE LONG REMEMBERED THUNDER

I

In his room at the Elsby Commercial Hotel, Tremaine opened his luggage and took out a small tool kit, used a screwdriver to remove the bottom cover plate from the telephone. He inserted a tiny aluminum cylinder, crimped wires and replaced the cover. Then he dialed a long-distance Washington number and waited half a minute for the connection.

"Fred, Tremaine here. Put the buzzer on." A thin hum sounded on the wire as the scrambler went into operation.

"Okay, can you read me all right? I'm set up in Elsby. Grammond's boys are supposed to keep me informed. Meantime, I'm not sitting in this damned room crouched over a dial. I'll be out and around for the rest of the afternoon."

"I want to see results," the thin voice came back over the filtered hum of the jamming device. "You spent a week with Grammond—I can't wait another. I don't mind telling you certain quarters are pressing me."

"Fred, when will you learn to sit on your news breaks until you've got some answers to go with the questions?"

"I'm an appointive official," Fred said sharply. "But never mind that. This fellow Margrave—General Margrave, Project Officer for the hyperwave program—he's been on my neck day and night. I can't say I blame him. An unauthorized transmitter interfering with a Top Secret project, progress slowing to a halt, and this Bureau—"

"Look, Fred. I was happy in the lab. Headaches, nightmares and all. Hyperwave is my baby, remember? You elected me to be a leg-man; now let me do it my way."

"I felt a technical man might succeed where a trained investigator could be misled. And since it seems to be pinpointed in your home area—"

"You don't have to justify yourself. Just don't hold out on

125

me. I sometimes wonder if I've seen the complete files on this—"

"You've seen all the files! Now I want answers, not questions! I'm warning you, Tremaine. Get that transmitter. I need someone to hang!"

Tremaine left the hotel, walked two blocks west along Commerce Street and turned in at a yellow brick building with the words ELSBY MUNICIPAL POLICE cut in the stone lintel above the door. Inside, a heavy man with a creased face and thick gray hair looked up from behind an ancient Underwood. He studied Tremaine, shifted a toothpick to the opposite corner of his mouth.

"Don't I know you, mister?" he said. His soft voice carried a note of authority.

Tremaine took off his hat. "Sure you do, Jess. It's been a while, though."

The policeman got to his feet. "Jimmy," he said, "Jimmy Tremaine." He came to the counter and put out his hand. "How are you, Jimmy? What brings you back to the boondocks?"

"Let's go somewhere and sit down, Jess."

In a back room Tremaine said, "To everybody but you this is just a visit to the old home town. Between us, there's more."

Jess nodded. "I heard you were with the guv'ment."

"It won't take long to tell; we don't know much yet." Tremaine covered the discovery of the powerful unidentified interference on the high-security hyperwave band, the discovery that each transmission produced not one but a pattern of "fixes" on the point of origin. He passed a sheet of paper across the table. It showed a set of concentric circles, overlapped by a similar group of rings.

"I think what we're getting is an echo effect from each of these points of intersection. The rings themselves represent the diffraction pattern—"

"Hold it, Jimmy. To me it just looks like a beer ad. I'll take your word for it."

"The point is this, Jess: we think we've got it narrowed down to this section. I'm not sure of a damn thing, but I think that transmitter's near here. Now, have you got any ideas?"

"That's a tough one, Jimmy. This is where I should come

up with the news that Old Man Whatchamacallit's got an attic full of gear he says is a time machine. Trouble is, folks around here haven't even taken to TV. They figure we should be content with radio, like the Lord intended."

"I didn't expect any easy answers, Jess. But I was hoping maybe you had something . . ."

"Course," said Jess, "there's always Mr. Bram . . ."

"Mr. Bram," repeated Tremaine. "Is he still around? I remember him as a hundred years old when I was a kid."

"Still just the same, Jimmy. Comes in town maybe once a week, buys his groceries and hikes back out to his place by the river."

"Well, what about him?"

"Nothing. But he's the town's mystery man. You know that. A little touched in the head."

"There were a lot of funny stories about him, I remember," Tremaine said. "I always liked him. One time he tried to teach me something; I've forgotten what. Wanted me to come out to his place and he'd teach me. I never did go. We kids used to play in the caves near his place, and sometimes he gave us apples."

"I've never seen any harm in Bram," said Jess. "But you know how this town is about foreigners, especially when they're a mite addled. Bram has blue eyes and blond hair—or did before it turned white—and he talks just like everybody else. From a distance he seems just like an ordinary American. But up close, you feel it. He's foreign, all right. But we never did know where he came from."

"How long's he lived here in Elsby?"

"Beats me, Jimmy. You remember old Aunt Tress, used to know all about ancestors and such as that? She couldn't remember about Mr. Bram. She was kind of senile, I guess. She used to say he'd lived in that same old place out on the Concord road when she was a girl. Well, she died five years ago . . . in her seventies. He still walks in town every Wednesday . . . or he did up till yesterday, anyway."

"Oh?" Tremaine stubbed out his cigarette, lit another. "What happened then?"

"You remember Soup Gaskin? He's got a boy, name of Hull. He's Soup all over again."

"I remember Soup," Tremaine said. "He and his bunch used to come in the drug store where I worked and perch on the stools and kid around with me, and Mr. Hempleman would watch them from over back of the prescription counter and look nervous. They used to raise Cain in the other drug store . . ."

"Soup's been in the pen since then. His boy Hull's the same kind. Him and a bunch of his pals went out to Bram's place one night and set it on fire."

"What was the idea of that?"

"Dunno. Just meanness, I reckon. Not much damage done. A car was passing by and called it in. I had the whole caboodle locked up here for six hours. Then the sob sisters went to work: poor little tyke routine, high spirits, you know the line. All of 'em but Hull are back in the streets playin' with matches by now. I'm waiting for the day they'll make jail age."

"Why Bram?" Tremaine persisted. "As far as I know, he never had any dealings to speak of with anybody here in town."

"Oh hoh, you're a little young, Jimmy," Jess chuckled. "You never knew about Mr. Bram—the young Mr. Bram—and Linda Carroll."

Tremaine shook his head.

"Old Miss Carroll. School teacher here for years; guess she was retired by the time you were playing hookey. But her dad had money, and in her day she was a beauty. Too good for the fellers in these parts. I remember her ridin by in a high-wheeled shay, when I was just a nipper. Sitting up proud and tall, with that red hair piled up high. I used to think she was some kind of princess . . ."

"What about her and Bram? A romance?"

Jess rocked his chair back on two legs, looked at the ceiling, frowning. "This would ha' been about nineteen-oh-one. I was no more'n eight years old. Miss Linda was maybe in her twenties—and that made her an old maid, in those times. The word got out she was setting her cap for Bram. He was a good-looking young feller then, over six foot, of course, broad backed, curly yellow hair—and a stranger to boot. Like I said, Linda Carroll wanted nothin to do with the local bucks. There was a big shindy planned. Now, you know Bram was funny about any kind of socializing; never would go any place at night. But this was a Sunday afternoon and someways or other they got Bram down there; and Miss Linda made her play, right there in front of the town, practically. Just before sundown they went off together in that fancy shay. And the next day, she was home again— alone. That finished off her reputation, as far as the biddies in Elsby was concerned. It was ten years 'fore she even landed the teaching job. By that time, she was already old. And nobody was ever fool enough to mention the name Bram in front of her."

Tremaine got to his feet. "I'd appreciate it if you'd keep your ears and eyes open for anything that might build into a lead on this, Jess. Meantime, I'm just a tourist, seeing the sights."

"What about that gear of yours? Didn't you say you had some kind of detector you were going to set up?"

"I've got an oversized suitcase," Tremaine said. "I'll be setting it up in my room over at the hotel."

"When's this bootleg station supposed to broadcast again?"

"After dark. I'm working on a few ideas. It might be an infinitely repeating logarithmic sequence, based on—"

"Hold it, Jimmy. You're over my head." Jess got to his feet. "Let me know if you want anything. And by the way—" he winked broadly—"I always did know who busted Soup Gaskin's nose and took out his front teeth."

II

Back in the street, Tremaine headed south toward the Elsby Town Hall, a squat structure of brownish-red brick, crouched under yellow autumn trees at the end of Sheridan Street. Tremaine went up the steps and past heavy double doors. Ten yards along the dim corridor, a hand-lettered cardboard sign over a black-varnished door said "MUNICIPAL OF-FICE OF RECORD." Tremaine opened the door and went in.

A thin man with garters above the elbow looked over his shoulder at Tremaine.

"We're closed," he said.

"I won't be a minute," Tremaine said. "Just want to check on when the Bram property changed hands last."

The man turned to Tremaine, pushed a drawer shut with his hip. "Bram? He dead?"

"Nothing like that. I just want to know when he bought the place."

The man came over to the counter, eyeing Tremaine. "He ain't going to sell, mister, if that's what you want to know."

"I want to know when he bought."

The man hesitated, closed his jaw hard. "Come back to-morrow," he said.

Tremaine put a hand on the counter, looked thoughtful. "I was hoping to save a trip." He lifted his hand and scratched the side of his jaw. A folded bill opened on the counter. The thin man's eyes darted toward it. His hand eased out, covered the bill. He grinned quickly.

"See what I can do," he said.

It was ten minutes before he beckoned Tremaine over to the table where a two-foot-square book lay open. An un-trimmed fingernail indicated a line written in faded ink:

"May 19, Acreage sold, One Dollar and other G&V con-sid. NW Quarter Section 24, Township Elsby. Bram. (see Vol. 9 & cet.)"

"Translated, what does that mean?" said Tremaine.

"That's the ledger for 1901; means Bram bought a quarter section on the nineteenth of May. You want me to look up the deed?"

"No, thanks," Tremaine said. "That's all I needed." He turned back to the door.

"What's up, mister?" the clerk called after him. "Bram in some kind of trouble?"

"No. No trouble."

The man was looking at the book with pursed lips. "Nine-teen-oh-one," he said. "I never thought of it before, but you know, old Bram must be dern near to ninety years old. Spry for that age."

"I guess you're right."

The clerk looked sideways at Tremaine. "Lots of funny stories about old Bram. Useta say his place was haunted. You know; funny noises and lights. And they used to say there was money buried out at his place."

"I've heard those stories. Just superstition, wouldn't you say?"

"Maybe so." The clerk leaned on the counter, assumed a knowing look. "There's one story that's not superstition . . ."

Tremaine waited.

"You—uh—paying anything for information?"

"Now why would I do that?" Tremaine reached for the door knob.

The clerk shrugged. "Thought I'd ask. Anyway—I can swear to this. Nobody in this town's ever seen Bram between sundown and sunup."

Untrimmed sumacs threw late-afternoon shadows on the discolored stucco facade of the Elsby Public Library. Inside, Tremaine followed a paper-dry woman of indeterminate age to a rack of yellowed newsprint.

"You'll find back to nineteen-forty here," the librarian said. "The older are there in the shelves."

"I want nineteen-oh-one, if they go back that far."

The woman darted a suspicious look at Tremaine. "You have to handle these old papers carefully."

"I'll be extremely careful." The woman sniffed, opened a drawer, leafed through it, muttering.

"What date was it you wanted?"

"Nineteen-oh-one; the week of May nineteenth."

The librarian pulled out a folded paper, placed it on the table, adjusted her glasses, squinted at the front page. "That's it," she said. "These papers keep pretty well, provided they're stored in the dark. But they're still flimsy, mind you."

"I'll remember." The woman stood by as Tremaine looked over the front page. The lead article concerned the opening of the Pan-American Exposition at Buffalo. Vice-President Roosevelt had made a speech. Tremaine leafed over, reading slowly.

On page four, under a column headed *County Notes* he saw the name Bram:

> Mr. Bram has purchased a quarter section of fine grazing land, north of town, together with a sturdy house, from J. P. Spivey of Elsby. Mr. Bram will occupy the home and will continue to graze a few head of stock. Mr. Bram, who is a newcomer to the county, has been a resident of Mrs. Stoate's Guest Home in Elsby for the past months.

"May I see some earlier issues; from about the first of the year?"

The librarian produced the papers. Tremaine turned the pages, read the heads, skimmed an article here and there. The librarian went back to her desk. An hour later, in the issue for July 7, 1900, an item caught his eye:

A Severe Thunderstorm. Citizens of Elsby and the country were much alarmed by a violent cloudburst, accompanied by lightning and thunder, during the night of the fifth. A fire set in the pine woods north of Spivey's farm destroyed a considerable amount of timber and threatened the house before burning itself out along the river.

The librarian was at Tremaine's side. "I have to close the library now. You'll have to come back tomorrow."

Outside, the sky was sallow in the west; lights were coming on in windows along the side streets. Tremaine turned up his collar against a cold wind that had risen, started along the street toward the hotel.

A block away a black late-model sedan rounded a corner with a faint squeal of tires and gunned past him, a heavy antenna mounted forward of the left rear tail fin whipping in the slipstream. Tremaine stopped short, stared after the car.

"Damn!" he said aloud. An elderly man veered, eyeing him sharply. Tremaine set off at a run, covered the two blocks to the hotel, yanked open the door to his car, slid into the seat, made a U-turn, and headed north after the police car.

Two miles into the dark hills north of the Elsby city limits, Tremaine rounded a curve. The police car was parked on the shoulder beside the highway just ahead. He pulled off the road ahead of it and walked back. The door opened. A tall figure stepped out.

"What's your problem, mister?" a harsh voice drawled.

"What's the matter? Run out of signal?"

"What's it to you, mister?"

"Are you boys in touch with Grammond on the car set?"

"We could be."

"Mind if I have a word with him? My name's Tremaine."

"Oh," said the cop, "you're the big shot from Washington." He shifted chewing tobacco to the other side of his jaw. "Sure, you can talk to him." He turned and spoke to the other cop, who muttered into the mike before handing it to Tremaine.

The heavy voice of the State Police chief crackled. "What's your beef, Tremaine?"

"I thought you were going to keep your men away from Elsby until I gave the word, Grammond."

"That was before I knew your Washington stuffed shirts were holding out on me."

"It's nothing we can go to court with, Grammond. And the job you were doing might have been influenced if I'd told you about the Elsby angle."

Grammond cursed. "I could have put my men in the town and taken it apart brick by brick in the time—"

"That's just what I don't want. If our bird sees cops cruising, he'll go underground."

"You've got it all figured, I see. I'm just the dumb hick you boys use for the spade work, that it?"

"Pull your lip back in. You've given me the confirmation I needed."

"Confirmation, hell! All I know is that somebody somewhere is punching out a signal. For all I know, it's forty midgets on bicycles, pedalling all over the damned state. I've got fixes in every county—"

"The smallest hyperwave transmitter Uncle Sam knows how to build weighs three tons," said Tremaine. "Bicycles are out."

Grammond snorted. "Okay, Tremaine," he said. "You're the boy with all the answers. But if you get in trouble, don't call me; call Washington."

Back in his room, Tremaine put through a call.

"It looks like Grammond's not willing to be left out in the cold, Fred. Tell him if he queers this—"

"I don't know but what he might have something," the voice came back over the filtered hum. "Suppose he smokes them out—"

"Don't go dumb on me, Fred. We're not dealing with West Virginia moonshiners."

"Don't tell me my job, Tremaine!" the voice snapped. "And don't try out your famous temper on me. I'm still in charge of this investigation."

"Sure. Just don't get stuck in some senator's hip pocket." Tremaine hung up the telephone, went to the dresser and poured two fingers of Scotch into a water glass. He tossed it down, then pulled on his coat and left the hotel.

He walked south two blocks, turned left down a twilit side street. He walked slowly, looking at the weathered frame houses. Number 89 was a once-stately three-storied mansion overgrown with untrimmed vines, its windows squares of sad yellow light. He pushed through the gate in the ancient picket fence, mounted the porch steps and pushed the button beside the door, a dark panel of cracked varnish. It was a long minute before the door opened. A tall woman with white hair and fine-boned face looked at him coolly.

"Miss Carroll," Tremaine said. "You won't remember me, but I—"

"There is nothing whatever wrong with my faculties, James," Miss Carroll said calmly. Her voice was still resonant, a deep contralto. Only a faint quaver reflected her age—close to ninety, Tremaine thought, startled.

"I'm flattered you remember me, Miss Carroll," he said.

"Come in." She led the way to a pleasant parlor set out with the furnishings of another era. She motioned Tremaine to a seat and took a straight chair across the room from him.

"You look very well, James," she said, nodding. "I'm pleased to see that you've amounted to something."

"Just another bureaucrat, I'm afraid."

"You were wise to leave Elsby. There is no future here for a young man."

"I often wondered why you didn't leave, Miss Carroll. I thought, even as a boy, that you were a woman of great ability."

"Why did you come today, James?" asked Miss Carroll.

"I . . ." Tremaine started. He looked at the old lady. "I want some information. This is an important matter. May I rely on your discretion?"

"Of course."

"How long has Mr. Bram lived in Elsby?"

Miss Carroll looked at him for a long moment. "Will what I tell you be used against him?"

"There'll be nothing done against him, Miss Carroll . . . unless it needs to be, in the national interest."

"I'm not at all sure I know what the term 'national interest' means, James. I distrust these glib phrases."

"I always liked Mr. Bram," said Tremaine. "I'm not out to hurt him."

"Mr. Bram came here when I was a young woman. I'm not certain of the year."

"What does he do for a living?"

"I have no idea."

"Why did a healthy young fellow like Bram settle out in that isolated piece of country? What's his story?"

"I'm ... not sure that anyone truly knows Bram's story."

"You called him 'Bram', Miss Carroll. Is that his first name ... or his last?"

"That is his only name. Just ... Bram."

"You knew him well once, Miss Carroll. Is there anything—"

A tear rolled down Miss Carroll's faded cheek. She wiped it away impatiently.

"I'm an unfulfilled old maid, James," she said. "You must forgive me."

Tremaine stood up. "I'm sorry. Really sorry. I didn't mean to grill you, Miss Carroll. You've been very kind. I had no right ..."

Miss Carroll shook her head. "I knew you as a boy, James. I have complete confidence in you. If anything I can tell you about Bram will be helpful to you, it is my duty to oblige you; and it may help him." She paused. Tremaine waited.

"Many years ago I was courted by Bram. One day he asked me to go with him to his house. On the way he told me a terrible and pathetic tale. He said that each night he fought a battle with evil beings, alone, in a cave beneath his house."

Miss Carroll drew a deep breath and went on. "I was torn between pity and horror. I begged him to take me back. He refused." Miss Carroll twisted her fingers together, her eyes fixed on the long past. "When we reached the house, he ran to the kitchen. He lit a lamp and threw open a concealed panel. There were stairs. He went down ... and left me there alone.

"I waited all that night in the carriage. At dawn he emerged. He tried to speak to me but I would not listen.

"He took a locket from his neck and put it into my hand. He told me to keep it and, if ever I should need him, to press it between my fingers in a secret way ... and he would come. I told him that until he would consent to see a doctor, I did not wish him to call. He drove me home. He never called again."

"This locket," said Tremaine, "do you still have it?"

Miss Carroll hesitated, then put her hand to her throat, lifted a silver disc on a fine golden chain. "You see what a foolish old woman I am, James."

"May I see it?"

She handed the locket to him. It was heavy, smooth. "I'd like to examine this more closely," he said. "May I take it with me?"

Miss Carroll nodded.

"There is one other thing," she said, "perhaps quite meaningless ..."

"I'd be grateful for any lead."

"Bram fears the thunder."

III

As Tremaine walked slowly toward the lighted main street of Elsby a car pulled to a stop beside him. Jess leaned out, peered at Tremaine and asked:

"Any luck, Jimmy?"

Tremaine shook his head. "I'm getting nowhere fast. The Bram idea's a dud, I'm afraid."

"Funny thing about Bram. You know, he hasn't showed up yet. I'm getting a little worried. Want to run out there with me and take a look around?"

"Sure. Just so I'm back by full dark."

As they pulled away from the curb Jess said, "Jimmy, what's this about State Police nosing around here? I thought you were playing a lone hand from what you were saying to me."

"I thought so too, Jess. But it looks like Grammond's a jump ahead of me. He smells headlines in this; he doesn't want to be left out."

"Well, the State cops could be mighty handy to have around. I'm wondering why you don't want 'em in. If there's some kind of spy ring working—"

"We're up against an unknown quantity. I don't know what's behind this and neither does anybody else. Maybe it's a ring of Bolsheviks ... and maybe it's something bigger. I have the feeling we've made enough mistakes in the last few years; I don't want to see this botched."

The last pink light of sunset was fading from the clouds to the west as Jess swung the car through the open gate, pulled up under the old trees before the square-built house. The windows were dark. The two men got out, circled the house once, then mounted the steps and rapped on the door. There was a black patch of charred flooring under the window, and the paint on the wall above it was bubbled. Somewhere a cricket set up a strident chirrup, suddenly cut off. Jess leaned down, picked up an empty shotgun shell. He looked at Tremaine. "This don't look good," he said. "You suppose those fool boys . . . ?"

He tried the door. It opened. A broken hasp dangled. He turned to Tremaine. "Maybe this is more than kid stuff," he said. "You carry a gun?"

"In the car."

"Better get it."

Tremaine went to the car, dropped the pistol in his coat pocket, rejoined Jess inside the house. It was silent, deserted. In the kitchen Jess flicked the beam of his flashlight around the room. An empty plate lay on the oilcloth-covered table.

"This place is empty," he said. "Anybody'd think he'd been gone a week."

"Not a very cozy—" Tremaine broke off. A thin yelp sounded in the distance.

"I'm getting jumpy," said Jess. "Dern hounddog, I guess."

A low growl seemed to rumble distantly. "What the devil's that?" Tremaine said.

Jess shone the light on the floor. "Look here," he said. The ring of light showed a spatter of dark droplets all across the plank floor.

"That's blood, Jess . . ." Tremaine scanned the floor. It was of broad slabs, closely laid, scrubbed clean but for the dark stains.

"Maybe he cleaned a chicken. This is the kitchen."

"It's a trail." Tremaine followed the line of drops across the floor. It ended suddenly near the wall.

"What do you make of it, Jimmy?"

A wail sounded, a thin forlorn cry, trailing off into silence. Jess stared at Tremaine. "I'm too damned old to start believing in spooks," he said. "You suppose those damn-fool boys are hiding here, playing tricks?"

"I think," Tremaine said, "that we'd better go ask Hull Gaskin a few questions."

At the station Jess led Tremaine to a cell where a lanky teenage boy lounged on a steel-framed cot, blinking up at the visitor under a mop of greased hair.

"Hull, this is Mr. Tremaine," said Jess. He took out a heavy key, swung the cell door open. "He wants to talk to you."

"I ain't done nothin," Hull said sullenly. "There ain't noth-in wrong with burnin out a Commie, is there?"

"Bram's a Commie, is he?" Tremaine said softly. "How'd you find that out, Hull?"

"He's a foreigner, ain't he?" the youth shot back. "Besides, we heard . . ."

"What did you hear?"

"They're lookin for the spies."

"Who's looking for spies?"

"Cops."

"Who says so?"

The boy looked directly at Tremaine for an instant, flicked his eyes to the corner of the cell. "Cops was talkin about 'em," he said.

"Spill it, Hull," the policeman said. "Mr. Tremaine hasn't got all night."

"They parked out east of town, on 302, back of the woodlot. They called me over and asked me a bunch of questions. Said I could help 'em get them spies. Wanted to know all about any funny-actin people around here."

"And you mentioned Bram?"

The boy darted another look at Tremaine. "They said they figured the spies was out north of town. Well, Bram's a foreigner, and he's out that way, ain't he?"

"Anything else?"

The boy looked at his feet.

"What did you shoot at, Hull?" Tremaine said. The boy looked at him sullenly.

"You know anything about the blood on the kitchen floor?"

"I don't know what you're talkin about," Hull said. "We was out squirrel-huntin."

"Hull, is Mr. Bram dead?"

"What you mean?" Hull blurted. "He was—"

"He was what?"

"Nothin."

"The Chief won't like it if you hold out on him, Hull," Tremaine said. "He's bound to find out."

Jess looked at the boy. "Hull's a pretty dumb boy," he said. "But he's not that dumb. Let's have it, Hull."

The boy licked his lips. "I had Pa's 30-30, and Bovey Lay had a twelve-gauge . . ."

"What time was this?"

"Just after sunset."

"About seven-thirty, that'd be," said Jess. "That was half an hour before the fire was spotted."

"I didn't do no shootin. It was Bovey. Old Bram jumped out at him, and he just fired off the hip. But he didn't kill him. He seen him run off . . ."

"You were on the porch when this happened. Which way did Bram go?"

"He . . . run inside."

"So then you set fire to the place. Whose bright idea was that?"

Hull sat silent. After a moment Tremaine and Jess left the cell.

"He must have gotten clear, Jimmy," said Jess. "Maybe he got scared and left town."

"Bram doesn't strike me as the kind to panic." Tremaine looked at his watch. "I've got to get on my way, Jess. I'll check with you in the morning."

Tremaine crossed the street to the Paradise Bar and Grill, pushed into the jukebox-lit interior, took a stool and ordered a Scotch and water. He sipped the drink, then sat staring into the dark reflection in the glass. The idea of a careful reconnoitre of the Elsby area was gone now, with police swarming everywhere. It was too bad about Bram. It would be interesting to know where the old man was . . . and if he was still alive. He'd always seemed normal enough in the old days: a big solid-looking man, middle-aged, always pleasant enough, though he didn't say much. He'd tried hard, that time, to interest Tremaine in learning whatever it was . . .

Tremaine put a hand in his jacket pocket, took out Miss Carroll's locket. It was smooth, the size and shape of a wrist-watch chassis. He was fingering it meditatively when a rough hand slammed against his shoulder, half knocking him from the stool. Tremaine caught his balance, turned, looked into the scarred face of a heavy-shouldered man in a leather jacket.

"I heard you was back in town, Tremaine," the man said.

The bartender moved up. "Looky here, Gaskin, I don't want no trouble—"

"Shove it!" Gaskin squinted at Tremaine, his upper lip curled back to expose the gap in his teeth. "You tryin to make more trouble for my boy, I hear. Been over to the jail, stickin your nose in."

Tremaine dropped the locket in his pocket and stood up. Gaskin hitched up his pants, glanced around the room. Half a dozen early drinkers stared, wide-eyed. Gaskin squinted at Tremaine. He smelled of unwashed flannel.

"Sicked the cops onto him. The boy was out with his friends, havin a little fun. Now there he sets in jail."

Tremaine moved aside from the stool, started past the man. Soup Gaskin grabbed his arm.

"Not so fast! I figger you owe me damages. I—"

"Damage is what you'll get," said Tremaine. He slammed a stiff left to Gaskin's ribs, drove a hard right to the jaw. Gaskin jackknifed backwards, tripped over a bar stool, fell on his back. He rolled over, got to hands and knees, shook his head.

"Git up, Soup!" someone called. "Hot dog!" offered another.

"I'm calling the police!" the bartender yelled.

"Never mind," a voice said from the door A blue-jacketed State Trooper strolled into the room, fingers hooked into his pistol belt, the steel caps on his boot heels clicking with each step. He faced Tremaine, feet apart.

"Looks like you're disturbin the peace, Mr. Tremaine," he said.

"You wouldn't know who put him up to it, would you?" Tremaine said.

"That's a dirty allegation," the cop grinned. "I'll have to get off a hot letter to my congressman."

Gaskin got to his feet, wiped a smear of blood across his cheek, then lunged past the cop and swung a wild right. Tremaine stepped aside, landed a solid punch on Gaskin's ear. The cop stepped back against the bar. Soup whirled, slammed out with lefts and rights. Tremaine lashed back with a straight left; Gaskin slammed against the bar, rebounded, threw a knockout right ... and Tremaine ducked, landed a right uppercut that sent Gaskin reeling back, bowled over a table, sent glasses flying. Tremaine stood over him.

"On your feet, jailbird," he said. "A workout is exactly what I needed."

"Okay, you've had your fun," the State cop said. "I'm taking you in, Tremaine."

Tremaine looked at him. "Sorry, copper," he said. "I don't have time right now." The cop looked startled, reached for his revolver.

"What's going on here, Jimmy?" Jess stood in the door, a huge .44 in his hand. He turned his eyes on the trooper.

"You're a little out of your jurisdiction," he said. "I think you better move on 'fore somebody steals your bicycle."

The cop eyed Jess for a long moment, then holstered his pistol and stalked out of the bar. Jess tucked his revolver into his belt, looked at Gaskin sitting on the floor, dabbing at his bleeding mouth. "What got into you, Soup?"

"I think the State boys put him up to it," Tremaine said. "They're looking for an excuse to take me out of the picture."

Jess motioned to Gaskin. "Get up, Soup. I'm lockin you up alongside that boy of yours."

Outside, Jess said, "You got some bad enemies there, Jimmy. That's a tough break. You ought to hold onto your temper with those boys. I think maybe you ought to think about getting over the state line. I can run you to the bus station, and send your car along . . ."

"I can't leave now, Jess. I haven't even started."

IV

In his room, Tremaine doctored the cut on his jaw, then opened his trunk, checked over the detector gear. The telephone rang.

"Tremaine? I've been on the telephone with Grammond. Are you out of your mind? I'm—"

"Fred," Tremaine cut in, "I thought you were going to get those state cops off my neck."

"Listen to me, Tremaine. You're called off this job as of now. Don't touch anything! You'd better stay right there in that room. In fact, that's an order!"

"Don't pick now to come apart at the seams, Fred," Tremaine snapped.

"I've ordered you off! That's all!" The phone clicked and the dial tone sounded. Tremaine dropped the receiver in its cradle, then walked to the window absently, his hand in his pocket.

He felt broken pieces and pulled out Miss Carroll's locket.

It was smashed, split down the center. It must have gotten it in the tussle with Soup, Tremaine thought. It looked—

He squinted at the shattered ornament. A maze of fine wires was exposed, tiny condensers, bits of glass.

In the street below, tires screeched. Tremaine looked down. A black car was at the curb, doors sprung. Four uniformed men jumped out, headed for the door. Tremaine whirled to the phone. The desk clerk came on.

"Get me Jess—fast!"

The police chief answered.

"Jess, the word's out I'm poison. A carful of State law is at the front door. I'm going out the back. Get in their way all you can." Tremaine dropped the phone, grabbed up the suitcase and let himself out into the hall. The back stairs were dark. He stumbled, cursed, made it to the service entry. Outside, the alley was deserted.

He went to the corner, crossed the street, thrust the suitcase into the back seat of his car and slid into the driver's seat. He started up and eased away from the curb. He glanced in the mirror. There was no alarm.

It was a four-block drive to Miss Carroll's house. The housekeeper let Tremaine in.

"Oh, yes, Miss Carroll is still up," she said. "She never retires until nine. I'll tell her you're here, Mr. Tremaine."

Tremaine paced the room. On his third circuit Miss Carroll came in.

"I wouldn't have bothered you if it wasn't important," Tremaine said. "I can't explain it all now. You said once you had confidence in me. Will you come with me now? It concerns Bram . . . and maybe a lot more than just Bram."

Miss Carroll looked at him steadily. "I'll get my wrap."

On the highway Tremaine said, "Miss Carroll, we're headed for Bram's house. I take it you've heard of what happened out there?"

"No, James. I haven't stirred out of the house. What is it?"

"A gang of teen-age toughs went out last night. They had guns. One of them took a shot at Bram. And Bram's disappeared. But I don't think he's dead."

Miss Carroll gasped. "Why? Why did they do it?"

"I don't think they know themselves."

"You say . . . you believe he still lives . . ."

"He must be alive. It dawned on me a little while ago ... a little late, I'll admit. The locket he gave you. Did you ever try it?"

"Try it? Why ... no. I don't believe in magic, James."

"Not magic. Electronics. Years ago Bram talked to me about radio. He wanted to teach me. Now I'm here looking for a transmitter. That transmitter was busy last night. I think Bram was operating it."

There was a long silence.

"James," Miss Carroll said at last, "I don't understand."

"Neither do I, Miss Carroll. I'm still working on finding the pieces. But let me ask you: that night that Bram brought you out to his place, you say he ran to the kitchen and opened a trapdoor in the floor—"

"Did I say floor? That was an error; the panel was in the wall."

"I guess I jumped to the conclusion. Which wall?"

"He crossed the room. There was a table, with a candlestick. He went around it and pressed his hand against the wall, beside the woodbox. The panel slid aside. It was very dark within. He ducked his head, because the opening was not large, and stepped inside ..."

"That would be the east wall ... to the left of the back door?"

"Yes."

"Now, Miss Carroll, can you remember exactly what Bram said to you that night? Something about fighting something, wasn't it?"

"I've tried for sixty years to put it out of my mind, James. But I remember every word, I think." She was silent for a moment.

"I was beside him on the buggy seat. It was a warm evening, late in spring. I had told him that I loved him, and ... he had responded. He said that he would have spoken long before, but that he had not dared. Now there was that which I must know.

"His life was not his own, he said. He was not ... native to this world. He was an agent of a mighty power, and he had trailed a band of criminals ..." She broke off. "I could not truly understand that part, James. I fear it was too incoherent. He raved of evil beings who lurked in the shadows of a cave. It was his duty to wage each night an unceasing battle with occult forces."

"What kind of battle? Were these ghosts, or demons, or what?"

"I don't know. Evil powers which would be unloosed on the world, unless he met them at the portal as the darkness fell and opposed them."

"Why didn't he get help?"

"Only he could stand against them. I knew little of abnormal psychology, but I understood the classic evidence of paranoia. I shrank from him. He sat, leaning forward, his eyes intent. I wept and begged him to take me back. He turned his face to me, and I saw the pain and anguish in his eyes. I loved him ... and feared him. And he would not turn back. Night was falling, and the enemy awaited him."

"Then, when you got to the house ... ?"

"He had whipped up the horses, and I remember how I clung to the top braces, weeping. Then we were at the house. Without a word he jumped down and ran to the door. I followed. He lit a lamp and turned to me. From somewhere there was a wailing call, like an injured animal. He shouted something—an unintelligible cry—and ran toward the back of the house. I took up the lamp and followed. In the kitchen he went to the wall, pressed against it. The panel opened. He looked at me. His face was white.

" 'In the name of the High God, Linda Carroll, I entreat you ...'

"I screamed. And he hardened his face, and went down ... and I screamed and screamed again ..." Miss Carroll closed her eyes, drew a shuddering breath.

"I'm sorry to have put you through this, Miss Carroll," Tremaine said. "But I had to know."

Faintly in the distance a siren sounded. In the mirror, headlights twinkled half a mile behind. Tremaine stepped on the gas. The powerful car leaped ahead.

"Are you expecting trouble on the road, James?"

"The State police are unhappy with me, Miss Carroll. And I imagine they're not too pleased with Jess. Now they're out for blood. But I think I can outrun them."

"James," Miss Carroll said, sitting up and looking behind. "If those are police officers, shouldn't you stop?"

"I can't, Miss Carroll. I don't have time for them now. If my idea means anything, we've got to get there fast ..."

Bram's house loomed gaunt and dark as the car whirled through the gate, ground to a stop before the porch. Tremaine jumped out, went around the car and helped Miss Carroll out. He was surprised at the firmness of her step. For a moment, in the fading light of dusk, he glimpsed her profile. *How beautiful she must have been ...*

He reached into the glove compartment for a flashlight.

"We haven't got a second to waste," he said. "That other car's not more than a minute behind us." He reached into the back of the car, hauled out the heavy suitcase. "I hope you remember how Bram worked that panel."

On the porch Tremaine's flashlight illuminated the broken hasp. Inside, he led the way along a dark hall, pushed into the kitchen.

"It was there," Miss Carroll said, pointing. Outside, an engine sounded on the highway, slowing, turning in. Headlights pushed a square of cold light across the kitchen wall. Tremaine jumped to the spot Miss Carroll had indicated, put the suitcase down, felt over the wall.

"Give me the light, James," Miss Carroll said calmly. "Press there." She put the spot on the wall. Tremaine leaned against it. Nothing happened. Outside, there was the thump of car doors; a muffled voice barked orders.

"Are you sure ... ?"

"Yes. Try again, James."

Tremaine threw himself against the wall, slapped at it, searching for a hidden latch.

"A bit higher; Bram was a tall man. The panel opened below ..."

Tremaine reached higher, pounded, pushed up, sideways—

With a click a three by four foot section of wall rolled silently aside. Tremaine saw greased metal slides and, beyond, steps leading down.

"They are on the porch now, James," said Miss Carroll.

"The light!" Tremaine reached for it, threw a leg over the sill. He reached back, pulled the suitcase after him. "Tell them I kidnapped you, Miss Carroll. And thanks."

Miss Carroll held out her hand. "Help me, James. I hung back once before. I'll not repeat my folly."

Tremaine hesitated for an instant, then reached out, handed Miss Carroll in. Footsteps sounded in the hall. The flashlight showed Tremaine a black pushbutton bolted to a two by four stud. He pressed it. The panel slid back in place.

Tremaine flashed the light on the stairs.

"Okay, Miss Carroll," he said softly. "Let's go down."

There were fifteen steps, and at the bottom, a corridor, with curved walls of black glass, and a floor of rough boards. It went straight for twenty feet and ended at an old-fashioned five-panel wooden door. Tremaine tried the brass knob. The door opened on a room shaped from a natural cave, with water-worn walls of yellow stone, a low uneven ceiling, and a packed-earth floor. On a squat tripod in the center of the chamber rested an apparatus of black metal and glass, vaguely gunlike, aimed at the blank wall. Beside it, in an ancient wooden rocker, a man lay slumped, his shirt blood-caked, a black puddle on the floor beneath him.

"Bram!" Miss Carroll gasped. She went to him, took his hand, staring into his face.

"Is he dead?" Tremaine said tightly.

"His hands are cold ... but there is a pulse."

A kerosene lantern stood by the door. Tremaine lit it, brought it to the chair. He took out a pocket knife, cut the coat and shirt back from Bram's wound. A shotgun blast had struck him in the side; there was a lacerated area as big as Tremaine's hand.

"It's stopped bleeding," he said. "It was just a graze at close range, I'd say." He explored further. "It got his arm too, but not as deep. And I think there are a couple of ribs broken. If he hasn't lost too much blood ..." Tremaine pulled off his coat, spread it on the floor.

"Let's lay him out here and try to bring him around."

Lying on his back on the floor, Bram looked bigger than his six-foot-four, younger than his near-century, Tremaine thought. Miss Carroll knelt at the old man's side, chafing his hands, murmuring to him.

Abruptly a thin cry cut the air.

Tremaine whirled, startled. Miss Carroll stared, eyes wide. A low rumble sounded, swelled louder, broke into a screech, cut off.

"Those are the sounds I heard that night," Miss Carroll breathed. "I thought afterwards I had imagined them, but I remember ... James, what does it mean?"

"Maybe it means Bram wasn't as crazy as you thought," Tremaine said.

Miss Carroll gasped sharply. "James! Look at the wall—"

Tremaine turned. Vague shadows moved across the stone, flickering, wavering.

"What the devil . . . !"

Bram moaned, stirred. Tremaine went to him. "Bram!" he said. "Wake up!"

Bram's eyes opened. For a moment he looked dazedly at Tremaine, then at Miss Carroll. Awkwardly he pushed himself to a sitting position.

"Bram . . . you must lie down," Miss Carroll said.

"Linda Carroll," Bram said. His voice was deep, husky.

"Bram, you're hurt . . ."

A mewling wail started up. Bram went rigid. "What hour is this?" he grated.

"The sun has just gone down; it's after seven—"

Bram tried to get to his feet. "Help me up," he ordered. "Curse the weakness . . ."

Tremaine got a hand under the old man's arm. "Careful, Bram," he said. "Don't start your wound bleeding again."

"To the Repellor," Bram muttered. Tremaine guided him to the rocking chair, eased him down. Bram seized the two black pistol-grips, squeezed them.

"You, young man," Bram said. "Take the circlet there; place it about my neck."

The flat-metal ring hung from a wire loop. Tremaine fitted it over Bram's head. It settled snugly over his shoulders, a flange at the back against his neck.

"Bram," Tremaine said. "What's this all about?"

"Watch the wall there. My sight grows dim. Tell me what you see."

"It looks like shadows: but what's casting them?"

"Can you discern details?"

"No. It's like somebody waggling their fingers in front of a slide projector."

"The radiation from the star is yet too harsh," Bram muttered. "But now the node draws close. May the High Gods guide my hand!"

A howl rang out, a raw blast of sound. Bram tensed. "What do you see?" he demanded.

"The outlines are sharper. There seem to be other shapes behind the moving ones. It's like looking through a steamy window . . ." Beyond the misty surface Tremaine seemed to see a high narrow chamber, bathed in white light. In the foreground creatures like shadowy caricatures of men paced to and fro. "They're like something stamped out of alligator hide," Tremaine whispered. "When they turn and I see them edge-on, they're thin . . ."

"An effect of dimensional attenuation. They strive now to match matrices with this plane. If they succeed, this earth you know will lie at their feet."

"What are they? Where are they? That's solid rock—"

"What you see is the Niss Command Center. It lies in another world than this, but here is the multihedron of intersection. They bring their harmonic generators to bear here in the hope of establishing an aperture of focus."

"I don't understand half of what you're saying, Bram. And the rest I don't believe. But with this staring me in the face, I'll have to act as though I did."

Suddenly the wall cleared. Like a surface of moulded glass the stone threw back ghostly highlights. Beyond it, the Niss technicians, seen now in sharp detail, worked busily, silently, their faces like masks of ridged red-brown leather. Directly opposite Bram's Repellor, an apparatus like an immense camera with a foot-wide silvered lens stood aimed, a black-clad Niss perched in a saddle atop it. The white light flooded the cave, threw black shadows across the floor. Bram hunched over the Repellor, face tensed in strain. A glow built in the air around the Niss machine. The alien technicians stood now, staring with tiny bright-red eyes. Long seconds passed. The black-clad Niss gestured suddenly. Another turned to a red-marked knife-switch, pulled. As suddenly as it had cleared, the wall went milky, then dulled to opacity. Bram slumped back, eyes shut, breathing hoarsely.

"Near were they then," he muttered, "I grow weak . . ."

"Let me take over," Tremaine said. "Tell me how."

"How can I tell you? You will not understand."

"Maybe I'll understand enough to get us through the night."

Bram seemed to gather himself. "Very well. This must you know . . .

"I am an agent in the service of the Great World. For centuries we have waged war against the Niss, evil beings who loot the continua. They established an Aperture here, on your Earth. We detected it, and found that a Portal could be set up here briefly. I was dispatched with a crew to counter their move—"

"You're talking gibberish," Tremaine said. "I'll pass the Great World and the continua . . . but what's an Aperture?"

"A point of material contact between the Niss world and this plane of space-time. Through it they can pump this rich planet dry of oxygen, killing it—then emerge to feed on the corpse."

"What's a Portal?"

"The Great World lies in a different harmonic series than do Earth and the Niss World. Only at vast intervals can we set up a Portal of temporary identity as the cycles mesh. We monitor the Niss emanations, and forestall them when we can, now in this plane, now in that."

"I see: denial to the enemy."

"But we were late. Already the multihedron was far advanced. A blinding squall lashed outside the river cave where the Niss had focused the Aperture, and the thunder rolled as the ionization effect was propagated in the atmosphere. I threw my force against the Niss Aperture, but could not destroy it . . . but neither could they force their entry."

"And this was sixty years ago? And they're still at it?"

"You must throw off the illusion of time! To the Niss only a few days have passed. But here—where I spend only minutes from each night in the engagement, as the patterns coincide—it has been long years."

"Why don't you bring in help? Why do you have to work alone?"

"The power required to hold the Portal in focus against the stresses of space-time is tremendous. Even then the cycle is brief. It gave us first a fleeting contact of a few seconds; it was through that that we detected the Niss activity here. The next contact was four days later, and lasted twenty-four minutes—long enough to set up the Repellor. I fought them then . . . and saw that victory was in doubt. Still, it was a fair world; I could not let it go without a struggle. A third identity was possible twenty days later; I elected to remain here until then, attempt to repel the Niss, then return home at the next contact. The Portal closed, and my crew and I settled down to the engagement.

"The next night showed us in full the hopelessness of the contest. By day, we emerged from where the Niss had focused the Aperture, and explored this land, and came to love its small warm sun, its strange blue sky, its mantle of green . . . and the small humble grass-blades. To us of an ancient world it seemed a paradise of young life. And then I ventured into the town ... and there I saw such a maiden as the Cosmos has forgotten, such was her beauty ...

"The twenty days passed. The Niss held their foothold— yet I had kept them back.

"The Portal reopened. I ordered my crew back. It closed. Since then, have I been alone ..."

"Bram," Miss Carroll said. "Bram ... you stayed when you could have escaped—and I—"

"I would that I could give you back those lost years, Linda Carroll," Bram said. "I would that we could have been together under a brighter sun than this."

"You gave up your world, to give this one a little time," Tremaine said. "And we rewarded you with a shotgun blast."

"Bram ... when will the Portal open again?"

"Not in my life, Linda Carroll. Not for ten thousand years."

"Why didn't you recruit help?" Tremaine said. "You could have trained someone ..."

"I tried, at first. But what can one do with frightened rustics? They spoke of witchcraft, and fled."

"But you can't hold out forever. Tell me how this thing works. It's time somebody gave you a break!"

V

Bram talked for half an hour, while Tremaine listened. "If I should fail," he concluded, "take my place at the Repellor. Place the circlet on your neck. When the wall clears, grip the handles and pit your mind against the Niss. Will that they do not come through. When the thunder rolls, you will know that you have failed."

"All right. I'll be ready. But let me get one thing straight: this Repellor of yours responds to thoughts, is that right? It amplifies them—"

"It serves to focus the power of the mind. But now let us make haste. Soon, I fear, will they renew the attack."

"It will be twenty minutes or so, I think," said Tremaine. "Stay where you are and get some rest."

Bram looked at him, his blue eyes grim under white brows. "What do you know of this matter, young man?"

"I think I've doped out the pattern; I've been monitoring

these transmissions for weeks. My ideas seemed to prove out okay the last few nights."

"No one but I in all this world knew of the Niss attack. How could you have analyzed that which you knew not of?"

"Maybe you don't know it, Bram, but this Repellor of yours has been playing hell with our communications. Recently we developed what we thought was a Top Secret project—and you're blasting us off the air."

"This is only a small portable unit, poorly screened," Bram said. "The resonance effects are unpredictable. When one seeks to channel the power of thought—"

"Wait a minute!" Tremaine burst out.

"What is it?" Miss Carroll said, alarmed.

"Hyperwave," Tremaine said. "Instantaneous transmission. And thought. No wonder people had headaches—and nightmares! We've been broadcasting on the same band as the human mind!"

"This 'hyperwave'," Bram said. "You say it is instantaneous?"

"That's supposed to be classified information."

"Such a device is new in the Cosmos," Bram said. "Only a protoplasmic brain is known to produce a null-lag excitation state."

Tremaine frowned. "Bram, this Repellor focuses what I'll call thought waves for want of a better term. It uses an interference effect to damp out the Niss harmonic generator. What if we poured more power to the Repellor?"

"No. The power of the mind cannot be amplified—"

"I don't mean amplification; I mean an additional source. I have a hyperwave receiver here. With a little rewiring, it'll act as a transmitter. Can we tie it in?"

Bram shook his head. "Would that I were a technician," he said. "I know only what is required to operate the device."

"Let me take a look," Tremaine said. "Maybe I can figure it out."

"Take care. Without it, we fall before the Niss."

"I'll be careful." Tremaine went to the machine, examined it, tracing leads, identifying components.

"This seems clear enough," he said. "These would be powerful magnets here; they give a sort of pinch effect. And these are refracting-field coils. Simple, and brilliant. With this idea, we could beam hyperwave—"

"First let us deal with the Niss!"

"Sure." Tremaine looked at Bram. "I think I can link my apparatus to this," he said. "Okay if I try?"

"How long?"

"It shouldn't take more than fifteen minutes."

"That leaves little time."

"The cycle is tightening," Tremaine said. "I figure the next transmissions ... or attacks ... will come at intervals of under five minutes for several hours now; this may be the last chance."

"Then try," said Bram.

Tremaine nodded, went to the suitcase, took out tools and a heavy black box, set to work. Linda Carroll sat by Bram's side, speaking softly to him. The minutes passed.

"Okay," Tremaine said. "This unit is ready." He went to the Repellor, hesitated a moment, then turned two nuts and removed a cover.

"We're off the air," he said. "I hope my formula holds."

Bram and Miss Carroll watched silently as Tremaine worked. He strung wires, taped junctions, then flipped a switch on the hyperwave set and tuned it, his eyes on the dials of a smaller unit.

"Nineteen minutes have passed since the last attack," Bram said. "Make haste."

"I'm almost done," Tremaine said.

A sharp cry came from the wall. Tremaine jumped. "What the hell makes those sounds?"

"They are nothing—mere static. But they warn that the harmonic generators are warming." Bram struggled to his feet. "Now comes the assault."

"The shadows!" Miss Carroll cried.

Bram sank into the chair, leaned back, his face pale as wax in the faint glow from the wall. The glow grew brighter; the shadows swam into focus.

"Hurry, James," Miss Carroll said. "It comes quickly."

Bram watched through half-closed eyes. "I must man the Repellor. I ..." He fell back in the chair, his head lolling.

"Bram!" Miss Carroll cried. Tremaine snapped the cover in place, whirled to the chair, dragged it and its occupant away from the machine, then turned, seized the grips. On the wall the Niss moved in silence, readying the attack. The black-clad figure was visible, climbing to his place. The wall cleared. Tremaine stared across at the narrow room, the gray-clad Niss. They stood now, eyes on him. One pointed. Others erected leathery crests.

Stay out, you ugly devils, Tremaine thought. *Go back, retreat, give up . . .*

Now the blue glow built in a flickering arc across the Niss machine. The technicians stood, staring across the narrow gap, tiny red eyes glittering in the narrow alien faces. Tremaine squinted against the brilliant white light from the high-vaulted Niss Command Center. The last suggestion of the sloping surface of the limestone wall was gone. Tremaine felt a draft stir; dust whirled up, clouded the air. There was an odor of iodine.

Back, Tremaine thought. *Stay back . . .*

There was a restless stir among the waiting rank of Niss. Tremaine heard the dry shuffle of horny feet against the floor, the whine of the harmonic generator. His eyes burned. As a hot gust swept around him he choked and coughed.

NO! he thought, hurling negation like a weightless bomb. *FAIL! RETREAT!*

Now the Niss moved, readying a wheeled machine, rolling it into place; Tremaine coughed rackingly, fought to draw a breath, blinking back blindness. A deep thrumming started up; grit particles stung his cheek, the backs of his hands. The Niss worked rapidly, their throat gills visibly dilated now in the unaccustomed flood of oxygen . . .

Our oxygen, Tremaine thought. *The looting has started already, and I've failed, and the people of Earth will choke and die . . .*

From what seemed an immense distance, a roll of thunder trembled at the brink of audibility, swelling.

The black-clad Niss on the alien machine half rose, erecting a black-scaled crest, exulting. Then, shockingly, his eyes fixed on Tremaine's, his trap-like mouth gaped, exposing a tongue like a scarlet snake, a cavernous pink throat set with a row of needle-like snow-white teeth. The tongue flicked out, a gesture of utter contempt.

And suddenly Tremaine was cold with deadly rage. *We have a treatment for snakes in this world,* he thought with savage intensity. *We crush 'em under our heels . . .* He pictured a writhing rattler, broken-backed, a club descending; a darting red coral snake, its venom ready, slashed in the blades of a power mower; a cottonmouth, smashed into red ruin by a shotgun blast . . .

BACK, SNAKE! he thought. *DIE! DIE!*

The thunder faded.

And atop the Niss Generator, the black-clad Niss snapped his mouth shut, crouched.

"DIE!" Tremaine shouted. "DIE!"

The Niss seemed to shrink in on himself, shivering. His crest went flaccid, twitched twice. The red eyes winked out and the Niss toppled from the machine. Tremaine coughed, gripped the handles, turned his eyes to a gray-uniformed Niss who scrambled up to replace the operator.

I SAID DIE, SNAKE!

The Niss faltered, tumbled back among his fellows, who darted about now like ants in a broached anthill. One turned red eyes on Tremaine, then scrambled for the red cut-out switch.

NO, YOU DON'T, Tremaine thought. *IT'S NOT THAT EASY, SNAKE. DIE!*

The Niss collapsed. Tremaine drew a rasping breath, blinked back tears of pain, took in a group of Niss in a glance.

Die!

They fell. The others turned to flee then, but like a scythe Tremaine's mind cut them down, left them in windrows. Hate walked naked among the Niss and left none living.

Now the machines, Tremaine thought. He fixed his eyes on the harmonic generator. It melted into slag. Behind it, the high panels set with jewel-like lights blackened, crumpled into wreckage. Suddenly the air was clean again. Tremaine breathed deep. Before him the surface of the rock swam into view.

NO! Tremaine thought thunderously. *HOLD THAT AP-ERTURE OPEN!*

The rock-face shimmered, faded. Tremaine looked into the white-lit room, at the blackened walls, the huddled dead. *No pity,* he thought. *You would have sunk those white teeth into soft human throats, sleeping in the dark ... as you've done on a hundred worlds. You're a cancer in the cosmos. And I have the cure.*

WALLS, he thought, *COLLAPSE!*

The roof before him sagged, fell in. Debris rained down from above, the walls tottered, went down. A cloud of roiled dust swirled, cleared to show a sky blazing with stars.

Dust, stay clear, Tremaine thought. *I want good air to breathe for the work ahead.* He looked out across a landscape of rock, ghostly white in the starlight.

LET THE ROCKS MELT AND FLOW LIKE WATER!

An upreared slab glowed, slumped, ran off in yellow rivulets that were lost in the radiance of the crust as it bubbled, belching released gasses. A wave of heat struck Tremaine. *Let it be cool here*, he thought. *Now, Niss world . . .*

"No!" Bram's voice shouted. "Stop, stop!"

Tremaine hesitated. He stared at the vista of volcanic fury before him.

I could destroy it all, he thought. *And the stars in the Niss sky . . .*

"Great is the power of your hate, man of Earth," Bram cried. "But curb it now, before you destroy us all!"

"Why?" Tremaine shouted. "I can wipe out the Niss and their whole diseased universe with them, with a thought!"

"Master yourself," Bram said hoarsely. "Your rage destroys you! One of the suns you see in the Niss sky is your Sol!"

"Sol?" Tremaine said. "Then it's the Sol of a thousand years ago. Light takes time to cross a galaxy. And the earth is still here . . . so it wasn't destroyed!"

"Wise are you," Bram said. "Your race is a wonder in the Cosmos, and deadly is your hate. But you know nothing of the forces you unloose now. Past time is as mutable as the steel and rock you melted but now."

"Listen to him, James," Miss Carroll pleaded. "Please listen."

Tremaine twisted to look at her, still holding the twin grips. She looked back steadily, her head held high. Beside her, Bram's eyes were sunken deep in his lined face.

"Jess said you looked like a princess once, Miss Carroll," Tremaine said, "when you drove past with your red hair piled up high. And Bram: you were young, and you loved her. The Niss took your youth from you. You've spent your life here, fighting them, alone. And Linda Carroll waited through the years, because she loved you . . . and feared you. The Niss did that. And you want me to spare them?"

"You have mastered them," said Bram. "And you are drunk with the power in you. But the power of love is greater than the power of hate. Our love sustained us; your hate can only destroy."

Tremaine locked eyes with the old man. He drew a deep breath at last, let it out shudderingly. "All right," he said. "I guess the God complex got me." He looked back once more at the devastated landscape. "The Niss will remember this encounter, I think. They won't try Earth again."

"You've fought valiantly, James, and won," Miss Carroll said. "Now let the power go."

Tremaine turned again to look at her. "You deserve better than this, Miss Carroll," he said. "Bram, you said time is mutable. Suppose—"

"Let well enough alone," Bram said. "Let it go!"

"Once, long ago, you tried to explain this to Linda Carroll. But there was too much against it; she couldn't understand. She was afraid. And you've suffered for sixty years. Suppose those years had never been. Suppose I had come that night ... instead of now—"

"It could never be!"

"It can if I will it!" Tremaine gripped the handles tighter. *Let this be THAT night,* he thought fiercely. *The night in 1901, when Bram's last contact failed. Let it be that night, five minutes before the portal closed. Only this machine and I remain as we are now; outside there are gas lights in the farm houses along the dirt road to Elsby, and in the town horses stand in the stables along the cinder alleys behind the houses; and President McKinley is having dinner in the White House ...*

There was a sound behind Tremaine. He whirled. The ravaged scene was gone. A great disc mirror stood across the cave, intersecting the limestone wall. A man stepped through it, froze at the sight of Tremaine. He was tall, with curly blond hair, fine-chiseled features, broad shoulders.

"Fdazh ha?" he said. Then his eyes slid past Tremaine, opened still wider in astonishment. Tremaine followed the stranger's glance. A young woman, dressed in a negligee of pale silk, stood in the door, a hairbrush in her hand, her red hair flowing free to her waist. She stood rigid in shock.

Then ...

"Mr. Bram ... !" she gasped. "What—"

Tremaine found his voice. "Miss Carroll, don't be afraid," he said. "I'm your friend, you must believe me."

Linda Carroll turned wide eyes to him. "Who are you?" she breathed. "I was in my bedroom—"

"I can't explain. A miracle has been worked here tonight ... on your behalf." Tremaine turned to Bram. "Look—" he started.

"What man are you?" Bram cut in in heavily accented English. "How do you come to this place?"

"Listen to me, Bram!" Tremaine snapped. "Time is mutable. You stayed here, to protect Linda Carroll—and Linda Carroll's world. You've just made that decision, right?" Tremaine went on, not waiting for a reply. "You were stuck here ... for sixty years. Earth technology developed fast. One day a man stumbled in here, tracing down the signal from your Repellor; that was me. You showed me how to use the device ... and with it I wiped out the Niss. And then I set the block back for you and Linda Carroll. The Portal closes in two minutes. Don't waste time ..."

"Mutable time?" Bram said. He went past Tremaine to Linda. "Fair lady of Earth," he said. "Do not fear ..."

"Sir, I hardly know you," Miss Carroll said. "How did I come here, hardly clothed—"

"Take her, Bram!" Tremaine shouted. "Take her and get back through that Portal—fast." He looked at Linda Carroll. "Don't be afraid," he said. "You know you love him; go with him now, or regret it all your days."

"Will you come?" asked Bram. He held out his hand to her. Linda hesitated, then put her hand in his. Bram went with her to the mirror surface, handed her through. He looked back at Tremaine.

"I do not understand, man of Earth," he said. "But I thank you." Then he was gone.

Alone in the dim-lit grotto Tremaine let his hands fall from the grips, staggered to the rocker and sank down. He felt weak, drained of strength. His hands ached from the strain of the ordeal. How long had it lasted? Five minutes? An hour? Or had it happened at all ... ?

But Bram and Linda Carroll were gone. He hadn't imagined that. And the Niss were defeated.

But there was still his own world to contend with. The police would be waiting, combing through the house. They would want to know what he had done with Miss Carroll. Maybe there would be a murder charge. There'd be no support from Fred and the Bureau. As for Jess, he was probably in a cell now, looking a stiff sentence in the face for obstructing justice ...

Tremaine got to his feet, cast a last glimpse at the empty room, the outlandish shape of the Repellor, the mirrored portal. It was a temptation to step through it. But this was his world, with all its faults. Perhaps later, when his strength returned, he could try the machine again ...

The thought appalled him. *The ashes of hate are worse than the ashes of love,* he thought. He went to the stairs, climbed them, pressed the button. Nothing happened. He pushed the panel aside by hand and stepped into the kitchen. He circled the heavy table with the candlestick, went along the hall and out onto the porch. It was almost the dawn of a fresh spring day. There was no sign of the police. He looked at the grassy lawn, the row of new-set saplings.

Strange, he thought. *I don't remember any saplings. I thought I drove in under a row of trees ...* He squinted into the misty early morning gloom. His car was gone. That wasn't too surprising; the cops had impounded it, no doubt. He stepped down, glanced at the ground ahead. It was smooth, with a faint footpath cut through the grass. There was no mud, no sign of tire tracks—

The horizon seemed to spin suddenly. *My God!!* Tremaine thought. *I've left myself in the year* 1901 ...!

He whirled, leaped up on the porch, slammed through the door and along the hall, scrambled through the still-open panel, bounded down the stairs and into the cave—

The Repellor was gone. Tremaine leaped forward with a cry—and under his eyes, the great mirror twinkled, winked out. The black box of the hyperwave receiver lay alone on the floor, beside the empty rocker. The light of the kerosene lamp reflected from the featureless wall.

Tremaine turned, stumbled up the steps, out into the air. The sun showed a crimson edge just peeping above distant hills.

1901, Tremaine thought. *The century has just turned. Somewhere a young fellow named Ford is getting ready to put the nation on wheels, and two boys named Wright are about to give it wings. No one ever heard of a World War, or the roaring Twenties, or Prohibition, or FDR, or the Dust*

*Bowl, or Pearl Harbor. And Hiroshima and Nagasaki are just
two cities in distant floral Japan . . .*

He walked down the path, stood by the rutted dirt road.
Placid cows nuzzled damp grass in the meadow beyond it. In
the distance a train hooted.

There are railroads, Tremaine thought. *But no jet planes,
no radio, no movies, no automatic dish-washers. But then
there's no TV, either. That makes up for a lot. And there are
no police waiting to grill me, and no murder charge, and no
neurotic nest of bureaucrats waiting to welcome me back . . .*

He drew a deep breath. The air was sweet. *I'm here*, he
thought. *I feel the breeze on my face and the firm sod
underfoot. It's real, and it's all there is now, so I might as
well take it calmly. After all, a man with my education ought
to be able to do well in this day and age!*

Whistling, Tremaine started the ten-mile walk into town.

COCOON

Sid Throndyke overrode his respirator to heave a deep sigh.

"Wow!" he said, flipping to his wife's personal channel. "A tough day on the Office channel."

The contact screens attached to his eyeballs stayed blank: Cluster was out. Impatiently, Sid toed the console, checking the channels: Light, Medium, and Deep Sitcom; autho-hypno; Light and Deep Narco; four, six and eight-party Social; and finally, muttering to himself, Psychan. Cluster's identity symbol appeared on his screens.

"There you are," he grieved. "Psychan again. After a hard day, the least a man expects is to find his wife tuned to his channel—"

"Oh, Sid; there's this wonderful analyst. A new model. It's doing so much for me, really wonderful. . . ."

"I know," Sid grumped. "That orgasm-association technique. That's all I hear. I'd think you'd want to keep in touch with the Sitcoms, so you know what's going on; but I suppose you've been tied into Psychan all day—while I burned my skull out on Office."

"Now, Sid; didn't I program your dinner and everything?"

"Um." Mollified, Sid groped with his tongue for the dinner lever, eased the limp plastic tube into his mouth. He sucked a mouthful of the soft paste—

"Cluster! You know I hate Vege-pap. Looks like you could at least dial a nice Prote-sim or Sucromash . . ."

"Sid, you ought to tune to Psychan. It would do you a world of good . . ." Her sub-vocalized voice trailed off in the earphones. Sid snorted, dialed a double Prote-sim AND a Sucromash, fuming at the delay. He gulped his dinner, not even noticing the rich gluey consistency, then in a somewhat better mood, flipped to the Light Sitcom.

It was good enough stuff, he conceded; the husband was a congenital psychopathic inferior who maintained his family

161

in luxury by a series of fantastic accidents. You had to chuckle when his suicide attempt failed at the last moment, after he'd lost all that blood. The look on his face when they dragged him back ...

But somehow it wasn't enough. Sid dialed the medium; it wasn't much better. The deep, maybe.

Sid viewed for a few minutes with growing impatience. Sure, you had to hand it to the Sitcom people; there was a lot of meat in the deep sitcom. It was pretty subtle stuff, the way the wife got the money the husband had been saving and spent it for a vacation trip for her chihuahua; had a real social content, too deep for most folks. But like the rest of the sitcoms, it was historical. Sure, using old-time settings gave a lot of scope for action. But how about something more pertinent to the contemporary situation? Nowadays, even though people led the kind of rich, full lives that Vital Programming supplied, there was still a certain lack. Maybe it was just a sort of atavistic need for gross muscular exertion. He'd viewed a discussion of the idea of a few nights earlier on the usual Wednesday night four-party hookup with the boys. Still, in his case, he had plenty of muscle tone. He'd spent plenty on a micro-spasm attachment for use with the narco channel ...

That was a thought. Sid didn't usually like narco; too synthetic, as he'd explained to the boys. They hadn't liked the remark, he remembered. Probably they were all narco fans. But what the hell, a man had a right to a few maverick notions.

Sid tuned to the Narco channel. It was a traditional sex fantasy, in which the familiar colorless hero repeatedly fended off the advances of coitus-seeking girls. It was beautifully staged, with plenty of action, but like the sitcoms, laid in one of those never-never historical settings. Sid flipped past with a sub-vocal grunt. It wasn't much better than Cluster's orgasm-association treatments.

The stylized identity-symbol of the Pubinf announcer flashed on Sid's screens, vibrating in resonance with the impersonal voice of the Official announcer:

"... cause for concern. CentProg states that control will have been re-established within the hour. Some discomfort may result from vibration in sectors north of Civic Center, but normalcy will be restored shortly. Now, a word on the food situation."

A hearty, gelatinous voice took over: "Say, folks, have you considered switching to Vege-pap? Vege-pap now comes in a variety of rich flavors, all, of course, equally nourishing, every big swallow loaded with the kind of molecule that keeps those metabolisms rocking along at the pace of today's more-fun-than-ever sitcoms—and today's stimulating narco and social channels, too!

"Starting with First Feeding tomorrow, you'll have that opportunity you've wanted to try Vege-pap. Old-fashioned foods, like Prote-sim and Sucromash, will continue to be available of course, where exceptional situations warrant. Now—"

"What's that!" Sid sub-vocalized. He toed the replay key, listened again. Then he dug a toe viciously against the tuning key, flipping to the Psychan monitor.

"Cluster!" he barked at his wife's identity pattern. "Have you heard about this nonsense? Some damn fool on Pubinf is blathering about Vege-pap for everybody! By God, this is a free country. I'd like to see anyone try—"

"Sid," Cluster's voice came faintly, imploring. "P-P-Please, S-S-Sid . . ."

"Damn it, Cluster . . . !" Sid stopped talking, coughed, gulped. His throat was burning. In his excitement he'd been vocalizing. The realization steadied him. He'd have to calm down. He'd been behaving like an animal . . .

"Cluster, darling. Kindly interrupt your treatment. I have to talk to you. Now. It's important." Confound it, if she didn't switch to his channel now—

"Yes, Sid." Cluster's voice had a ragged undertone. Sid half-suspected she was vocalizing then too . . .

"I was listening to Pubinf," he said, aware of a sense of dignity in the telling. No narco-addict he, but a mature-minded auditor of a serious channel like Pubinf. "They're raving about cutting off Prote-sim. Never heard of such nonsense. Have you heard anything about this?"

"No, Sid. You should know I never—"

"I know! But I thought maybe you'd heard something . . ."

"Sid, I've been under treatment all day—except the time I spent programming your dinner."

"You can get Prote-sim in exceptional situations, they said!

I wonder what that's supposed to mean? Why, I've been a Prote-sim man for years . . ."

"Maybe it will do you good, Sid. Something different . . ."

"Different? What in the world do I want with something different? I have a comfortable routine, well-balanced, creative. I'm not interested in having any government fat-head telling me what to eat."

"But Vege-sim might be good; build you up or something."

"Build me up? What are you talking about? I view sports regularly; and aren't you forgetting my Micro-spasm accessory? Hah! I'm a very physically-minded man, when it comes to that."

"I know you are, Sid. I didn't mean . . . I only meant, maybe a little variety . . ."

Sid was silent, thinking. Variety. Hmmmm. Might be something in that. Maybe he WAS in a rut, a little.

"Cluster," he said suddenly. "You know, it's a funny thing; I've kind of gotten out of touch. Oh, I don't mean with important affairs. Heck, I hardly ever tune in Narco, or auto-hypno, for that matter. But I mean, after all, it's been quite a while now I guess, since we gave up well, you know, physical contact."

"Sid! If you're going to be awful, I'm switching right back to my Psychan—"

"I don't mean to be getting personal, Cluster. I was just thinking . . . By golly, how long has it been since that first contract with CentProg?"

"Why . . . I haven't any idea. That was so long ago. I can't see what difference it makes. Heavens, Sid, life today is so rich and full—"

"Don't get me wrong, I'm not talking about wanting to change, or anything idiotic. Just wondering. You know."

"Poor Sid. If you could spend more time with wonderful channels like Psychan, and not have to bother with that boring old Office . . ."

Sid chuckled sub-vocally. "A man needs the feeling of achievement he gets from doing a job, Cluster. I wouldn't be happy, just relaxing with Sitcom all the time. And after all, Indexing is an important job. If we fellows in the game all quit, where'd CentProg be? Eh?"

"I hadn't thought of it like that, Sid. I guess it is pretty important."

"Darn right kid. They haven't built the computer yet that can handle Indexing—or Value Judgment, or Criticism—. It'll be a while yet before the machine replaces man." Sid chuckled again. Cluster was such a kid in a lot of ways.

Still, it had been a long time. Funny, how you didn't think much about time, under Vital Programming. After all, your program was so full, you didn't have time to moon over the past. You popped out of Dream-stim, had a fast breakfast (Vege-pap; hah! He'd see about that!), then over to Office channel. That kept a fellow on his toes, right up till quitting time. Then dinner with Cluster, and right into the evening's round of Sitcoms, Socials, Narcos—whatever you wanted.

But how long had it been? A long time, no doubt. Measured in, say, years, the way folks used to be in the habit of thinking.

Years and years. Yes, by golly. Years and years.

Quite suddenly, Sid was uneasy. How long had it been? He had been about twenty-eight—the term came awkwardly to mind—twenty-eight when he and Cluster first met. Then there was that first anniversary—a wild time that had been, with friends over for TV. And then Vital Programming had come along. He and Cluster had been among the first to sign up.

God, what a long time it had been. TV. Imagine sitting. The thought of being propped up against coarse chairs, out in the open, made Sid wince. And other people around—faces right out in the open and everything. Staring at a little screen no more than five feet square. How in the world had people stood it? Still, it was all in what you were used to. People were adaptable. They had had to be to survive in those primitive conditions. You had to give the old-timers credit. He and Cluster were a pretty lucky couple to have lived in the era when Vital Programming was developed. They could see the contrast right in their own lives. The younger folks, now—

"Sid," Cluster broke in plaintively. "May I finish my treatment now?"

Sid dialed off, annoyed. Cluster wasn't interested in his problems. She was so wrapped up in Psychan these days, she couldn't even discuss the sitcoms intelligently. Well, Sid Throndyke wasn't a man to be pushed around. He nudged the 'fone switch, gave a number. An operator answered.

"I want the Pubinf office."

There was a moment's silence. "That number is unavailable," the recorded voice said.

"Unavailable, hell! I want to talk to them down there! What's all this about cutting off Prote-sim?"

"That information is not available."

"Look," Sid said, calming himself with an effort. "I want to talk to someone at Pubinf—"

"The line is available now."

An unfamiliar identity pattern appeared on Sid's screens.

"I want to find out about this food business," Sid began—

"A temporary measure," a harassed voice said. "Due to the emergency."

"What emergency?" Sid stared at the pattern belligerently. As he watched, it wavered, almost imperceptibly. A moment later, he felt a distinct tremor through the form-hugging plastic cocoon.

"What . . . !" he gasped, "what was that?!"

"There's no cause for alarm," the Pubinf voice said. "You'll be kept fully informed through regular—"

A second shock rumbled. Sid gasped. "What the devil's going on . . . ?"

The Pubinf pattern was gone. Sid blinked at the blank screens, then switched to his monitor channel. He had to talk to someone. Cluster would be furious at another interruption, but—

"Sid!" Cluster's voice rasped in Sid's hemispherical canals. She was vocalizing now for sure, he thought wildly.

"They broke right in!" Cluster cried. "Just as I was ready to climax—"

"Who?" Sid demanded. "What's going on here? What are you raving about?"

"Not an identity pattern, either," Cluster wailed. "Sid, it was a—a—face."

"What?" Sid blinked. He hadn't heard Cluster use obscenity before. This must be serious.

"Calm yourself," he said. "Now tell me exactly what happened."

"I told you: a—face. It was horrible, Sid. On the Psychan channel. And he was shouting—"

"Shouting what?"

"I don't know. Something about 'Get out'. Oh, Sid, I've never been so humiliated . . ."

"Listen, Cluster," Sid said. "You tune in to a nice narco now, and get some rest. I'll deal with this."

"A face," Cluster sobbed. "A great, nasty, *hairy* face—"

"That's enough!" Sid snapped. He cut Cluster's identity pattern with an impatient gouge of his toe. Sometimes it seemed like women enjoyed obscenity . . .

Now what? He was far from giving up on the Vege-pap issue, and now this: a respectable married woman insulted right in her own cocoon. Things were going to hell. But he'd soon see about that. With a decisive twist of the ankle, Sid flipped to the Police channel.

"I want to report an outrage."

The police identity pattern blanked abruptly. For a moment Sid's contact screens were blank. Then a face appeared.

Sid sucked in a breath out of phase with his respirator. THIS wasn't the police channel. The face stared at him, mouth working: a pale face, with whiskers sprouting from hollow cheeks, lips sunken over toothless gums. Then the audio came in, in midsentence:

". . . to warn you. You've got to listen, you fools! You'll all die here! It's already at the north edge of the city. The big barrier wall's holding, but—"

The screen blanked; the bland police pattern reappeared.

"The foregoing interruption was the result of circumstances beyond the control of CentProg," a taped voice said smoothly. "Normal service will now be resumed."

"Police!" Sid yelled. He was vocalizing now, and be damned to it! There was just so much a decent citizen would stand for—

The screen flickered again. The police pattern disappeared. Sid held his breath—

A face appeared. This was a different one, Sid was sure. It was hairier than the other one, but not as hollow-cheeked. He watched in dumb shock as the mouth opened—

"Listen," a hoarse voice said. "Everybody, listen. We're blanketing all the channels this time—I hope. This is our last try. There's only a few of us. It wasn't easy getting into here—and there's no time left. We've got to move fast."

The voice stopped as the man on the screen breathed hoarsely, swallowed. Then he went on:

"It's the ice; it's moving down on us, fast, a god-awful big glacier. The walls can't stand much longer. It'll either wipe the city off the map or bury it. Either way, anybody that stays is done for.

"Listen; it won't be easy, but you've got to try. Don't try to go down. You can't get out below because of the drifts. Go up, onto the roofs. It's your only chance—you must go up."

The image on Sid's contact screens trembled violently, then blanked. Moments later, Sid felt a tremor—worse, this time. His cocoon seemed to pull at him. For a moment he was aware of the drag of a hundred tiny contacts grafted to the skin, a hundred tiny conductors penetrating to nerve conduits—

An almost suffocating wave of claustrophobia swept over him. The universe seemed to be crushing in on him, immobile, helpless, a grub buried in an immense anthill—

The shock passed. Slowly, Sid regained a grip on himself. His respirator was cycling erratically, attempting to match to his ragged breathing impulses. His chest ached from the strain. He groped with a toe, keyed in Cluster's identity pattern.

"Cluster! Did you feel it? Everything was rocking . . ."

There was no reply. Sid called again. No answer. Was she ignoring him, or—

Maybe she was hurt, alone and helpless—

Sid fought for calm. No need for panic. Dial CentProg, report the malfunction. He felt with trembling toes, and punched the keys . . .

CentProg's channel was dark, lifeless. Sid stared, unbelieving. It wasn't possible. He switched wildly to the light sitcom—

Everything normal here. The husband fell down the stairs, smashing his new camera . . .

But this was no time to get involved. Sid flipped through the medium and deep Sitcoms: all normal. Maybe he could get through to the police now—

Mel Goldfarb's pattern blinked on the personal call code. Sid tuned him in.

"Mel! What's it all about? My God, that earthquake—"

"I don't like it, Sid. I felt it, over here in South Sector. The . . . uh . . . face . . . said the North Sector. You're over that side. What did you—"

"My God, I thought the roof was going to fall in, Mel. It

was terrible! Look, I'm trying to get through to the police. Keep in touch, hey?"

"Wait, Sid; I'm worried—"

Sid cut the switch, flipped to the police channel. If that depraved son of a bitch showed his face again—

The police pattern appeared. Sid paused to gather his thoughts. First things first . . .

"That earthquake," he said. "What's happening? And the maniac who's been exposing his face. My wife—"

"The foregoing interruption was the result of circumstances beyond the control of CentProg. Normal service will now be resumed."

"What are you talking about? NOTHING is beyond the control of CentProg—"

"The foregoing interruption was the result of circumstances beyond the control of CentProg. Normal service will now be resumed."

"That's enough of your damned nonsense! What about this crazy guy showing his bare face? How do I know that he won't—"

"The foregoing interruption was the result of circumstances beyond the control of CentProg. Normal service will now be resumed."

Sid stared, aghast. A taped voice! A brush-off! He was supposed to settle for that? Well, by God, he had a contract . . .

Mel's code flashed again. Sid tuned him in. "Mel, this is a damned outrage. I called police channel and do you know what I got? A canned announcement—"

"Sid," Mel cut in. "Do you suppose it meant anything? I mean the . . . uh . . . guy with the . . . uh . . . face. All that about getting out, and the glacier wiping out the city."

"What?" Sid stared at Mel's pattern, trying to make sense of what he was saying. "Glacier?" he said. "Wipe out what?"

"You saw him, didn't you? The crazy bird, cut in on all channels. He said the ice was going to wipe out the city . . ."

Sid thought back. The damned obscene face. He hadn't really listened to what it was raving about. But it was something about getting out . . .

"Tell me that again, Mel."

Mel repeated the bare-faced man's warning. "Do you suppose there's anything in it? I mean, the shocks, and everything. And you can't get police channel. And I tried to tune in to Pubinf just now and I got a canned voice, just like you did . . ."

"It's crazy, Mel. It can't . . ."

"I don't know. I've tried to reach a couple of the fellows; I can't get through . . ."

"Mel," Sid asked suddenly. "How long has it been? I mean, how long since CentProg has been handling things?"

"What? My God, Sid, what a question. I don't know."

"A long time, eh, Mel? A lot could have happened outside."

"My contract—"

"But how do we know? I was talking to Cluster just now; we couldn't remember. I mean, how can you gauge a thing like that? We have our routine, and everything goes along, and nobody thinks about anything like . . . outside. Then all of a sudden—"

"I'm trying Pubinf again," Mel said. "I don't like this—"

Mel was gone. Sid tried to think. Pubinf was handing out canned brush-offs, just like Police Channel. CentProg . . . maybe it was okay now . . .

CentProg was still dark. Sid was staring at the blank screens when a new shock sent heavy vibrations through his cocoon. Sid gasped, tried to keep cool. It would pass; it wasn't anything, it couldn't be . . .

The vibrations built, heavy, hard shocks that drove the air from Sid's lungs, yanked painfully at arms, legs, neck, and his groin . . .

It was a long time before the nausea passed. Sid lay, drawing breath painfully, fighting down the vertigo. The pain—it was a help, in a way. It helped to clear his head. Something was wrong, badly wrong. He had to think now, do the right thing. It wouldn't do to panic. If only there wouldn't be another earthquake . . .

Something wet splattered against Sid's half-open mouth. He recoiled, automatically spitting the mucky stuff, snorting—

It was Vege-pap, gushing down from the feeding tube. Sid averted his face, felt the cool semi-liquid pattering against the cocoon, spreading over it, sloshing down the sides. Something was broken . . .

Sid groped for the cut-off with his tongue, gagging at the viscous mess pouring over his face. Of course, it hadn't actually touched his skin, except for his lips; the cocoon protected him. But he could feel the thick weight of it, awash in the fluid that supported the plastic cocoon. He could sense it quite clearly, flowing under him, forcing him up in the chamber as the hydrostatic balance was upset. With a shock of pain, Sid felt a set of neuro contacts along his spinal cord come taut. He gritted his teeth, felt searing agony as the contacts ripped loose.

Half the world went dark and cold. Sid was only dimly aware of the pressure against his face and chest as he pressed against the cell roof. All sensation was gone from his legs now, from his left arm, his back. His left contact screen was blank, unseeing. Groaning with the effort, Sid strained to reach out with a toe, key the emergency signal—

Hopeless. Without the boosters he could never make it. His legs were dead, paralyzed. He was helpless.

He tried to scream, choked, fought silently in the swaddling cocoon, no longer a euphorically caressing second skin but a dead, clammy weight, binding him. He twisted, feeling unused muscles cramp at the effort, touched the lever that controlled the face-plate. It had been a long time since Sid had opened the plate. He'd had a reputation as an open-air fiend once—but that had been—he didn't know how long. The lever was stiff. Sid lunged against it again. It gave. There was a sudden lessening of pressure as the burden of Vege-pap slopped out through the opening. Sid sank away from the ceiling of the tiny cubicle, felt his cocoon ground on the bottom.

For a long time Sid lay, dazed by pain and shock, not even thinking, waiting for the agony to subside . . .

Then the itching began. It penetrated Sid's daze, set him twitching in a frenzy of discomfort. The tearing loose of the dorsal contacts had opened dozens of tiny rents in the cocoon; a sticky mixture of the supporting water bath and Vege-pap seeped in, irritating the tender skin. Sid writhed, struggled to scratch—and discovered that, miraculously, the left arm responded now. The motor nerves which had been stunned by the electroneural trickle-flow through the contacts were recovering control. Feebly, Sid's groping hand reached his inflamed hip—and scrabbled against the smooth sheath of plastic.

He had to get out. The cocoon was a confining nightmare,

a dead husk that had to be shed. The face-plate was open. Sid felt upward, found the edge, tugged—

Slippery as an eel, he slithered from the cocoon, hung for an instant as the remaining contacts came taut, then slammed to the floor a foot below. Sid didn't feel the pain of the fall; as the contacts ripped free, he fainted.

When Sid recovered consciousness, his first thought was that the narco channel was getting a little TOO graphic. He groped for a tuning switch—

Then he remembered. The earthquake, Mel, the canned announcement—

And he had opened his face-plate and fought to get out— and here he was. He blinked dully, then moved his left hand. It took a long time, but he managed to peel the contact screens from his eyes. He looked around. He was lying on the floor in a rectangular tunnel. A dim light came from a glowing green spot along the corridor. Sid remembered seeing it before, a long time ago ... the day he and Cluster had entered their cocoons.

Now that he was detached from the stimuli of the cocoon, it seemed to Sid, he was able to think a little more clearly. It had hurt to be torn free from the security of the cocoon, but it wasn't so bad now. A sort of numbness had set in. But he couldn't lie here and rest; he had to do something, fast. First, there was Cluster. She hadn't answered. Her cocoon was situated right next to his—

Sid tried to move; his leg twitched; his arm fumbled over the floor. It was smooth and wet, gummy with the Vege-pap that was still spilling down from the open face-plate. The smell of the stuff was sickening. Irrationally, Sid had a sudden mouth-watering hunger for Prote-sim.

Sid fixed his eyes on the green light, trying to remember. He and Cluster had been wheeled along the corridor, laughing and talking gaily. Somehow, out here, things took on a different perspective. That had been—God! YEARS ago. How long? Maybe—twenty years? Longer. Fifty, maybe. Maybe longer. How could you know? For a while they had tuned to Pubinf, followed the news, kept up with friends on the outside. But more and more of their friends had signed contracts with CentProg. The news sort of dried up. You lost interest.

But what mattered now wasn't how long, it was what he

was going to do. Of course, an attendant would be along soon in any case to check up, but meanwhile, Cluster might be in trouble—

The tremor was bad this time. Sid felt the floor rock, felt the hard paving under him ripple like the surface of a pond. Somewhere, a rumbling sound rolled, and somewhere something heavy fell. The green light flickered, then burned steadily again.

A shape moved in the gloom of the corridor; there was the wet slap of footsteps. Sid sub-vocalized a calm 'Hi, fellows'— The silence rang in his ears. My God, of course they couldn't hear him. He tried again, consciously vocalizing, a tremendous shout—

A feeble croak, and a fit of coughing. When he recovered his breath, a bare and hairy face, greenish white, was bending over him.

". . . this poor devil," the man was saying in a thin choked voice.

Another face appeared over the first face's shoulder. Sid recognized them both. They were the two that had been breaking into decent channels, with their wild talk about a glacier . . .

"Listen, fellow," one of the bare-faced men said. Sid stared with fascinated disgust at the clammy pale skin, the sprouting hairs, the loose toothless mouth, the darting pink tongue. God, people were horrible to look at!

". . . be along after a while. Didn't mean to stir up anybody in your shape. You been in too long, fellow. You can't make it."

"I'm . . . good . . . shape . . ." Sid whispered indignantly.

"We can't do anything for you. You'll have to wait till the maintenance unit comes along. I'm pretty sure you'll be okay. The ice's piled itself up in a wall now, and split around the city walls. I think they'll hold. Course, the ice will cover the city, but that won't matter. CentProg will still handle everything. Plenty of energy from the pile and the solar cells, and the recycling will handle the food okay . . ."

". . . Cluster . . ." Sid gasped. The bare-faced man leaned closer. Sid explained about his wife. The man checked nearby face-plates. He came back and knelt by Sid. "Rest easy, fellow," he said. "They all look all right. Your wife's okay. Now, we're going to have to go on. But you'll be okay.

Plenty of Vege-pap around, I see. Just eat a little now and then. The Maintenance machine will be along and get you tucked back in."

"Where . . . ?" Sid managed.

"Us? We're heading south. Matt here knows where we can get clothes and supplies, maybe even a flier. We never were too set on this Vital Programming. We've only been in maybe a few years and we always did a lot of auto-gym work, keeping in shape. Didn't like the idea of wasting away . . . Matt's the one found out about the ice. He came for me . . ."

Sid was aware of the other man talking. It was hard to hear him.

A sudden thought struck Sid. ". . . how . . . long . . . ?" he asked.

It took three tries, but the bare-faced man got the idea at last.

"I'll take a look, fellow," he said. He went to Sid's open face-plate, peered at it, called the other man over. Then he came back, his feet spattering in the puddled Vege-pap.

"Your record says . . . 2043," he said. He looked at Sid with wide eyes. They were red and irritated, Sid saw. It made his own eyes itch.

"If that's right, you been here since the beginning. My God, that's over . . . two hundred years . . ."

The second bare-faced man, Matt, was pulling the other away. He was saying something, but Sid wasn't listening. Two hundred years. It seemed impossible. But after all, why not? In a controlled environment, with no wear and tear, no disease, you could live as long as CentProg kept everything running. But two hundred years . . .

Sid looked around. The two men were gone. He tried to remember just what had happened, but it was too hard. The ice, they had said, wouldn't crush the city. But it would flow around it, encase it in ice, and the snow would fall, and cover it, and the city would lie under the ice.

Ages might pass. In the cells, the cocoons would keep everyone snug and happy. There would be the traditional sitcoms, and Narco, and Psychan . . .

And up above, the ice.

Sid remembered the awful moments in the cocoon, when

the shock waves had rocked him; the black wave of fear that had closed in; the paralyzing claustrophobia.

The ice would build up and build up. Ice, two miles thick . . .

Why hadn't they waited? Sid groped, pushed himself up, rolled over. He was stronger already. Why hadn't they waited? He'd used the micro-spasm unit regularly—every so often. He had good muscle tone. It was just that he was a little stiff. He scrabbled at the floor, moved his body a few inches. Nothing to it. He remembered the reason for the green light; it was the elevator. They had brought him and Cluster down in it. All he had to do was get to it, and—

What about Cluster? He could try to bring her along. It would be lonely to be without her. But she wouldn't want to leave. She'd been here—two hundred years. Sid almost chuckled. Cluster wouldn't like the idea of being as old as that . . .

No, he'd go alone. He couldn't stay, of course. It would never be the same again for him. He pulled himself along, an inch, another. He rested, sucked up some Vege-pap from where it spread near his mouth . . .

He went on. It was a long way to the green light, but if you took it an inch at a time, an inch at a time . . .

He reached the door. There hadn't been any more shocks. Along the corridor, the glass face-plates stood closed, peaceful, orderly. The mess on the floor was the only thing. But the maintenance units would be along. The bare-faced man had said so.

You opened the door to the elevator by breaking a beam of light; Sid remembered that. He raised his arm; it was getting strong, all right. It was hardly any effort to lift it right up—

The door opened with a whoosh of air. Sid worked his way inside. Half way in, the door tried to close on him; his weight must have triggered the door-closing mechanism. But it touched him and flew open again. It was working fine, Sid thought.

He pulled his legs in, then rested. He would have to get up to the switch, somehow, and that was going to be tricky. Still, he had gotten this far okay. Just a little farther, and he'd catch up with the bare-faced men, and they'd set out together.

It took Sid an hour of hard work, but he managed to

reach, first, the low stool, then the chrome-plated control button. With a lurch the car started up. Sid fell back to the floor and fought back wave on wave of vertigo. It was hectic, being outside. But he wouldn't go back now; not even to see Cluster's familiar identity pattern again. Never again. He had to get out.

The elevator came to a stop. The door slid open—and a blast of sub-arctic air struck Sid like a blow from a giant hammer. His naked body—mere flaccid skin over atrophied bones—curled like a grub in the flames. For a long moment all sensation was washed away in the shock of the cold. Then there was pain; pain that went on and on . . .

And then the pain went, and it was almost like being back again, back in the cocoon, warm and comfortable, secure and protected and safe. But not quite the same. A thought stirred in Sid's mind. He pushed at the fog of cotton-wool, fought to grasp the thought that bobbed on the surface of the blissful warmth.

He opened his eyes. Out across the white expanse of roof-tops, beyond the last rim of the snow, the glittering jagged shape of the ice-face reared up, crystal-blue, gigantic; and in the high arched blue-black sky, a star burned with a brilliant fire.

This was what he wanted to tell Cluster, Sid thought. This, about the deep sky, and the star, so far away—and yet a man could see it.

But it was too late now to tell Cluster, too late to tell anyone. The bare-faced men were gone. Sid was alone; alone now under the sky.

Long ago, Sid thought, on the shore of some warm and muddy sea, some yearning sea-thing had crawled out to blink at the open sky, gulp a few breaths of burning oxygen, and die.

But not in vain. The urge to climb out was the thing. That was the force that was bigger than all the laws of nature, greater than all the distant suns blazing in their meaningless lonely splendor.

The other ones, the ones below, the secure and comfortable ones in their snug cocoons under the snow, they had lost the great urge. The thing that made a man.

But he, Sid Throndyke—he had made it.

Sid lay with his eyes on the star and the silent snow drifted over him to form a still small mound; and then the mound was buried, and then the city.

And only the ice and the star remained.

A TRIP TO THE CITY

"She'll be pulling out in a minute, Brett," Mr. Phillips said. He tucked his railroader's watch back in his vest pocket. "You better get aboard—if you're still set on going."

"It was reading all them books done it," Aunt Haicey said. "Thick books, and no pictures in them. I knew it'd make trouble." She plucked at the faded hand-embroidered shawl over her thin shoulders, a tiny bird-like woman with bright anxious eyes.

"Don't worry about me," Brett said. "I'll be back."

"The place'll be yours when I'm gone," Aunt Haicey said. "Lord knows it won't be long."

"Why don't you change your mind and stay on, boy?" Mr. Phillips said, blinking up at the young man. "If I talk to Mr. J.D., I think he can find a job for you at the plant."

"So many young people leave Casperton," Aunt Haicey said. "They never come back."

Mr. Phillips clicked this teeth. "They write, at first," he said. "Then they gradually lose touch."

"All your people are here, Brett," Aunt Haicey said. "Haven't you been happy here?"

"Why can't you young folks be content with Casperton?" Mr. Phillips said. "There's everything you need here."

"It's that Pretty-Lee done it," Aunt Haicey said. "If it wasn't for that girl—"

A clatter rán down the line of cars. Brett kissed Aunt Haicey's dry cheek, shook Mr. Phillips' hand, and swung aboard. His suitcase was on one of the seats. He put it up above in the rack, and sat down, turned to wave back at the two old people.

It was a summer morning. Brett leaned back and watched the country slide by. It was nice country, Brett thought; mostly in corn, some cattle, and away in the distance the hazy blue hills. Now he would see what was on the other side

179

of them: the cities, the mountains, and the ocean. Up until now all he knew about anything outside of Casperton was what he'd read or seen pictures of. As far as he was concerned, chopping wood and milking cows back in Casperton, they might as well not have existed. They were just words and pictures printed on paper. But he didn't want to just read about them. He wanted to see for himself.

Pretty-Lee hadn't come to see him off. She was probably still mad about yesterday. She had been sitting at the counter at the Club Rexall, drinking a soda and reading a movie magazine with a big picture of an impossibly pretty face on the cover—the kind you never see just walking down the street. He had taken the next stool and ordered a coke.

"Why don't you read something good, instead of that pap?" he asked her.

"Something good? You mean something dry, I guess. And don't call it . . . that word. It doesn't sound polite."

"What does it say? That somebody named Doll Starr is fed up with glamor and longs for a simple home in the country and lots of kids? Then why doesn't she move to Casperton?"

"You wouldn't understand," said Pretty-Lee.

He took the magazine, leafed through it. "Look at this: all about people who give parties that cost thousands of dollars, and fly all over the world having affairs with each other and committing suicide and getting divorced. It's like reading about Martians."

"I still like to read about the stars. There's nothing wrong with it."

"Reading all that junk just makes you dissatisfied. You want to do your hair up crazy like the pictures in the magazines and wear weird-looking clothes—"

Pretty-Lee bent her straw double. She stood up and took her shopping bag. "I'm very glad to know you think my clothes are weird—"

"You're taking everything I say personally. Look." He showed her a full-color advertisement on the back cover of the magazine. "Look at this. Here's a man supposed to be cooking steaks on some kind of back-yard grill. He looks like a movie star; he's dressed up like he was going to get married; there's not a wrinkle anywhere. There's not a spot on that apron. There isn't even a grease spot on the frying pan. The lawn is as smooth as a billiard table. There's his son; he looks just like his pop, except that he's not grey at the temples. Did you ever really see a man that handsome, or hair that was just silver over the ears and the rest glossy black? The daughter looks like a movie starlet, and her mom is exactly the same, except that she has that grey streak in front to match her husband. You can see the car in the drive; the treads of the tires must have just been scrubbed; they're not even dusty. There's not a pebble out of place; all the flowers are in full bloom; no dead ones. No leaves on the lawn; no dry twigs showing on the trees. That other house in the background looks like a palace, and the man with the rake, looking over the fence: he looks like this one's twin brother, and he's out raking leaves in brand new clothes—"

Pretty-Lee grabbed her magazine. "You just seem to hate everything that's nicer than this messy town—"

"I don't think it's nicer. I like you; your hair isn't always perfectly smooth, and you've got a mended place on your dress, and you feel human, you smell human—"

"Oh!" Pretty-Lee turned and flounced out of the drug store.

Brett shifted in the dusty plush seat and looked around. There were a few other people in the car. An old man was reading a newspaper; two old ladies whispered together. There was a woman of about thirty with a mean-looking kid; and some others. They didn't look like magazine pictures, any of them. He tried to picture them doing the things you read in newspapers: the old ladies putting poison in somebody's tea; the old man giving orders to start a war. He thought about babies in houses in cities, and airplanes flying over, and bombs falling down: huge explosive bombs. Blam! Buildings fall in, pieces of glass and stone fly through the air. The babies are blown up along with everything else—

But the kind of people he knew couldn't do anything like that. They liked to loaf and eat and talk and drink beer and buy a new tractor or refrigerator and go fishing. And if they ever got mad and hit somebody—afterwards they were embarrassed and wanted to shake hands. . . .

The train slowed, came to a shuddery stop. Through the window he saw a cardboardy-looking building with the words BAXTER'S JUNCTION painted across it. There were a few faded posters on a bulletin board. An old man was sitting on a bench, waiting. The two old ladies got off and a boy in blue jeans got on. The train started up. Brett folded his jacket and tucked it under his head and tried to doze off. . . .

Brett awoke, yawned, sat up. The train was slowing. He remembered you couldn't use the toilets while the train was stopped. He got up and went to the end of the car. The door was jammed. He got it open and went inside and closed the door behind him. The train was going slower, clack-clack . . . clack-clack . . . clack . . . clack . . . cuh-lack . . .

He washed his hands, then pulled at the door. It was stuck. He pulled harder. The handle was too small; it was hard to get hold of. The train came to a halt. Brett braced himself and strained against the door. It didn't budge.

He looked out the grimy window. The sun was getting lower. It was about three-thirty, he guessed. He couldn't see anything but some dry-looking fields.

Outside in the corridor there were footsteps. He started to call, but then didn't. It would be too embarrassing, pounding on the door and yelling, "Let me out! I'm stuck in the toilet . . ."

He tried to rattle the door. It didn't rattle. Somebody was dragging something heavy past the door. Mail bags, maybe. He'd better yell. But dammit, the door couldn't be all that hard to open. He studied the latch. All he had to do was turn it. He got a good grip and twisted. Nothing.

He heard the mail bag bump-bump, and then another one. To heck with it; he'd yell. He'd wait until he heard the footsteps pass the door again and then he'd make some noise.

Brett waited. It was quiet now. He rapped on the door anyway. No answer. Maybe there was nobody left in the car. In a minute the train would start up and he'd be stuck here until the next stop. He banged on the door. "Hey! The door is stuck!"

It sounded foolish. He listened. It was very quiet. He pounded again. The car creaked once. He put his ear to the door. He couldn't hear anything. He turned back to the window. There was no one in sight.

He turned around and gave the door a good kick. If he damaged it, it was too bad; the railroad shouldn't have defective locks on the doors. If they tried to make him pay for it, he'd tell them they were lucky he didn't sue the railroad . . .

He braced himself against the opposite wall, drew his foot back, and kicked hard at the lock. Something broke. He pulled the door open.

He was looking out the open door and through the window beyond. There was no platform, just the same dry fields he could see on the other side. He came out and went along to his seat. The car was empty now.

He looked out the window. Why had the train stopped here? Maybe there was some kind of trouble with the engine. It had been sitting here for ten minutes or so now. Brett got up and went along to the door, stepped down onto the iron step. Leaning out, he could see the train stretching along ahead, one car, two cars—

There was no engine.

Maybe he was turned around. He looked the other way. There were three cars. No engine there either. He must be on some kind of siding . . .

Brett stepped back inside, and pushed through into the next car. It was empty. He walked along the length of it, into the next car. It was empty too. He went back through the two cars and his own car and on, all the way to the end of the train. All the cars were empty. He stood on the platform at the end of the last car, and looked back along the rails. They ran straight, through the dry fields, right to the horizon. He stepped down to the ground, went along the cindery bed to the front of the train, stepping on the ends of the wooden ties. The coupling stood open. The tall, dusty coach stood silently on its iron wheels, waiting. Ahead the tracks went on—

And stopped.

He walked along the ties, following the iron rails, shiny on top, and brown with rust on the sides. A hundred feet from the train they ended. The cinders went on another ten feet and petered out. Beyond, the fields closed in. Brett looked up at the sun. It was lower now in the west, its light getting yellow and late-afternoonish. He turned and looked back at the train. The cars stood high and prim, empty, silent. He walked back, climbed in, got his bag down from the rack, pulled on his jacket. He jumped down to the cinders, followed them to where they ended. He hesitated a moment, then pushed between the knee-high stalks. Eastward across the field he could see what looked like a smudge on the far horizon.

He walked until dark, then made himself a nest in the dead stalks, and went to sleep.

He lay on his back, looking up at pink dawn clouds. Around him, dry stalks rustled in a faint stir of air. He felt crumbly earth under his fingers. He sat up, reached out and broke off a stalk. It crumbled into fragile chips. He wondered what it was. It wasn't any crop he'd ever seen before.

He stood, looked around. The field went on and on, dead flat. A locust came whirring toward him, plumped to earth at his feet. He picked it up. Long elbowed legs groped at his fingers aimlessly. He tossed the insect into the air. It fluttered away. To the east the smudge was clearer now; it seemed to be a grey wall, far away. A city? He picked up his bag and started on.

He was getting hungry. He hadn't eaten since the previous morning. He was thirsty too. The city couldn't be more than three hours' walk. He tramped along, the dry plants crackling under his feet, little puffs of dust rising from the dry ground. He thought about the rails, running across the empty fields, ending . . .

He had heard the locomotive groaning up ahead as the train slowed. And there had been feet in the corridor. Where had they gone?

He thought of the train, Casperton, Aunt Haicey, Mr. Phillips. They seemed very far away, something remembered from long ago. Up above, the sun was hot. That was real. The rest seemed unimportant. Ahead there was a city. He would walk until he came to it. He tried to think of other things: television, crowds of people, money: the tattered paper and the worn silver—

Only the sun and the dusty plain and the dead plants were real now. He could see them, feel them. And the suitcase. It was heavy; he shifted hands, kept going.

There was something white on the ground ahead, a small shiny surface protruding from the earth. Brett dropped the suitcase, went down on one knee, dug into the dry soil, pulled out a china teacup, the handle missing. Caked dirt crumbled away under his thumb, leaving the surface clean. He looked at the bottom of the cup. It was unmarked. Why just one teacup, he wondered, here in the middle of nowhere? He dropped it, took up his suitcase, and went on.

After that he watched the ground more closely. He found a shoe; it was badly weathered, but the sole was good. It was a high-topped work shoe, size 10½-C. Who had dropped it here? He thought of other lone shoes he had seen, lying at the roadside or in alleys. How did they get there . . . ?

Half an hour later he detoured around the rusted front fender of an old-fashioned car. He looked around for the rest of the car but saw nothing. The wall was closer now; perhaps five miles more. A scrap of white paper fluttered across the field in a stir of air. He saw others blowing along in the fitful gusts. He ran a few steps, caught one, smoothed it out.

BUY NOW—PAY LATER!

He picked up another.

PREPARE TO MEET GOD

A third said:

WIN WITH WILLKIE

The wall loomed above him, smooth and grey. Dust was caked on his skin and clothes, and as he walked he brushed at himself absently. The suitcase dragged at his arm, thumped against his skin. He was very hungry and thirsty. He sniffed the air, instinctively searching for the odors of food. He had been following the wall for a long time, searching for an opening. It curved away from him, rising vertically from the level earth. Its surface was porous, unadorned, too smooth to climb. It was, Brett estimated, twenty feet high. If there were anything to make a ladder from—

Ahead he saw a wide gate, flanked by grey columns. He came up to it, put the suitcase down, and wiped at his forehead with his handkerchief. Through the opening in the wall a paved street was visible, and the facades of buildings. Those on the street before him were low, not more than one or two stories, but behind them taller towers reared up. There were no people in sight; no sounds stirred the hot noon-time air. Brett picked up his bag and passed through the gate.

For the next hour he walked empty pavements listening to the echoes of his footsteps against brownstone fronts, empty shop windows, curtained glass doors, and here and there a vacant lot, weed-grown and desolate. He paused at cross streets, looked down long vacant ways. Now and then a distant sound came to him: the lonely honk of a horn, a faintly tolling bell, a clatter of hooves.

He came to a narrow alley that cut like a dark canyon between blank walls. He stood at its mouth, listening to a distant murmur, like a crowd at a funeral. He turned down the narrow way.

It went straight for a few yards, then twisted. As he followed its turnings the crowd noise gradually grew louder. He could make out individual voices now, an occasional word above the hubbub. He started to hurry, eager to find someone to talk to.

Abruptly the voices—hundreds of voices, he thought—rose in a roar, a long-drawn Yaaayyyyy . . . ! Brett thought of a stadium crowd as the home team trotted onto the field. He could hear a band now, a shrilling of brass, the clatter and thump of percussion instruments. Now he could see the mouth of the alley ahead, a sunny street hung with bunting, the backs of people, and over their heads the rhythmic bobbing of a passing procession, tall shakos and guidons in almost-even rows. Two tall poles with a streamer between them swung into view. He caught a glimpse of tall red letters:

. . . For Our Side!

He moved closer, edged up behind the grey-backed crowd. A phalanx of yellow-tuniced men approached, walking stiffly, fez tassles swinging. A small boy darted out into the street, loped along at their side. The music screeched and wheezed. Brett tapped the man before him.

"What's it all about . . . ?"

He couldn't hear his own voice. The man ignored him. Brett moved along behind the crowd, looking for a vantage point or a thinning in the ranks. There seemed to be fewer people ahead. He came to the end of the crowd, moved on a few yards, stood at the curb. The yellow-jackets had passed now, and a group of round-thighed girls in satin blouses and black boots and white fur caps glided into view, silent, expressionless. As they reached a point fifty feet from Brett, they broke abruptly into a strutting prance, knees high, hips flirting, tossing shining batons high, catching them, twirling them, and up again . . .

Brett craned his neck, looking for TV cameras. The crowd

lining the opposite side of the street stood in solid ranks, drably clad, eyes following the procession, mouths working. A fat man in a rumpled suit and a panama hat squeezed to the front, stood picking his teeth. Somehow, he seemed out of place among the others. Behind the spectators, the store fronts looked normal, dowdy brick and mismatched glass and oxidizing aluminum, dusty windows and cluttered displays of cardboard, a faded sign that read TODAY ONLY—PRICES SLASHED. To Brett's left the sidewalk stretched, empty. To his right the crowd was packed close, their shouts rising and falling. Now a rank of blue-suited policemen followed the majorettes, swinging along silently. Behind them, over them, a piece of paper blew along the street. Brett turned to the man on his right.

"Pardon me. Can you tell me the name of this town?"

The man ignored him. Brett tapped the man's shoulder. "Hey! What town is this?"

The man took off his hat, whirled it overhead, then threw it up. It sailed away over the crowd, lost. Brett wondered briefly how people who threw their hats ever recovered them. But then, nobody he knew would throw his hat . . .

"You mind telling me the name of this place?" Brett said, as he took the man's arm, pulled. The man rotated toward Brett, leaning heavily against him. Brett stepped back. The man fell, lay stiffly, his arms moving, his eyes and mouth open.

"Ahhhhh," he said. "Whum-whum-whum. Awww, jawww . . ."

Brett stooped quickly. "I'm sorry," he cried. He looked around. "Help! This man . . ."

Nobody was watching. The next man, a few feet away, stood close against his neighbor, hatless, his jaw moving.

"This man's sick," said Brett, tugging at the man's arm. "He fell."

The man's eyes moved reluctantly to Brett. "None of my business," he muttered.

"Won't anybody give me a hand?"

"Probably a drunk."

Behind Brett a voice called in a penetrating whisper: "Quick! You! Get into the alley . . . !"

He turned. A gaunt man of about thirty with sparse reddish hair, perspiration glistening on his upper lip, stood at the mouth of a narrow way like the one Brett had come through. He wore a grimy pale yellow shirt with a wide-flaring collar, limp and sweat-stained, dark green knee-breeches, soft leather boots, scuffed and dirty, with limp tops that drooped over his ankles. He gestured, drew back into the alley. "In here."

Brett went toward him. "This man . . ."

"Come on, you fool!" The man took Brett's arm, pulled him deeper into the dark passage. Brett resisted. "Wait a minute. That fellow . . ." He tried to point.

"Don't you know yet?" The red-head spoke with a strange accent. "Golems . . . You got to get out of sight before the—"

The man froze, flattened himself against the wall. Automatically Brett moved to a place beside him. The man's head was twisted toward the alley mouth. The tendons in his weathered neck stood out. He had a three-day stubble of beard. Brett could smell him, standing this close. He edged away. "What—"

"Don't make a sound! Don't move, you idiot!" His voice was a thin hiss.

Brett followed the other's eyes toward the sunny street. The fallen man lay on the pavement, moving feebly, eyes open. Something moved up to him, a translucent brownish shape, like muddy water. It hovered for a moment, then dropped on the man like a breaking wave, flowed around him. The body shifted, rotating stiffly, then tilted upright. The sun struck through the fluid shape that flowed down now, amber highlights twinkling, to form itself into the crested wave, flow away.

"What the hell . . . !"

"Come on!" The red-head turned, trotted silently toward the shadowy bend under the high grey walls. He looked back, beckoned impatiently, passed out of sight around the turn—

Brett came up behind him, saw a wide avenue, tall trees with chartreuse springtime leaves, a wrought-iron fence, and beyond it, rolling green lawns. There were no people in sight.

"Wait a minute! What is this place?!"

His companion turned red-rimmed eyes on Brett. "How long have you been here?" he asked. "How did you get in?"

"I came through a gate. Just about an hour ago."

"I knew you were a man as soon as I saw you talking to the golem," said the red-head. "I've been here two months;

maybe more. We've got to get out of sight. You want food? There's a place ..." He jerked his thumb. "Come on. Time to talk later."

Brett followed him. They turned down a side street, pushed through the door of a dingy cafe. It banged behind them. There were tables, stools at a bar, a dusty juke box. They took seats at a table. The red-head groped under the table, pulled off a shoe, hammered it against the wall. He cocked his head, listening. The silence was absolute. He hammered again. There was a crash of crockery from beyond the kitchen door. "Now don't say anything," the red-head said. He eyed the door behind the counter expectantly. It flew open. A girl with red cheeks and untidy hair, dressed in a green waitress' uniform appeared, swept up to the table, pad and pencil in hand.

"Coffee and a ham sandwich," said the red-head. Brett said nothing. The girl glanced at him briefly, jotted hastily, whisked away.

"I saw them here the first day," the red-head said. "It was a piece of luck. I saw how the Gels started it up. They were big ones—not like the tidiers-up. As soon as they were finished, I came in and tried the same thing. It worked. I used the golem's lines—"

"I don't know what you're talking about," Brett said. "I'm going to ask that girl—"

"Don't say anything to her; it might spoil everything. The whole sequence might collapse; or it might call the Gels. I'm not sure. You can have the food when it comes back with it."

"Why do you say 'when "it" comes back'?"

"Ah." He looked at Brett strangely. "I'll show you."

Brett could smell food now. His mouth watered. He hadn't eaten for twenty-four hours.

"Care, that's the thing," the red-head said. "Move quiet, and stay out of sight, and you can live like a County Duke. Food's the hardest, but here—"

The red-cheeked girl reappeared, a tray balanced on one arm, a heavy cup and saucer in the other hand. She clattered them down on the table.

"Took you long enough," the red-head said. The girl sniffed, opened her mouth to speak—and the red-head darted out a stiff finger, jabbed her under the ribs. She stood, mouth open, frozen.

Brett half rose. "He's crazy, miss," he said. "Please accept—"

"Don't waste your breath." Brett's host was looking at him triumphantly. "Why do I call it 'it'?" He stood up, reached out and undid the top buttons of the green uniform. The waitress stood, leaning slightly forward, unmoving. The blouse fell open, exposing round white breasts—unadorned, blind.

"A doll," said the red-head. "A puppet; a golem."

Brett stared at her, the damp curls at her temple, the tip of her tongue behind her teeth, the tiny red veins in her round cheeks, and the white skin curving ...

"That's a quick way to tell 'em," said the red-head. "The teat is smooth." He rebuttoned the uniform, then jabbed again at the girl's ribs. She straightened, patted her hair.

"No doubt a gentleman like you is used to better," she said carelessly. She went away.

"I'm Awalawon Dhuva," the red-head said.

"My name's Brett Hale." Brett took a bite of the sandwich.

"Those clothes," Dhuva said. "And you have a strange way of talking. What county are you from?"

"Jefferson."

"Never heard of it. I'm from Wavly. What brought you here?"

"I was on a train. The tracks came to an end out in the middle of nowhere. I walked ... and here I am. What is this place?"

"Don't know." Dhuva shook his head. "I knew they were lying about the Fire River, though. Never did believe all that stuff. Religious hokum, to keep the masses quiet. Don't know what to believe now. Take the roof. They say a hundred kharfads up; but how do we know? Maybe it's a thousand— or only ten. By Grat, I'd like to go up in a balloon, see for myself."

"What are you talking about?" Brett said. "Go where in a balloon? See what?"

"Oh, I've seen one at the Tourney. Big hot-air bag, with a basket under it. Tied down with a rope. But if you cut the rope ...! But you can bet the priests will never let that happen, no, sir." Dhuva looked at Brett speculatively. "What about your county: Fession, or whatever you called it. How high do they tell you it is there?"

"You mean the sky? Well, the air ends after a few miles and space just goes on—millions of miles—"

Dhuva slapped the table and laughed. "The people in Fesseron must be some yokels! Just goes on up; now who'd swallow that tale?" He chuckled.

"Only a child thinks the sky is some kind of tent," said Brett. "Haven't you ever heard of the Solar System, the other planets?"

"What are those?"

"Other worlds. They all circle around the sun, like the Earth."

"Other worlds, eh? Sailing around up under the roof? Funny: I never saw them." Dhuva snickered. "Wake up, Brett. Forget all those stories. Just believe what you see."

"What about that brown thing?"

"The Gels? They run this place. Look out for them, Brett. Stay alert. Don't let them see you."

"What do they do?"

"I don't know—and I don't want to find out. This is a great place—I like it here. I have all I want to eat, plenty of nice rooms for sleeping. There's the parades and the scenes. It's a good life—as long as you keep out of sight."

"How do you get out of here?" Brett asked, finishing his coffee.

"Don't know how to get out; over the wall, I suppose. I don't plan to leave through. I left home in a hurry. The Duke—never mind. I'm not going back."

"Are all the people here . . . golems?" Brett said. "Aren't there any more real people?"

"You're the first I've seen. I spotted you as soon as I saw you. A live man moves different than a golem. You see golems doing things like knitting their brows, starting back in alarm, looking askance, and standing arms akimbo. And they have things like pursed lips and knowing glances and mirthless laughter. You know: all the things you read about, that real people never do. But now that you're here, I've got somebody to talk to. I did get lonesome, I admit. I'll show you where I stay and we'll fix you up with a bed."

"I won't be around that long."

"What can you get outside that you can't get here? There's everything you need here in the city. We can have a great time."

"You sound like my Aunt Haicey," Brett said. "She said I had everything I needed back in Casperton. How does she know what I need? How do you know? How do I know myself? I can tell you I need more than food and a place to sleep—"

"What more?"

"Everything. Things to think about and something worth doing. Why, even in the movies—"

"What's a movie?"

"You know, a play, on film. A moving picture."

"A picture that moves?"

"That's right."

"This is something the priests told you about?" Dhuva seemed to be holding in his mirth.

"Everybody's seen movies."

Dhuva burst out laughing. "Those priests," he said. "They're the same everywhere. The stories they tell, and people believe them. What else?"

"Priests have nothing to do with it."

Dhuva composed his features. "What do they tell you about Grat, and the Wheel?"

"Grat? What's that?"

"The Over-Being. The Four-eyed One." Dhuva made a sign, caught himself. "Just habit," he said. "I don't believe that rubbish. Never did."

"I suppose you're talking about God," Brett said.

"I don't know about God. Tell me about it."

"He's the creator of the world. He's ... well, superhuman. He knows everything that happens, and when you die, if you've led a good life, you meet God in Heaven."

"Where's that?"

"It's ..." Brett waved a hand vaguely, "up above."

"But you said there was just emptiness up above," Dhuva recalled. "And some other worlds whirling around, like islands adrift in the sea."

"Well—"

"Never mind," Dhuva held up his hands. "Our priests are liars too. All that balderdash about the Wheel and the River of Fire. It's just as bad as your Hivvel or whatever you

:alled it. And our Grat and your Mud, or Gog: they're the
.ame—" Dhuva's head went up. "What's that?"

"I didn't hear anything."

Dhuva got to his feet, turned to the door. Brett rose. A
towering brown shape, glassy and transparent, hung in the
door, its surface rippling. Dhuva whirled, leaped past Brett,
dived for the rear door. Brett stood frozen. The shape
flowed—swift as quick-silver—caught Dhuva in mid-stride,
engulfed him. For an instant Brett saw the thin figure, legs
kicking, upended within the muddy form of the Gel. Then
the turbid wave swept across to the door, sloshed it aside,
disappeared. Dhuva was gone.

Brett stood rooted, staring at the doorway. A bar of
sunlight fell across the dusty floor. A brown mouse ran along
the baseboard. It was very quiet. Brett went to the back door
through which the Gel had disappeared, hesitated a moment,
then thrust it open.

He was looking down into a great dark pit, acres in extent,
its sides riddled with holes, the amputated ends of water and
sewage lines and power cables dangling. Far below light
glistened from the surface of a black pool. A few feet away
the waitress stood unmoving in the dark on a narrow strip of
linoleum. At her feet the chasm yawned. The edge of the
door was ragged, as though it had been gnawed away by
rats. There was no sign of Dhuva.

Brett stepped back into the dining room, let the door swing
shut. He took a deep breath, picked up a paper napkin from
a table and wiped his forehead, dropped the napkin on the
floor and went out into the street, his suitcase forgotten now.
At the corner he turned, walked along past silent shop
windows crowded with home permanents, sun glasses, fingernail polish, suntan lotion, paper cartons, streamers, plastic
toys, vari-colored garments of synthetic fiber, home reme-
dies, beauty aids, popular music, greeting cards . . .

At the next corner he stopped, looking down the silent
streets. Nothing moved. Brett went to a window in a grey
concrete wall, pulled himself up to peer through the dusty
pane, saw a room filled with tailor's forms, garment racks, a
bicycle, bundled back issues of magazines without covers.

He went along to a door. It was solid, painted shut. The
next door looked easier. He wrenched at the tarnished brass
knob, then stepped back and kicked the door. With a hollow

sound the door fell inward, taking with it the jamb. Brett stood staring at the gaping opening. A fragment of masonry dropped with a dry clink. Brett stepped through the breach in the grey facade. The black pool at the bottom of the pit winked a flicker of light at him in the deep gloom.

Around him, the high walls of the block of buildings loomed in silhouette; the squares of the windows were ranks of luminous blue against the dark. Dust motes danced in shafts of sunlight. Far above, the roof was dimly visible, a spidery tangle of trusswork. And below was the abyss.

At Brett's feet the stump of a heavy brass rail projected an inch from the floor. It was long enough, Brett thought, to give firm anchor to a rope. Somewhere below, Dhuva—a stranger who had befriended him—lay in the grip of the Gels. He would do what he could—but he needed equipment and help. First he would find a store with rope, guns, knives. He would—

The broken edge of masonry where the door had been caught his eye. The shell of the wall, exposed where the door frame had torn away, was wafer-thin. Brett reached up, broke off a piece. The outer face—the side that showed on the street—was smooth, solid-looking. The back was porous, nibbled. Brett stepped outside, examined the wall. He kicked at the grey surface. A great piece of wall, six feet high, broke into fragments, fell on the sidewalk with a crash, driving out a puff of dust. Another section fell. One piece of it skidded away, clattered down into the depths. Brett heard a distant splash. He looked at the great jagged opening in the wall—like a jigsaw picture with a piece missing. He turned and started off at a trot, his mouth dry, his pulse thumping painfully in his chest.

Two blocks from the hollow building, Brett slowed to a walk, his footsteps echoing in the empty street. He looked into each store window as he passed. There were artificial legs, bottles of colored water, immense dolls, wigs, glass eyes—but no rope. Brett tried to think. What kind of store would handle rope? A marine supply company, maybe. But where would he find one?

Perhaps it would be easiest to look in a telephone book. Ahead he saw a sign lettered HOTEL. Brett went up to the revolving door, pushed inside. He was in a dim, marble-panelled lobby, with double doors leading into a beige-carpeted bar on his right, the brass-painted cage of an elevator directly before him, flanked by tall urns of sand and an ascending staircase. On the left was a dark mahogany-finished reception desk. Behind the desk a man stood silently, waiting. Brett felt a wild surge of relief.

"Those things, those Gels!" he called, starting across the room. "They got my friend—"

He broke off. The clerk stood, staring over Brett's shoulder, holding a pen poised over a book. Brett reached out, took the pen. The man's finger curled stiffly around nothing. A golem.

Brett turned away, went into the bar. Vacant stools were ranged before a dark mirror. At the tables empty glasses stood before empty chairs. Brett started as he heard the revolving door thump-thump. Suddenly soft light bathed the lobby behind him. Somewhere a piano tinkled *More Than You Know*. With a distant clatter of closing doors the elevator came to life.

Brett hugged a shadowed corner, saw a fat man in a limp seersucker suit cross to the reception desk. He had a red face, a bald scalp blotched with large brown freckles. The clerk inclined his head blandly.

"Ah, yes, sir, a nice double with bath . . ." Brett heard the unctuous voice of the clerk as he offered the pen. The fat man took it, scrawled something in the register. ". . . at fourteen dollars," the clerk murmured. He smiled, dinged the bell. A boy in tight green tunic and trousers and a pillbox cap with a chin strap pushed through a door beside the desk, took the key, led the way to the elevator. The fat man entered. Through the openwork of the shaft Brett watched as the elevator car rose, greasy cables trembling and swaying. He started back across the lobby—and stopped dead.

A wet brown shape had appeared in the entrance. It flowed across the rug to the bellhop. Face blank, the golem turned back to its door. Above, Brett heard the elevator stop. Doors clashed. The clerk stood poised behind the desk. The Gel hovered, then flowed away. The piano was silent now. The lights burned, a soft glow, then winked out. Brett thought about the fat man. He had seen him before . . .

He went up the stairs. In the second floor corridor Brett felt his way along in near-darkness, guided by the dim light coming through transoms. He tried a door. It opened. He stepped into a large bedroom with a double bed, an easy chair, a chest of drawers. He crossed the room, looked out across an alley. Twenty feet away white curtains hung at windows in a brick wall. There was nothing behind the windows.

There were sounds in the corridor. Brett dropped to the floor behind the bed.

"All right, you two," a drunken voice bellowed. "And may all your troubles be little ones." There was laughter, squeals, a dry clash of beads flung against the door. A key grated. The door swung wide. Lights blazed in the hall, silhouetting the figures of a man in black jacket and trousers, a woman in a white bridal dress and veil, flowers in her hand.

"Take care, Mel!"

". . . do anything I wouldn't do!"

". . . kiss the bride, now!"

The couple backed into the room, pushed the door shut, stood against it. Brett crouched behind the bed, not breathing, waiting. The couple stood silently at the door, in the dark . . .

Brett stood, rounded the foot of the bed, approached the two unmoving figures. The girl looked young, sleek, perfect-featured, with soft dark hair. Her eyes were half-open; Brett caught a glint of light reflected from the eyeball. The man was bronzed, broad-shouldered, his hair wavy and blond. His lips were parted, showing even white teeth. The two stood, not breathing, sightless eyes fixed on nothing.

Brett took the bouqet from the woman's hand. The flowers seemed real—except that they had no perfume. He dropped them on the floor, pulled at the male golem to clear the door. The figure pivoted, toppled, hit with a heavy thump. Brett raised the woman in his arms and propped her against the bed. Back at the door he listened. All was quiet now. He started to open the door, then hesitated. He went back to the bed, undid the tiny pearl buttons down the front of the bridal gown, pulled it open. The breasts were rounded, smooth, an unbroken creamy white . . .

In the hall, he started toward the stair. A tall Gel rippled into view ahead, its shape flowing and wavering, now billowing out, then rising up. The shifting form undulated toward Brett. He made a move to run, then remembered Dhuva, stood motionless. The Gel wobbled past him, slumped suddenly, flowed under a door. Brett let out a breath. Never mind the fat man. There were too many Gels here. He started back along the corridor.

Soft music came from double doors which stood open on a landing. Brett went to them, risked a look inside. Graceful couples moved sedately on a polished floor, diners sat at tables, black-clad waiters moving among them. At the far side of the room, near a dusty rubber plant, sat the fat man, studying a menu. As Brett watched he shook out a napkin, ran it around inside his collar, then mopped his face.

Never disturb a scene, Dhuva had said. But perhaps he could blend with it. Brett brushed at his suit, straightened his tie, stepped into the room. A waiter approached, eyed him dubiously. Brett got out his wallet, took out a five-dollar bill.

"A quiet table in the corner," he said. He glanced back. There were no Gels in sight. He followed the waiter to a table near the fat man.

Seated, he looked around. He wanted to talk to the fat man, but he couldn't afford to attract attention. He would watch, and wait his chance.

At the nearby tables men with well-pressed suits, clean collars, and carefully shaved faces murmured to sleekly gowned women who fingered wine glasses, smiled archly. He caught fragments of conversation:

"My dear, have you heard . . ."

". . . in the low eighties . . ."

". . . quite impossible. One must . . ."

". . . for this time of year."

The waiter returned with a shallow bowl of milky soup. Brett looked at the array of spoons, forks, knives, glanced sideways at the diners at the next table. It was important to follow the correct ritual. He put his napkin in his lap, careful to shake out all the folds. He looked at the spoons again, picked a large one, glanced at the waiter. So far so good . . .

"Wine, sir?"

Brett indicated the neighboring couple. "The same as they're having." The waiter turned away, returned holding a wine bottle, label toward Brett. He looked at it, nodded. The waiter busied himself with the cork, removing it with many flourishes, setting a glass before Brett, pouring half an inch of wine. He waited expectantly.

Brett picked up the glass, tasted it. It tasted like wine. He nodded. The waiter poured. Brett wondered what would have happened if he had made a face and spurned it. But it would be too risky to try. No one ever did it.

Couples danced, resumed their seats; others rose and took the floor. A string ensemble in a distant corner played restrained tunes that seemed to speak of the gentle faded melancholy of decorous tea dances on long-forgotten afternoons. Brett glanced toward the fat man. He was eating soup noisily, his napkin tied under his chin.

The waiter was back with a plate. "Lovely day, sir," he said.

"Great," Brett agreed.

The waiter placed a covered platter on the table, removed the cover, stood with carving knife and fork poised.

"A bit of the crispy, sir?"

Brett nodded. He eyed the waiter surreptitiously. He looked real. Some golems seemed realer than others; or perhaps it merely depended on the parts they were playing. The man who had fallen at the parade had been only a sort of extra, a crowd member. The waiter, on the other hand, was able to converse. Perhaps it would be possible to learn something from him . . .

"What's . . . uh . . . how do you spell the name of this town?" Brett asked.

"I was never much of a one for spelling, sir," the waiter said.

"Try it."

"Gravy, sir?"

"Sure. Try to spell the name."

"Perhaps I'd better call the headwaiter, sir," the golem said stiffly.

From the corner of an eye Brett caught a flicker of motion. He whirled, saw nothing. Had it been a Gel?

"Never mind," he said. The waiter served potatoes, peas, refilled the wine glass, moved off silently. The question had been a little too unorthodox, Brett decided. Perhaps if he led up to the subject more obliquely . . .

When the waiter returned Brett said, "Nice day."

"Very nice, sir."

"Better than yesterday."

"Yes indeed, sir."

"I wonder what tomorrow'll be like."

"Perhaps we'll have a bit of rain, sir."

Brett nodded toward the dance floor. "Nice orchestra."

"They're very popular, sir."

"From here in town?"

"I wouldn't know as to that, sir."

"Lived here long yourself?"

"Oh, yes, sir." The waiter's expression showed disapproval. "Would there be anything else, sir?"

"I'm a newcomer here," Brett said. "I wonder if you could tell me—"

"Excuse me, sir." The waiter was gone. Brett poked at the mashed potatoes. Quizzing golems was hopeless. He would have to find out for himself. He turned to look at the fat man. As Brett watched he took a large handkerchief from a pocket, blew his nose loudly. No one turned to look. The orchestra played softly. The couples danced. Now was as good a time as any . . .

Brett rose, crossed to the other's table. The man looked up.

"Mind if I sit down?" Brett said. "I'd like to talk to you."

The fat man blinked, motioned to a chair. Brett sat down, leaned across the table. "Maybe I'm wrong," he said quietly, "but I think you're real."

The fat man blinked again. "What's that?" he snapped. He had a high petulant voice.

"You're not like the rest of them. I think I can talk to you. I think you're another outsider."

The fat man looked down at his rumpled suit. "I . . . ah . . . was caught a little short today. Didn't have time to change. I'm a busy man. And what business is it of yours?" He clamped his jaw shut, eyed Brett warily.

"I'm a stranger here," Brett said. "I want to find out what's going on in this place—"

"Buy an amusement guide. Lists all the shows—"

"I don't mean that. I mean these dummies all over the place, and the Gels—"

"What dummies? Jells? Jello? You don't like Jello?"

"I love Jello. I don't—"

"Just ask the waiter. He'll bring you your Jello. Any flavor you like. Now if you'll excuse me . . ."

"I'm talking about the brown things; they look like muddy water. They come around if you interfere with a scene."

The fat man looked nervous. "Please. Go away."

"If I make a disturbance, the Gels will come. Is that what you're afraid of?"

"Now, now. Be calm. No need for you to get excited."

"I won't make a scene," Brett said. "Just talk to me. How long have you been here?"

"I dislike scenes. I dislike them intensely."

"When did you come here?"

"Just ten minutes ago. I just sat down. I haven't had my dinner yet. Please, young man. Go back to your table." The fat man watched Brett warily. Sweat glistened on his bald head.

"I mean this town. How long have you been here? Where did you come from?"

"Why, I was born here. Where did I come from? What sort of question is that? Just consider that the stork brought me."

"You were born here?"

"Certainly."

"What's the name of the town?"

"Are you trying to make a fool of me?" The fat man was getting angry. His voice was rising.

"Shhh," Brett cautioned. "You'll attract the Gels."

"Blast the Jilts, whatever that is!" the fat man snapped. "Now, get along with you. I'll call the manager."

"Don't you know?" Brett said, staring at the fat man. "They're all dummies; golems, they're called. They're not real."

"Who're not real?"

"All these imitation people at the tables and on the dance floor. Surely you realize—"

"I realize you're in need of medical attention." The fat man pushed back his chair and got to his feet. "You keep the table," he said. "I'll dine elsewhere."

"Wait!" Brett got up, seized the fat man's arm.

"Take your hands off me—" The fat man went toward the door. Brett followed. At the cashier's desk Brett turned suddenly, saw a fluid brown shape flicker—

"Look!" He pulled at the fat man's arm—

"Look at what?" The Gel was gone.

"It was there: a Gel."

The fat man flung down a bill, hurried away. Brett fumbled out a ten, waited for change. "Wait!" he called. He heard the fat man's feet receding down the stairs.

"Hurry," he said to the cashier. The woman sat glassy-eyed, staring at nothing. The music died. The lights flickered, went off. In the gloom Brett saw a fluid shape rise up—

He ran, pounding down the stairs. The fat man was just rounding the corner. Brett opened his mouth to call—and went rigid, as a translucent shape of mud shot from the door, rose up to tower before him. Brett stood, mouth half open, eyes staring, leaning forward with hands outflung. The Gel loomed, its surface flickering—waiting. Brett caught an acrid odor of geraniums.

A minute passed. Brett's cheek itched. He fought a desire to blink, to swallow—to turn and run. The high sun beat down on the silent street, the still window displays.

Then the Gel broke form, slumped, flashed away. Brett tottered back against the wall, let his breath out in a harsh sigh.

Across the street he saw a window with a display of camping equipment, portable stoves, boots, rifles. He crossed the street, tried the door. It was locked. He looked up and down the street. There was no one in sight. He kicked in the glass beside the latch, reached through and turned the knob. Inside he looked over the shelves, selected a heavy coil of nylon rope, a sheath knife, a canteen. He examined a Winchester repeating rifle with a telescopic sight, then put it back and strapped on a .22 revolver. He emptied two boxes of long rifle cartridges into his pocket, then loaded the pistol. He coiled the rope over his shoulder and went back out into the empty street.

The fat man was standing in front of a shop in the next block, picking at a blemish on his chin and eyeing the window display. He looked up with a frown, started away as Brett came up.

"Wait a minute," Brett called. "Didn't you see the Gel? the one that cornered me back there?"

The fat man looked back suspiciously, kept going.

"Wait!" Brett caught his arm. "I know you're real. I've seen you belch and sweat and scratch. You're the only one I can call on—and I need help. My friend is trapped—"

The fat man pulled away, his face flushed an even deeper red. "I'm warning you, you maniac: get away from me ... !"

Brett stepped close, rammed the fat man hard in the ribs. He sank to his knees, gasping. The panama hat rolled away. Brett grabbed his arm, steadied him.

"Sorry," he said. "I had to be sure. You're real, all right. We've got to rescue my friend, Dhuva—"

The fat man leaned against the glass, rolling terrified eyes, rubbing his stomach. "I'll call the police!" he gasped.

"What police?" Brett waved an arm. "Look. Not a car in sight. Did you ever see the street that empty before?"

"Wednesday afternoon," the fat man gasped.

"Come with me. I want to show you. It's all hollow. There's nothing behind these walls—"

"Why doesn't somebody come along?" the fat man moaned.

"The masonry is only a quarter-inch thick," Brett said. "Come on; I'll show you."

"I don't like it," said the fat man. His face was pale and moist. "You're mad. What's wrong? It's so quiet . . ."

"We've got to try to save him. The Gel took him down into this pit—"

"Let me go," the man whined. "I'm afraid. Can't you just let me lead my life in peace?"

"Don't you understand? The Gel took a man. They may be after you next."

"There's no one after me! I'm a business man . . . a respectable citizen. I mind my own business, give to charity, go to church. All I want is to be left alone!"

Brett dropped his hands from the fat man's arms, stood looking at him: the blotched face, pale now, the damp forehead, the quivering jowls. The fat man stooped for his hat, slapped it against his leg, clamped it on his head.

"I think I understand now," said Brett. "This is your place, this imitation city. Everything's faked to fit your needs—like in the hotel. Wherever you go, the scene unrolls in front of you. You never see the Gels, never discover the secret of the golems—because you conform. You never do the unexpected."

"That's right. I'm law-abiding. I'm respectable. I don't pry. I don't nose into other people's business. Why should I? Just let me alone . . ."

"Sure," Brett said. "Even if I dragged you down there and

showed you, you wouldn't believe it. But you're not in the scene now. I've taken you out of it—"

Suddenly the fat man turned and ran a few yards, then looked back to see whether Brett was pursuing him. He shook a round fist.

"I've seen your kind before," he shouted. "Troublemakers."

Brett took a step toward him. The fat man yelped and ran another fifty feet, his coat tails bobbing. He looked back, stopped, a fat figure alone in the empty sunny street.

"You haven't seen the last of me!" he shouted. "We know how to deal with your kind." He tugged at his vest, went off along the sidewalk. Brett watched him go, then started back toward the hollow building.

The jagged fragments of masonry Brett had knocked from the wall lay as he had left them. Hs stepped through the opening, peered down into the murky pit, trying to judge its depth. A hundred feet at least. Perhaps a hundred and fifty.

He unslung the rope from his shoulder, tied one end to the brass stump, threw the coil down the precipitous side. It fell away into darkness, hung swaying. It was impossible to tell whether the end reached any solid footing below. He couldn't waste any more time looking for help. He would have to try it alone.

There was a scrape of shoe leather on the pavement outside. He turned, stepped out into the white sunlight. The fat man rounded the corner, recoiled as he saw Brett. He flung out a pudgy forefinger, his protruding eyes wide in his blotchy red face.

"There he is! I told you he came this way!" Two uniformed policemen came into view. One eyed the gun at Brett's side, put a hand on his own.

"Better take that off, sir."

"Look!" Brett said to the fat man. He stooped, picked up a crust of masonry. "Look at this—just a shell—"

"He's blasted a hole right in that building, officer!" the fat man shrilled. "He's dangerous."

The cop ignored the gaping hole in the wall. "You'll have to come along with me, sir. This gentleman registered a complaint . . ."

Brett stood staring into the cop's eyes. They were pale blue eyes, looking steadily back at him from a bland face. Could the cop be real? Or would he be able to push him over, as he had other golems?

"The fellow's not right in the head," the fat man was saying to the cop. "You should have heard his crazy talk. A troublemaker. His kind have got to be locked up!"

The cop nodded. "Can't have anyone causing trouble."

"Only a young fellow," said the fat man. He mopped at his forehead with a large handkerchief. "Tragic. But I'm sure that you men know how to handle him."

"Better give me the gun, sir." The cop held out a hand. Brett moved suddenly, rammed stiff fingers into the cop's ribs. He stiffened, toppled, lay rigid, staring up at nothing.

"You .. you killed him," the fat man gasped, backing. The second cop tugged at his gun. Brett leaped at him, sent him down with a blow to the ribs. He turned to face the fat man.

"I didn't kill them! I just turned them off. They're not real, they're just golems."

"A killer! And right in the city, in broad daylight."

"You've got to help me!" Brett cried. "This whole scene: don't you see? It has the air of something improvised in a hurry, to deal with the unexpected factor; that's me. The Gels know something's wrong, but they can't quite figure out what. When you called the cops the Gels obliged—"

Startlingly the fat man burst into tears. He fell to his knees.

"Don't kill me . . . oh, don't kill me . . ."

"Nobody's going to kill you, you fool!" Brett snapped. "Look! I want to show you!" He seized the fat man's lapel, dragged him to his feet and across the sidewalk, through the opening. The fat man stopped dead, stumbled back—

"What's this? What kind of place is this?" He scrambled for the opening.

"It's what I've been trying to tell you. This city you live in—it's a hollow shell. There's nothing inside. None of it's real. Only you . . . and me. There was another man: Dhuva. I was in a cafe with him. A Gel came. He tried to run. It caught him. Now he's . . . down there."

"I'm not alone," the fat man babbled. "I have my friends, my clubs, my business associates. I'm insured. Lately I've been thinking a lot about Jesus—"

He broke off, whirled, and jumped for the doorway. Brett leaped after him, caught his coat. It ripped. The fat man stumbled over one of the cop-golems, went to hands and knees. Brett stood over him.

"Get up, damn it!" he snapped. "I need help and you're going to help me!" He hauled the fat man to his feet. "All you have to do is stand by the rope. Dhuva may be unconscious when I find him. You'll have to help me haul him up. If anybody comes along, any Gels, I mean—give me a signal. A whistle ... like this—" Brett demonstrated. "And if I get in trouble, do what you can. Here ..." Brett started to offer the fat man the gun, then handed him the hunting knife. "If anybody interferes, this may not do any good, but it's something. I'm going down now."

The fat man watched as Brett gripped the rope, let himself over the edge. Brett looked up at the glistening face, the damp strands of hair across the freckled scalp. Brett had no assurance that the man would stay at his post, but he had done what he could.

"Remember," said Brett. "It's a real man they've got, like you and me ... not a golem. We owe it to him." The fat man's hands trembled. He watched Brett, licked his lips. Brett started down.

The descent was easy. The rough face of the excavation gave footholds. The end of a decaying timber projected; below it was the stump of a crumbling concrete pipe two feet in diameter. Brett was ten feet below the rim of floor now. Above, the broad figure of the fat man was visible in silhouette against the jagged opening in the wall.

Now the cliff shelved back; the rope hung free. Brett eased past the cut end of a rusted water pipe, went down hand over hand. If there were nothing at the bottom to give him footing, it would be a long climb back.

Twenty feet below he could see the still black water, pock-marked with expanding rings where bits of debris dislodged by his passage peppered the surface.

There was a rhythmic vibration in the rope. Brett felt it through his hands, a fine sawing sensation ...

He was falling, gripping the limp rope ...

He slammed on his back in three feet of oily water. The coils of rope collapsed around him with a sustained splashing. He got to his feet, groped for the end of the rope. The glossy nylon strands had been cleanly cut.

For half an hour Brett waded in waist-deep water beside a

wall of damp clay that rose sheer above him. Far above, bars of dim sunlight crossed the upper reaches of the cavern. He had seen no sign of Dhuva ... or the Gels.

He encountered a sodden timber that projected above the surface of the pool, clung to it to rest. Bits of flotsam—a plastic pistol, bridge tallies, a golf bag—floated in the black water. A tunnel extended through the clay wall ahead; beyond, Brett could see a second great cavern rising. He pictured the city, silent and empty above, and the honeycombed earth beneath. He moved on.

An hour later Brett had traversed the second cavern. Now he clung to an outthrust spur of granite directly beneath the point at which Dhuva had disappeared. Far above he could see the green-clad waitress standing stiffly on her ledge. He was tired. Walking in water, his feet floundering in soft mud, was exhausting. He was no closer to escape, or to finding Dhuva, than he had been when the fat man cut the rope.

He would have to find another way out. Endlessly wading at the bottom of the pit was useless. He would have to climb. One spot was as good as another. He stepped back and scanned the wall of clay looming over him. Twenty feet up, water dripped from the broken end of a four-inch water main. Brett uncoiled the rope from his shoulder, tied a loop in the end, whirled it and cast upward. On the third try it caught. He tested it, then started up. His hands were slippery with mud and water. He twined the rope around his legs, inched upward.

After the first ten feet he found toe-holds in the muddy wall. He worked his way up, his hands aching and raw. A projecting tangle of power cable gave a secure purchase for a foot. He rested. Nearby, an opening two feet in diameter gaped in the clay: a tunnel. It might be possible to swing sideways across the face of the clay and reach the opening. It was worth a try. His stiff, clay-slimed hands would pull him no higher.

He gripped the rope, kicked off sideways, hooked a foot in the tunnel mouth, half jumped, half fell into the mouth of the tunnel. He clung to the rope, shook it loose from the pipe above, coiled it and looped it over his shoulder. On hands and knees he started into the narrow passage.

The tunnel curved left, then right, dipped, then angled up. Brett crawled steadily, the smooth, stiff clay yielding and cold against his hands and sodden knees. Another smaller tunnel joined from the left. Another angled in from above. The tunnel widened to three feet, then four. Brett got to his feet, walked in a crouch. Here and there, barely visible in the near-darkness, objects lay imbedded in the mud: a silver-plated spoon, its handle bent; the rusted engine of an electric train, a portable radio, green with corrosion from burst batteries.

At a distance, Brett estimated, of a hundred yards from the pit, the tunnel opened into a vast cave, greenlit from tiny discs of frosted glass set in the ceiling far above. A row of discolored concrete piles, the foundations of the building above protruded against the near wall, their surfaces nibbled and pitted. Between Brett and the concrete columns the floor was littered with pale sticks and stones, gleaming dully in the gloom.

Brett started across the floor. One of the sticks snapped underfoot. He kicked a melon-sized stone. It rolled lightly, came to rest with hollow eyes staring toward him. A human skull.

The floor of the cave covered an area the size of a city block. It was blanketed with human bones, with here and there a small cat skeleton or the fanged snout-bones of a dog. There was a constant rustling of rats that played among the rib cages, sat atop crania, scuttled behind shin-bones. Brett picked his way, stepping over imitation pearl necklaces, zircon rings, plastic buttons, hearing aids, lipsticks, compacts, corset stays, prosthetic devices, rubber heels, wrist watches, lapel watches, pocket watches with corroded brass chains.

Ahead Brett saw a patch of color: a blur of pale yellow. He hurried, stumbling over bone heaps, crunching eyeglasses underfoot. He reached the still figure where it lay slackly, face down. Gingerly he squatted, turned it on its back. It was Dhuva.

Brett slapped the cold wrists, rubbed the clammy hands. Dhuva stirred, moaned weakly. Brett pulled him to a sitting position. "Wake up!" he whispered. "Wake up!"

Dhuva's eyelids fluttered. He blinked dully at Brett.

"The Gels may turn up any minute," Brett hissed. "We have to get away from here. Can you walk?"

"I saw it," said Dhuva faintly. "But it moved so fast . . ."

"You're safe here for the moment," Brett said. "There are

none of them around. But they may be back. We've got to find a way out!"

Dhuva started up, staring around. "Where am I?" he said hoarsely. Brett seized his arm, steadied him on his feet.

"We're in a hollowed-out cave," he said. "The whole city is undermined with them. They're connected by tunnels. We have to find one leading back to the surface."

Dhuva gazed around at the acres of bones. "It left me here for dead."

"Or to die," said Brett.

"Look at them," Dhuva breathed. "Hundreds ... thousands ..."

"The whole population, it looks like. The Gels must have whisked them down here one by one."

"But why?"

"For interfering with the scenes. But that doesn't matter now. What matters is getting out. Come on. I see tunnels on the other side."

They crossed the broad floor, around them the white bones, the rustle of rats. They reached the far side of the cave, picked a six-foot tunnel which trended upward, a trickle of water seeping out of the dark mouth. They started up the slope.

"We have to have a weapon against the Gels," said Brett.

"Why? I don't want to fight them." Dhuva's voice was thin, frightened. "I want to get away from here ... even back to Wavly. I'd rather face the Duke."

"This was a real town, once," said Brett. "The Gels have taken it over, hollowed out the buildings, mined the earth under it, killed off the people, and put imitation people in their place. And nobody ever knew. I met a man who's lived here all his life. He doesn't know. But we know ... and we have to do something about it."

"It's not our business. I've had enough. I want to get away."

"The Gels must stay down below, somewhere in that maze of tunnels. For some reason they try to keep up appearances ... but only for the people who belong here. They play out scenes for the fat man, wherever he goes. And he never goes anywhere he isn't expected to."

"We'll get over the wall somehow," said Dhuva. "We may starve, crossing the dry fields, but that's better than this."

They emerged from the tunnel into a coal bin, crossed to a sagging door, found themselves in a boiler room. Stairs led up to sunlight. In the street, in the shadow of tall buildings, a boxy sedan was parked at the curb. Brett went to it, tried the door. It opened. Keys dangled from the ignition switch. He slid into the dusty seat. Behind him there was a hoarse scream. Brett looked up. Through the streaked windshield he saw a mighty Gel rear up before Dhuva, who crouched back against the blackened brick front of the building.

"Don't move, Dhuva!" Brett shouted. Dhuva stood frozen, flattened against the wall. The Gel towered, its surface rippling.

Brett eased from the seat. He stood on the pavement, fifteen feet from the Gel. The rank Gel odor came in waves from the creature. Beyond it he could see Dhuva's white terrified face.

Silently Brett turned the latch of the old-fashioned auto hood, raised it. The copper fuel line curved down from the firewall to a glass sediment cup. The knurled retaining screw turned easily; the cup dropped into Brett's hand. Gasoline ran down in an amber stream. Brett pulled off his damp coat, wadded it, jammed it under the flow. Over his shoulder he saw Dhuva, still rigid—and the Gel, hovering, uncertain.

The coat was saturated with gasoline now. Brett fumbled a match box from his pocket. Wet. He threw the sodden container aside. The battery caught his eye, clamped in a rusted frame under the hood. He jerked the pistol from its holster, used it to short the terminals. Tiny blue sparks jumped. He jammed the coat near, rasped the gun against the soft lead poles. With a whoosh! the coat caught; yellow flames leaped, soot-rimmed. Brett snatched at a sleeve, whirled the coat high. The great Gel, attracted by the sudden motion, rushed at him. He flung the blazing garment over the monster, leaped aside.

The creature went mad. It slumped, lashed itself against the pavement. The burning coat was thrown clear. The Gel threw itself across the pavement, into the gutter, sending a splatter of filthy water over Brett. From the corner of his eye, Brett saw Dhuva seize the burning coat, hurl it into the pooled gasoline in the gutter. Fire leaped twenty feet high; in its center the great Gel bucked and writhed. The ancient car shuddered as the frantic monster struck it. Black smoke boiled up; an unbelievable stench came to Brett's nostrils. He

backed, coughing. Flames roared around the front of the car.
Paint blistered and burned. A tire burst. In a final frenzy,
the Gel whipped clear, lay, a great blackened shape of
melting rubber, twitching, then still.

"They've tunneled under everything," Brett said. "They've
cut through power lines and water lines, concrete, steel,
earth; they've left the shell, shored up with spidery-looking
truss work. Somehow they've kept water and power flowing
to wherever they needed it—"

"I don't care about your theories," Dhuva said; "I only
want to get away."

"It's bound to work, Dhuva. I need your help."

"No."

"Then I'll have to try alone." He turned away.

"Wait," Dhuva called. He came up to Brett. "I owe you a
life; you saved mine. I can't let you down now. But if this
doesn't work . . . or if you can't find what you want—"

"Then we'll go."

Together they turned down a side street, walking rapidly.
At the next corner Brett pointed.

"There's one!" They crossed to the service station at a run.
Brett tried the door. Locked. He kicked at it, splintered the
wood around the lock. He glanced around inside. "No good,"
he called. "Try the next building. I'll check the one behind."

He crossed the wide drive, battered in a door, looked in at
a floor covered with wood shavings. It ended ten feet from
the door. Brett went to the edge, looked down. Diagonally,
forty feet away, the underground fifty-thousand-gallon storage tank which supplied the gasoline pumps of the station
perched, isolated, on a column of striated clay, ribbed with
chitinous Gel buttresses. The truncated feed lines ended six
feet from the tank. From Brett's position, it was impossible
to say whether the ends were plugged.

Across the dark cavern a square of light appeared. Dhuva
stood in a doorway looking toward Brett.

"Over here, Dhuva!" Brett uncoiled his rope, arranged a
slip-noose. He measured the distance with his eye, tossed the
loop. It slapped the top of the tank, caught on a massive
fitting. He smashed the glass from a window, tied the end of
the rope to the center post. Dhuva arrived, watched as Brett
went to the edge, hooked his legs over the rope, and started
across to the tank, hand over hand.

It was an easy crossing. Brett's feet clanged against the tank. He straddled the six-foot cylinder, worked his way to the end, then clambered down to the two two-inch feed lines. He tested their resilience, then lay flat, eased out on them. There were plugs of hard waxy material in the cut ends of the pipes. Brett poked at them with the pistol. Chunks loosened and fell. He worked for fifteen minutes before the first trickle came. Two minutes later, two thick streams of gasoline were pouring down into the darkness.

Brett and Dhuva piled sticks, scraps of paper, shavings, and lumps of coal around a core of gasoline-soaked rags. Directly above the heaped tinder a taut rope stretched from the window post to a child's wagon, the steel bed of which contained a second heap of combustibles. The wagon hung half over the ragged edge of the floor.

"It should take about fifteen minutes for the fire to burn through the rope," Brett said. "Then the wagon will fall and dump the hot coals in the gasoline. By then it will have spread all over the surface and flowed down side tunnels into other parts of the cavern system."

"But it may not get them all."

"It will get some of them. It's the best we can do right now. You get the fire going in the wagon; I'll start this one up."

Dhuva sniffed the air. "That fluid," he said. "We know it in Wavly as phlogistoneum. The wealthy use it for cooking."

"We'll use it to cook Gels." Brett struck a match. The fire leaped up, smoking. Dhuva watched, struck his match awkwardly, started his blaze. They stood for a moment watching. The nylon curled and blackened, melting in the heat.

"We'd better get moving," Brett said. "It doesn't look as though it will last fifteen minutes."

They stepped out into the street. Behind them wisps of smoke curled from the door. Dhuva seized Brett's arm. "Look!"

Half a block away the fat man in the panama hat strode toward them at the head of a group of men in grey flannel. "That's him!" the fat man shouted, "the one I told you about. I knew the scoundrel would be back!" He slowed, eyeing Brett and Dhuva warily.

"You'd better get away from here, fast!" Brett called. "There'll be an explosion in a few minutes—"

"Smoke!" the fat man yelped. "Fire! They've set fire to the

city! There it is! pouring out of the window...and the door!" He started forward. Brett yanked the pistol from the holster, thumbed back the hammer.

"Stop right there," he barked. "For your own good I'm telling you to run. I don't care about that crowd of golems you've collected, but I'd hate to see a real human get hurt—even a cowardly one like you."

"These are honest citizens," the fat man gasped, standing, staring at the gun. "You won't get away with this. We all know you. You'll be dealt with . . ."

"We're going now. And you're going too."

"You can't kill us all," the fat man said. He licked his lips. "We won't let you destroy our city."

As the fat man turned to exhort his followers Brett fired, once, twice, three times. Three golems fell on their faces. The fat man whirled.

"Devil!" he shrieked. "A killer is abroad!" He charged, mouth open. Brett ducked aside, tripped the fat man. He fell heavily, slamming his face against the pavement. The golems surged forward. Brett and Dhuva slammed punches to the sternum, took clumsy blows on the shoulder, back, chest. Golems fell. Brett ducked a wild swing, toppled his attacker, turned to see Dhuva deal with the last of the dummies. The fat man sat in the street, dabbing at his bleeding nose, the panama still in place.

"Get up," Brett commanded. "There's no time left."

"You've killed them. Killed them all . . ." The fat man got to his feet, then turned suddenly and plunged for the door from which a cloud of smoke poured. Brett hauled him back. He and Dhuva started off, dragging the struggling man between them. They had gone a block when their prisoner, with a sudden frantic jerk, freed himself, set off at a run for the fire.

"Let him go!" Dhuva cried. "It's too late to go back!"

The fat man leaped fallen golems, wrestled with the door, disappeared into the smoke. Brett and Dhuva sprinted for the corner. As they rounded it a tremendous blast shook the street. The pavement before them quivered, opened in a wide crack. A ten-foot section dropped from view. They skirted the gaping hole, dashed for safety as the facades along the street cracked, fell in clouds of dust. The street trembled under a second explosion. Cracks opened, dust rising in puffs from the long wavering lines. Masonry collapsed around them. They put their heads down and ran.

Winded, Brett and Dhuva walked through the empty streets of the city. Behind them, smoke blackened the sky. Embers floated down around them. The odor of burning Gel was carried on the wind. The late sun shone on the blank pavement. A lone golem in a tasseled fez, left over from the morning's parade, leaned stiffly against a lamp post, eyes blank. Empty cars sat in driveways. TV antennae stood forlornly against the sunset.

"That place looks lived-in," said Brett, indicating an open apartment window with a curtain billowing above a potted geranium. "I'll take a look."

He came back shaking his head. "They were all in the TV room. They looked so natural at first; I mean, they didn't look up or anything when I walked in. I turned the set off. The electricity is still working anyway. Wonder how long it will last?"

They turned down a residential street. Underfoot the pavement trembled at a distant blast. They skirted a crack, kept going. Occasional golems stood in awkward poses or lay across sidewalks. One, clad in black, tilted awkwardly in a Gothic entry of fretted stone work. "I guess there won't be any church this Sunday," said Brett.

He halted before a brown brick apartment house. An untended hose welled on a patch of sickly lawn. Brett went to the door, stood listening, then went in. Across the room the still figure of a woman sat in a rocker. A curl stirred on her smooth forehead. A flicker of expression seemed to cross the lined face. Brett started forward. "Don't be afraid. You can come with us—"

He stopped. A flapping window-shade cast restless shadows on the still golem features on which dust was already settling. Brett turned away, shaking his head.

"All of them," he said. "It's as though they were snipped out of paper. When the Gels died their dummies died with them."

"Why?" said Dhuva. "What does it all mean?"

"Mean?" said Brett. He shook his head, started off again along the street. "It doesn't mean anything. It's just the way things are."

Brett sat in a deserted Cadillac, tuning the radio.

"... anybody hear me?" said a plaintive voice from the speaker. "This is Ab Gullorian, at the Twin Spires. Looks like I'm the only one left alive. Can anybody hear me?"

Brett tuned. "... been asking the wrong questions ... looking for the Final Fact. Now these are strange matters, brothers. But if a flower blooms, what man shall ask why? What lore do we seek in a symphony ... ?"

He twisted the knob again. "... Kansas City. Not more than half a dozen of us. And the dead! Piled all over the place. But it's a funny thing: Doc Potter started to do an autopsy—"

Brett turned the knob. ". . . CQ, CQ, CQ. This is Hollip Quate, calling CQ, CQ. There has been a disaster here at Port Wanderlust. We need—"

"Take Jesus into your hearts," another station urged.

"... to base," the radio said faintly, with much crackling. "Lunar Observatory to base. Come in, Lunar Control. This is Commander McVee of the Lunar Detachment, sole survivor—"

"... hello, Hollip Quate? Hollip Quate? This is Kansas City calling. Say, where did you say you were calling from ... ?"

"It looks as though both of us had a lot of mistaken ideas about the world outside," said Brett. "Most of these stations sound as though they might as well be coming from Mars."

"I don't understand where the voices come from," Dhuva said. "But all the places they name are strange to me ... except the Twin Spires."

"I've heard of Kansas City," Brett said, "but none of the other ones."

The ground trembled. A low rumble rolled. "Another one," Brett said. He switched off the radio, tried the starter. It groaned, turned over. The engine caught, sputtered, then ran smoothly.

"Get in, Dhuva. We might as well ride. Which way do we go to get out of this place?"

"The wall lies in that direction," said Dhuva. "But I don't know about a gate."

"We'll worry about that when we get to it," said Brett. "This whole place is going to collapse before long. We really started something. I suppose other underground storage tanks caught—and gas lines, too."

A building ahead cracked, fell in a heap of pulverized plaster. The car bucked as a blast sent a ripple down the street. A manhole cover popped up, clattered a few feet, dropped from sight. Brett swerved, gunned the car. It leaped over rubble, roared along the littered pavement. Brett looked in the rearview mirror. A block behind them the street ended. Smoke and dust rose from the immense pit.

"We just missed it that time!" he called. "How far to the wall?"

"Not far! Turn here . . ."

Brett rounded the corner with a shrieking of tires. Ahead the grey wall rose up, blank, featureless.

"This is a dead end!" Brett shouted.

"We'd better get out and run for it—"

"No time! I'm going to ram the wall! Maybe I can knock a hole in it."

Dhuva crouched; teeth gritted, Brett held the accelerator to the floor, roared straight toward the wall. The heavy car shot across the last few yards, struck—

And burst through a curtain of canvas into a field of dry stalks.

Brett steered the car in a wide curve to halt and look back. A blackened panama hat floated down, settled among the stalks. Smoke poured up in a dense cloud from behind the canvas wall. A fetid stench pervaded the air.

"That finishes that, I guess," Brett said.

"I don't know. Look there."

Brett turned. Far across the dry field columns of smoke rose from the ground.

"The whole thing's undermined," Brett said. "How far does it go?"

"No telling. But we'd better be off. Perhaps we can get beyond the edge of it. Not that it matters. We're all that's left . . ."

"You sound like the fat man," Brett said. "But why should we be so surprised to find out the truth? After all, we never saw it before. All we knew—or thought we knew—was what they told us. The moon, the other side of the world, a distant city . . . or even the next town. How do we really know what's there . . . unless we go and see for ourselves? Does a goldfish in his bowl know what the ocean is like?"

"Where did they come from, those Gels? How much of the world have they undermined? What about Wavly? Is it a golem country too? The Duke . . . and all the people I knew?"

"I don't know, Dhuva. I've been wondering about the people in Casperton. Like Doc Welch. I used to see him in the street with his little black bag. I always thought it was full of pills and scalpels; but maybe it really had zebra's tails and toad's eyes in it. Maybe he's really a magician on his way to cast spells against demons. Maybe the people I used to see hurrying to catch the bus every morning weren't really going to the office. Maybe they go down into caves and chip away at the foundations of things. Maybe they go up on rooftops and put on rainbow-colored robes and fly away. I used to pass by a bank in Casperton: a big grey stone building with little curtains over the bottom half of the windows. I never go in there. I don't have anything to do in a bank. I've always thought it was full of bankers, banking . . . Now I don't know. It could be anything . . ."

"That's why I'm afraid," Dhuva said. "It could be anything."

"Things aren't really any different than they were," said Brett, ". . . except that now we know." He turned the big car out across the field toward Casperton.

"I don't know what we'll find when we get back. Aunt Haicey, Pretty-Lee . . . But there's only one way to find out."

The moon rose as the car bumped westward, raising a trail of dust against the luminous sky of evening.

J. G. BALLARD

THE CRYSTAL WORLD	(X1380—60¢)
THE DROWNED WORLD	(F1266—50¢)
THE VOICES OF TIME	(F1243—50¢)
THE IMPOSSIBLE MAN	(F1204—50¢)

CHARLES L. HARNESS

THE ROSE	(X1648—60¢)
THE RING OF RITORNEL	(X1630—60¢)

FRANK HERBERT

THE SANTAROGA BARRIER	(S1615—75¢)
THE EYES OF HEISENBERG	(F1283—50¢)
DESTINATION: VOID	(F1249—50¢)

Send for a free list of all our books in print

These books are available at your local newsstand, or send price indicated plus 10¢ per copy to cover mailing costs to Berkley Publishing Corporation, 200 Madison Avenue, New York, N.Y. 10016.